Shattered Perfection

Heather R. Guimond

Dedication:

For the Captain of Team Awesome, without whom this book would have forever remained a first draft on my hard drive; and for the love of my life, my wonderful husband, who is my indefatigable champion, no matter what hair-brained idea I have.

Acknowledgments:

Several wonderful people helped me bring this effort to fruition through their generosity of time and spirit. Without their help and support, this book would never see the light of day, and a dream of mine would remain unfulfilled. For this reason, my undying gratitude belongs to:

John Grace, Meg Martin, and Christina Patz for answering the call when I needed readers.

Polett Villalta, for being the honest voice I could rely upon without question, always knowing she would give it to me straight. Look, Pol, no salad!

Vicki Lowe-Johnson, for making me feel like a rock-star while reading and giving me feedback. Your criticism, if I can even call it that, kept me editing like a fiend because I couldn't wait to hear what you'd say next.

Nick Marsh, for being everything I needed and then some. Beta reader, editor, qualifier ninja, cheerleader, ego-booster, walrus slapper, Oreo thief, and the best friend I could ever have hoped to have.

Nickii Fowler, for being more to this book, and to me, than this page could ever possibly contain. Reader, editor, guide, assistant, inspiration, role-model, hero, and the best Aunt in the world, if even the old bat gets me lost every time we get in the car together.

My husband, Joe, for being my support, my love, my partner for nearly two decades (I guess I'll be keeping you after all) and encouraging me through this process every step of the way.

The three most awesome and attractive children ever to grace the face of this planet. You make my life worthwhile every day. No matter how many times I threaten to sell you, I promise I never will.

@TheEnderBookshelf on Wattpad.com who is currently taking the fan fiction world by storm. Check out this amazing young author and give her a follow. She is on her way to big things. She may be young, but the quality of her description inspires me to do better and to work harder.

Finally, I want to thank a certain group of women who have become my personal "Justice League" of Superhero authors: **Mimi Jean Pamfiloff, Alice Clayton, Christina Lauren, Emma Chase, Chloe Neill and Darynda Jones.** Each one has delighted and entertained me through some very dark time and made me hope that maybe, just maybe I might someday be able to brush the hems of their capes (and in my wildest fantasies share a

cocktail or six). Thank you from the bottom of the
heart of one grateful and eternal fan.⸱

Table of Contents

One

"You're a stupid, worthless bitch!" Vance screams as he throws his dinner plate at the kitchen wall. I wince as I watch the gravy drip down the stark white wall and leak between it and the baseboard before pooling onto the floor while Vance rants and raves about how inedible my cooking is.

"All this time and you still haven't learned to serve anything at the proper temperature. Your potatoes are lumpy and the broccoli tastes like it was steamed with a sweaty gym sock," he sneers. "I don't know why I continue to put up with you. Everything about you is inferior. The way you dress, the way you behave... you're a total bitch to my coworkers and friends... hell Mimi, even the way you fuck. You're absolutely worthless."

I sit there calmly, listening to words I have heard dozens, maybe hundreds of times before.

"What are you waiting for?" he asks in a mocking tone, that infuriating smirk on his handsome face. "Go on, clean up this mess."

I take a few seconds to indulge in the fantasy of grabbing him by his wavy dark hair and driving my index and middle fingers into his piercing blue eyes. It's gruesome, I know. However, I've spent the last six months of our year and a half marriage enduring scenes like this. I think anyone would be driven to graphic, if not homicidal, imaginings by now. I know it's crazy to put up with the abuse, but there are a couple of reasons why I do. First, he wasn't always like this. He used to be attentive and caring. He was kind, loving and generous. He is intelligent, has always had a playful sense of humor that never failed to make me laugh before, and we almost never disagreed. Until recently, I still saw snippets of that man. The second, I suppose, is my pride. I married Vance only a few short months after meeting him in a chance encounter at Los Angeles International Airport. We had an intense, passionate love affair, both of us falling head over heels from almost the moment we met. Logic told me not to rush headlong into things, to back off and take my time getting to know him before making such a serious commitment, but he was the one. I don't want to admit to myself that I was wrong.

Sighing, I rise and move to the closet by the sink and grab the mop and the dustpan.

"No. I want you down on your hands and knees with a sponge, like the dog you are," he spits out.

I can't take anymore. The anger flares inside me, rising like a tsunami of venom. Months and months of suppressed emotion bubbles up and out of me, seemingly spilling onto the tile floor, splashing over every surface of the room, and coating us in its hatred.

"I am not a dog, you vicious mother fucker. Nor am I lazy, stupid, or worthless. You have been right about one thing recently though. I am a real bitch." Lost to the emotions flooding my system, I grab a glass from the drain board on the counter and pitch it at his head. He swiftly dodges it, lunges out of his chair and is on me in an instant. The breath rushes out of my lungs as my back hits the floor and stars burst behind my eyes as my head slams against the tile. His hand presses against the base of my throat and he squeezes tightly.

"Do you think you can smart mouth me, Mimi? Throw things at me? You must have lost your mind. I should kill you for this." His grip tightens, causing my vision to dim around the edges. For the first time, I am genuinely afraid. I clutch at his wrist, my nails scratching futilely at the skin. I writhe beneath his heavy body, my legs trying to find purchase on the slick tile floor, but his weight keeps me pinned.

Suddenly, he releases my neck and I gasp in heavy gulps of air. His hand twists into my blonde hair, wrapping it around his fist and tugging my head to the side. He buries his face into my neck and bites down hard. I cry out at the sharp pain as his other hand grabs ahold of the collar of my blouse and rips it down the front. I pummel his shoulders and back with my fists, trying to get him to stop, but he is completely out of his mind. He raises up off me slightly and reaches for the front of my pants, tearing those wide open too. In desperation, I drive the tips of my long fingernails into his ear canals.

His full weight crushes me as he drops down, gasping in pain or surprise, I'm not sure which. His breaths come fast and hard, but he is no longer savagely pawing at me. He inhales deeply and rolls off, sprawling out on the hard floor, his arms and legs splayed wide. I curl away from him into the fetal position, my body shaking from the adrenaline pumping through my veins. We lay like that for five, ten minutes, an hour. I don't really know. Eventually, my trembling subsides, but I'm afraid to move. Vance finally stands and nudges me with his foot.

"Clean this room up." He says quietly before exiting the room on soft feet.

Once I know he is in the back of the house and well away from me, I rise and test my muscles. I'm bruised in spots, there is a knot at the back of my head, and I know I will most likely be sore as hell tomorrow morning. Given the gravity of the situation, things could have turned out a lot worse.

I walk through the kitchen to the adjoining laundry room and sort through the basket of clean clothes I have not yet taken to the bedroom. It's a stroke of good luck, under the circumstances. I quickly shed my ruined clothing and don a pair of leggings and a sweatshirt from the load that I folded earlier in the day. I find a pair of flip flops by the back door and slip them on. Traveling back into the kitchen, I grab the mop and dustpan once again and head to the sink.

I fill the sink with warm water and absently watch the bubbles form after I add a few squirts of dish detergent. I look down at my unsteady hands, wringing them together to still them. I know I provoked him, but Vance has never been violent before. I don't even want to think about where he was headed before I was able to stop him. What if I hadn't? What if... what if... what if... It doesn't bear thinking about.

I can't stay any longer. Suffering the verbal abuse was enough to make any sane person leave long before now. I know I shouldn't have tolerated it for as long as I have already, but there is no way to delude myself into believing there is a reason to endure physical confrontations between us. Physical abuse, possibly attempted rape, and death threats? Even my love and pride can't overcome those things.

I set about mopping up the now congealed gravy, chicken and other detritus from my failed meal and push it into the dustpan. I dump it into the garbage can, along with the cold contents of my plate. I rinse out the mop, drain the sink and scour it out well, all the while planning to start a new life. Sure, I had considered leaving him before. I'd be lying if I said I'd never thought about it, but I'd always somehow convinced myself that the good outweighed the bad, or that things would magically get better. Assuming that was even possible, I can't stick around and wait for it to happen now.

First things first. I need a place to go. A hotel would do fine for a couple days, but I'm going to need an apartment. I have a good job as a corporate paralegal, but Vance's salary from his work as a mergers and acquisitions attorney paid all our bills. I don't have a realistic perspective as to how far my wages will go to support me in Los Angeles anymore. I had done fairly well before I married

Vance, so I suppose I shouldn't worry too much. It would only mean saying goodbye to our charming bungalow in the Fairfax District, a quiet enclave flanked by West Hollywood, the Miracle Mile, and Beverly Grove. It was Vance's house, where he had lived before I met him. Prior to our marriage, I had been living in a small studio apartment in the San Fernando Valley. I wasn't much of a social climber or status whore, so this would be no great loss to me. I didn't have a problem doing a little extra driving to my job downtown again.

As I finish cleaning up the kitchen, I make a list in my head of things I need to do the following day. I plan to call work and take a week off. I have plenty of time off stored up, so even though it is short notice, it shouldn't be a problem. I'll pack up my clothes after Vance has gone to work and find a hotel over the hill to stay for a few days. I could go to my friend Grace's house. I'm sure she'd let me stay in her spare bedroom, but I know Vance will come looking for me and that's the first place he'll go. I don't want to involve her in this mess any more than crying on her shoulder if I can help it.

After I get settled, I'll start my search for an apartment. No, wait. I should apply for a restraining order. As I realize this that's when the night's events truly hit me. He attacked me. He bit me, he choked me, and it seemed like he was getting ready to rape me. This man, the man who once swept me away on a wave of passion and overwhelming love, threatened to end my life tonight. My chest expands and contracts involuntarily, forcing a heavy sob out of my throat. I hang my head and cry tears I have not allowed myself in all this time. I cry for all the suffering I have refused to acknowledge, for all the humiliation I have endured through his words, but mostly for the death of my love for him. I know all this must make him seem like a monster, but it wasn't always this way.

Eighteen months earlier

Standing in line at the security checkpoint at LAX, I pushed my carry-on bag ahead of me with my toe as the line shuffled forward. I scanned the ticket in my hand as I heard a deep but seductive voice coming from just over my shoulder.

"Headed home?" the honeyed, but masculine voice dripped in my ear.

A tingling sensation began at the back of my neck and moved to encompass my entire scalp, culminating in a ringing in my ears as I turned to see a very tall, very handsome man, about thirty years old, standing over me, smiling. He had a dark mop of hair, somewhere between dark brown and black (I wasn't sure which but would have been thrilled to get up close and personal, running my fingers through it to make a well-informed determination). He had thickly lashed blue eyes, the kind that seem to glow when the light hit them just right, just as they were doing at that moment.

He also had those high cheekbones that all demi-gods have, and full sensuous lips I imagined would have been at home on just about any inch of my skin, surrounded by just the right amount of scruff. He also had what my mom would have called a Pepsodent smile, probably the product of years of orthodontic work (which, somewhere in the back of my mind, I felt was reassuring; perhaps he wasn't actually born completely perfect).

All that was missing from the picture was a halo, a sunbeam, and a pair of white wings. Perhaps also a bare, oiled chest and a white drapery covering over his hips, but who was I to be so choosy when I already had this Adonis speaking to me. Being the extremely cool and confident young woman I was, I'm sure I gave him a slightly deranged looking smile in response.

"Uhhh.... leaving home. Short trip to New York. Going to visit an old childhood friend," I said with all the wit and brilliance of a canned ham. Undaunted by my own awkwardness I blundered forward. "How about you? Leaving L.A. after working on your tan?" I said with what I hoped was a saucy wink but probably looked more like a nervous tic.

He laughed outright (to my great relief) and shook his head. "Nope. I'm leaving home just like you. I'm also headed to New York." The line inched ahead again, and we moved forward with it.

"Wow, that's a coincidence," I said. "Business or pleasure?" That sounded like a fairly normal question a fairly normal person would ask, I told

8

myself. I cleared my throat and stood a little straighter, hoping it wasn't too late to salvage my image.

"It's a business trip, but I'll be there a couple of weeks so I'm hoping to fit in some fun while I'm there." His eyes lit up a little. "I love the city, you know? If it were all work... well, that would just suck. I want to do it all, take in the sights, see the shows, eat the food, and watch the people..." He looked at me sheepishly. "I suppose that's expecting a little too much for a work trip though. They're paying me to actually get a job done."

"They must be some crazy bastards to bring you to a place like that, then expecting you to work around the clock for two weeks straight, resisting the temptations of New York. What nerve." I said, shaking my head in mock disgust.

"It could be worse, I guess. They could be sending me somewhere in Kansas."

"Ah, but then you could visit the world's biggest ball of twine." I offered earnestly.

He looked at me skeptically. "I think I'm afraid to ask how you know that."

"Sadly, I'm filled with a million useless facts. The good news is I'm a great partner for Trivial Pursuit."

"I didn't know that game was played with a partner," he said.

"Err... well that's usually the only way anyone will play with me," I said looking at my feet.

He laughed silently for a moment, one hand pressed against his midsection, which appeared to be extremely taut beneath his tight black t-shirt. Although it was probably a very bad idea, given my already embarrassingly strong physical attraction to the man, I took a moment to look at his lean physique. His shoulders were broad and muscular, and his pectorals were clearly defined beneath the cotton clinging to his form. His chest tapered to a trim waist, and his faded denim jeans were slung low on his hips. A pair of scuffed black boots completed his look. I wondered what he really did for a living, because all he needed was a leather jacket, and I could easily imagine him on a motorcycle riding from town to town doing odd jobs for pocket money.

His eyes twinkled with amusement as he looked at me. "Don't look so sad. Nobody plays Trivial Pursuit anymore, anyway."

I smiled at him as the line continued to move forward at a snail's pace. "So, what do you do for these horrible people who send you to New York to do nothing but slave away for them while the city pulses with life and atmosphere?"

"I'm a suit, unfortunately. I sold out and went to work for The Man after law school," he said, looking a little ashamed.

"Oh wow, you're an attorney?" I said, slightly surprised.

He winced a little, before saying "Please, don't be too impressed. It's just a way to earn a living."

"Oh, I'm not impressed," I said, then hurried to add, "I mean, I am. It's great. All that school, now you have a good job that pays well, and I'm sure you had to work hard to get it too, and oh shit, I'm really fucking this up." I stopped and took a deep breath while he looked at me with an uncomfortable expression on his face, clearly clocking the nearest escape route from the crazy gold digger in front of him. "What I mean is, it's just that we have something in common. I'm a paralegal."

"Oh hey, okay." He let out his own relieved sigh. "What area of law do you work in?"

"I work for a large practice downtown that houses many specialties, but I work in the corporate department," I said. "Pretty boring stuff, but it pays the bills."

He laughed and shook his head. "Which firm?" he asked.

I looked at him skeptically and slowly said "Miller and Dickerson. Why?"

He grinned and said, "Because I work for the competition, DuPont, Browerson, and Ajax. As a mergers and acquisitions specialist."

I couldn't help the wide grin that split my face. "Your building is just two streets away from mine. We literally work within a mile of each other, and yet we meet here?"

"Life can be random that way," he said continuing to smile at me.

On impulse, and in what was probably the most awkward move in the history of meetings between young men and women in airports, I thrust my hand out in front of him. "I'm Mimi Bishop."

He gently took my smaller hand in his large one and held it firmly, enveloping it with his warmth.

He didn't shake, just simply held it, while looking deep into my eyes. "Hello, Mimi Bishop. My name is Vance Ashcroft. Will you marry me?"

Something electric happened between us for a split second. At that moment, my vision tunneled, the cacophony of the airport faded into the distance and the world just stopped. In an instant, it was over, and we both dissolved into a massive fit of laughter. It wasn't the nervous tittering of a joke gone awry but great big whoops and belly laughs.

"What the hell was that, Vance? Do you use that line often?" I said as I wiped a stray tear from my eye.

"I always wanted to, but it's the first time I ever felt I had the right audience," he said grinning at me like a fool.

We approached the security scanners and I hefted my carry-on from the floor to put it into one of the security tubs. Vance reached in front of me and placed it on the conveyor belt, where I tossed my purse, as well. Slipping out of my shoes, I told him, "Well, it was brilliant. Best laugh I've had in a long time." I placed my tennies in another tub and moved through the security scanner toward the waiting TSA agent for my pat-down and highly impersonal groping. I was almost looking forward to it since I hadn't seen any action in months, except the TSA agent was a large and formidable looking woman.

I was putting my shoes back on at the end of the conveyor when Vance joined me.

"I really think someone should buy me dinner after that man-handling." He said as we both reached for our bags.

"Did you ask her to marry you, too? She might have gone a bit easier on you if you had. You know, maybe skipped the whole cavity search in public," I said with a sweet smile.

He gasped. "Mimi! I am saving myself for you. You are the only one for me. Although...," he put a finger to his lips in thought. "Bertha back there might be able to show me the merits of having over-developed grip strength. That could prove interesting for some private time in a secluded parking space."

I'm sure I looked at him like his hair was on fire.

With the smuggest smirk I have ever seen, he put a finger to my chin and slowly pushed my mouth closed. "I think I may have done the impossible and rendered you speechless. Tell me, was it what I said that shocked you, or the image it put in your brain?"

I groaned and pressed my fingertips to my eyelids as we turned and walked from the security checkpoint.

"Did you really have to say that? I wasn't picturing it, thank you very much, but now I have the lovely image of "Bertha" with her manly hand, scraggly, half-bitten fingernails and all, wrapped around your..."

"Enough! No more! No more! You win. I hadn't pictured it either, but now I am as traumatized as you," he said as he shook his head in distress. "My own humor turned against me like a weapon. Why are you a paralegal? You should be a lawyer. You would be lethal in a courtroom." He looked at me with a sideways grin and bumped my shoulder with his as we walked along the concourse.

I grinned up at him, enjoying how easy things had become between us, how my nervousness had vanished. Vance may have been a pretty face, but he sure didn't act like it. Too bad our time was coming to an end. I checked my watch. Sure enough, my flight was scheduled to leave in twenty short minutes.

"I'm flying out of here on American. How about you?" I asked, crossing my fingers behind my back. Given that we were at the airport at the same time, with the same destination and walking in the same direction through the airport, the odds were better than average that we were on the same flight. While it was highly unlikely we'd be seated together, we would at least have the next twenty minutes.

"Yes, Flight 330. Same as you?"

I nodded, beaming brightly at him.

"Score!" He exclaimed, pumping his fist exaggeratedly.

I rolled my eyes. "You really are a dork, you know that?"

"Now that hurt, Mimi. I'm just a man who happens to show enthusiasm when things go his way. I am happy that I get to continue with the pleasure of your company." He dropped his voice to a sinful growl. "Would you deny me my pleasure?" he asked arching that brow at me again.

I shoved him away from me by the shoulder playfully. "Pervert and a dork."

He grabbed my hand as we reached our gate and pulled me to a couple empty seats. We fell into them and looked at each other for a moment. Slowly, he lifted my hand to his lips, pressing a quick kiss to the backs of my fingers and whispered, "Yeah, but I'm thinking that's just your type."

I was stunned. Sure, we had been having a very fun and friendly conversation to this point, perhaps even mildly flirtatious, what with the whole faux marriage proposal and all, but this? This was a thunderbolt. No, a starburst. Fuck that, a freaking rocket ship to Mars. I opened my mouth to say something, not that I would have been able to come up with anything at the moment, clever or otherwise, but the attendant called for pre-boarding for our flight. Puffing out a sigh, Vance stood and shouldered his carry-on, while giving me a slightly embarrassed look.

"I'm in first class," he said with a grimace. So much for those twenty minutes.

An inexplicable tightening in my chest made it hard to speak, but I managed a surprisingly bright tone of voice. "Well, it's been quite an experience meeting you, Mr. Ashcroft. Don't let the slave drivers work you too hard over the next two weeks."

He looked at me like he wanted to say something, but simply put out his hand. I took it as he said, "It was an absolute honor, Miss Bishop." Then I watched quietly as he turned and walked toward the gate. Resting my chin in my hand, I kept watching as he disappeared through the doorway to the gangway and continued staring after he was long gone until they called my seating section.

As I embarked, I scanned the first-class area hoping to catch another glimpse of him, even if it was just to see another one of his smiles. I didn't see him sitting in any of the seats though. It seemed curious, but I didn't spend too much time thinking about it as the stream of people behind me propelled me forward.

I made my way to my seat, near the back of the plane. After cramming my carry-on in the already stuffed overhead compartment, I stumbled over the rotund, gentleman with the six-hair comb-over sitting in the aisle seat to reach mine next to the window. Evidently, common courtesy had deserted this fellow in the face of his fear of flying. At least, I assumed that was the cause of his shaking hands and profuse sweating. I tried to shrink against the window as he mopped his face with a handkerchief that had seen better days, making myself as small a target as possible, just in case any stray bullets of sweat came flying my way. I pulled the flight safety card out of the pocket of the seatback in front of me and studied it closely it for lack of anything better to do.

"Excuse me, sir," a familiar voice carried over to my seat. "How would you like to sit in first class for this flight?"

I looked up to see Vance looking expectantly at my seatmate, who appeared somewhat startled and confused.

"I'm offering to switch seats with you, sir. My seat is 3B, up in the first-class section." Vance spoke slowly as if the man were learning impaired. "I would like to change seats with you and sit here, with the lovely lady next to you, while you enjoy the fine service and legroom first class has to offer." He pressed his hands together in front of him, bowing slightly. I just refrained from rolling my eyes.

The nervous flyer struggled out of his seat, his shirt buttons straining mightily at his waist, and popped open the overhead compartment without a word. He grabbed a gray laptop bag out of it and hustled down the aisle, presumably before Vance could change his mind.

Vance stowed his gear and closed the compartment before flopping in the seat beside me. He leaned his head back against the seat and turned toward me with a wide grin.

I smiled back innocently and asked, "Are you sure you want to sit there? It might be a little... moist."

The horrified look on his face was priceless and my resulting laugh was loud and wild, provoking many dirty looks in my direction. Vance lifted his hands from the armrests, pretending to shake them dry. He looked around questioningly before calling out, "Does anyone happen to have any hand sanitizer?"

I was reduced to another laughing fit as the elderly woman across the aisle produced a small, travel size bottle from her handbag and offered it to him with a warm, grandmotherly smile. Vance squirted a small amount into his palm and handed the bottle back with a wink and what I was coming to realize was his signature charming grin.

As he rubbed his hands together, he turned to me and gave a wicked smile just for me. "That was not very nice, Mimi."

"Yes, it was. I was trying to warn you of the hazards of occupying the same seat as Captain von Sweatyballs."

Vance groaned painfully and squirmed uncomfortably in the seat. "Now, how do you know that his balls were, in fact, sweaty?"

"Well, not having actually inspected them personally, I can't say with a one hundred percent degree of certainty, but I think it is fair to say that in all likelihood, they were indeed sweaty."

His face lit up with barely concealed hope. "Aha! You concede that you could not possibly be, without a doubt, certain. It is possible they could have been as dry as the Sahara."

"Let me ask you this since you have balls, I presume." He nodded and motioned with his hand for me to continue.

"Have you ever, at any time, had your entire body be covered in a sheen of perspiration, yet had your balls remain as dry as the Sahara?"

He leaned back in the seat, his fingers threaded over his abdomen, and a thoughtful look on his face, as if contemplating numerous sweaty occasions, and the condition of his private parts. "You know, Mimi, a bit of antiperspirant works wonders under such conditions."

Once again, my mouth dropped open. "Do you put antiperspirant on your balls, Vance?"

"Now, that's a very personal question, Mimi. We've only just met. You can hardly expect me to tell you something like that."

I sputtered, "You're the one who brought it up! You can't back out now!"

"Actually, I think you're the one who instigated this whole gonadal conversation."

"Quit dodging the question. I'm going to assume you must, or you wouldn't have suggested it."

"Even men like to have that 'fresh' feeling every now and then." He stopped and looked in the direction the unfortunate sweaty man had lumbered off toward. "Well, most men."

We quieted down as the airline attendant began his safety speech. Shortly thereafter we were in the air and sipping flat soda from little plastic cups. We managed to get our silliness under control and spent the entire six hours lost in conversation, covering a wide variety of subjects. It turned out we had a great deal in common. We both enjoyed the outdoors, preferring to spend a day hiking and biking than even an hour in the gym. We liked to read though our tastes in literature were very different. He was a fan of the classics while I favored contemporary works. We learned we were both liberal in our politics, with strong feelings about social issues since we each grew up under less than ideal economic circumstances, he with his single mother and never knowing his dad. My own father died when I was very small, so I knew the hardships of living in a single income household and had felt the absence of a father figure too. Neither of us had siblings. The more we talked, the longer the list grew. Big things, little things, we ticked so many of the same boxes it was eerie.

As we talked, I found that I genuinely liked Vance. He was incredibly handsome, but beneath all that physical perfection was a rather naughty silliness, underscored further by an intelligent and thoughtful person who was completely unaware of his own attractiveness.

As our flight circled John F. Kennedy International Airport, Vance turned to me with a serious expression. He opened his mouth to speak, but nothing came out at first, giving his face something of the appearance of a gasping fish. He took my hand and for the first time since I met him, he looked slightly unsure of himself.

"Mimi, this was probably the best time I've had in a long time, and it was only a plane ride. I can't even imagine what a date with you would be like, but I'd really like to find out. I know this is a vacation for you, and you probably have your itinerary all planned, but do you think we could get together one night this week? I really want to see you again, and I am positive it will kill me if I have to wait the two weeks before I am back in Los Angeles."

The most incredible sense of relief washed over me. In the back of my mind, I had been dreading our landing, the uncertainty of any future time spent with Vance looming on the edges of my consciousness. It didn't matter what plans my friend, Laurel, had in store for me while I visited. I would carve out time for this man on any day he wanted to see me. She would just have to understand.

"I'd really like that too. I'll give you my information, and as soon as you know your schedule, give me a call and we'll figure something out this week," I said, still trying to play it cool when all I really wanted to do was throw myself into his lap and squeal like an over-excited fangirl.

Once the plane landed, we gathered our belongings and disembarked hand in hand. We continued to tease each other playfully as we made our way to baggage claim, but I was aware of a new vibe humming between us, just below the surface. I wondered if he felt it too, or if my imagination was running away with me.

The carousel was already turning as we approached and searched for our bags. Vance found his quickly, a silver wheeled case, and a simple black garment bag with shoulder strap that had frankly seen better days. His luggage was a study in opposites, from each side of the economic spectrum and I was puzzled by the dichotomy.

Before I could make a comment, I heard a feminine voice calling my name.

"Mimi, girl! Over here!" I looked over my shoulder to see Laurel hopping up and down and waving her arms as if she were trying to take flight. Her auburn hair was swirling about her head, getting caught in her mouth and her chic but nerdy glasses slipping down the bridge of her nose as she made a spectacle of herself. Standing all of five feet tall, she had huge green eyes, a pert little nose, and a lithe figure. She was wearing a conservative navy suit with a high collared white blouse, a short skirt, and five-inch spike heels. She looked something between a sexy librarian and a wood sprite on meth.

I waved back at her letting her know I saw her before she fell and broke an ankle or something. She smiled and gave me the best jazz hands she could, considering she was holding her smartphone in one of them. Assured she'd been clocked and identified, she shoved the phone in front of her face and began furiously texting someone.

I turned to Vance and laughed. "That's Laurel," I said, hitching a thumb over my left shoulder. "She's a little..."

"Enthusiastic?" He offered.

"Yes, that's one way to describe her. Out of her ever-loving mind would be another."

"I can't wait to meet her. You're planning to introduce me, right?" he asked.

I saw my suitcase come around on the carousel and attempted to heave it off, nearly knocking the passenger next to me down to the ground. Vance stepped in, grabbing the handle, and fluidly lifting it over the lip, and lowering it to the ground beside me. He raised the telescopic handle and waved his hand toward it with a flourish. I just rolled my eyes.

"I totally had that, you know," I huffed. I wheeled the case around and headed towards Laurel with Vance and his stuff right behind me. Laurel didn't look up until I stood right in front of her, tapping my foot. When she looked over my shoulder and saw Vance, her eyes immediately darted back to me. She leaned in and whispered loudly, "You know you have a slice of mancake stuck to your backside, right?"

Nodding, I deadpanned, "When they asked me if I wanted nuts on the flight, I said yes. This is what I got."

Laurel checked Vance out shamelessly for a moment, then turned to me. "Well, let's go. We've got stuff to do." She strutted off and I heard her mumbling to herself, "Man, I really gotta start flying American."

We followed her out of baggage claim and onto the sidewalk. Cars were moving aggressively down the street before us, cutting each other off and honking like crazy. Insults and hand gestures were tossed out the windows at dizzying speeds and I wondered why anyone willingly chose to drive in this city. Especially cab drivers.

Vance and I pulled up alongside Laurel as we headed toward the taxi stand. I nudged her in the arm to get her attention and pointed to Vance.

"This guy is actually a friend of mine. While we established on the plane that he does have nuts, he also has a name. This is Vance Ashcroft. Vance, this is Laurel O'Malley, my old childhood friend." They quickly shook hands as I explained, "Vance and I are going to have dinner sometime this week, and no, you are not invited. Hopefully, it won't interfere with any plans you have lined up for us."

Laurel gave Vance another long look as we queued up for the taxi. She shrugged and said, "Fine with me. Any day but Wednesday. We've got tickets to see Wicked that day. Any other day we can move our plans around, but under no circumstances can we move Wednesday, and you will not be bailing out on me that day. Capisce?"

"I got it, Dona O'Malley. You got a ring I need to kiss now?"

"No, just had a little Al Pacino marathon with Stevie the other day. Don't mind me. Things get a little sideways sometimes, Vance. Don't worry though, you'll catch on quick staying quiet like you do."

Vance just chuckled. "Between the two of you, I don't see where there's much of an opportunity to do anything else."

Laurel leaned in and patted him on his chest a few times. By the look in her eye, we were about two-and-a-half seconds from her copping a feel. I growled softly enough that only she could hear, so she backed off, but not before purring "I do so love a man who catches on quickly," then cackled unattractively as she approached the taxi that pulled up in front of us.

I turned to Vance while shaking my head. "Please do not judge me by my friends. I have an eclectic group of people in my life. You know how some people collect odd things? Well, I kind of do that with people. Laurel is one of my prize oddities."

"So, if I'm hearing you correctly... Laurel is your pig fetus in a jar?"

"Ew... no. Well, maybe."

"Fair enough. So where are you headed? Do you want to share a cab?" he asked hopefully.

"I think we're heading to the East Village. How about you?"

"Ah, well I'm headed to the Upper West Side. I'll catch the next cab. I'll give you a call once I've got everything nailed down and we'll plan our dinner. I'm really looking forward to it, Mimi." He leaned in and placed a soft kiss on my cheek just as Laurel started banging on the roof of the cab.

"We ain't got all night you two. Let's go, Mimi. The party awaits!" She shouted.

I wrapped my arms around Vance's neck and pulled him in for a quick but tight hug. I couldn't resist a little more contact than that polite cheek kiss. He hugged me back, placing his hands on my waist and resting his cheek on top of my head. He whispered to me, "Soon, little Mimi. Very soon."

We smiled goofily at each other as we parted, lingering for only a second more, then I jumped into the cab next to a squealing Laurel. The driver lurched into the erratic and noisy traffic of the airport, leaving me feeling dazed and giddy at the same time.

Two

I didn't have to wait long to hear from Vance. That evening, while sitting in a little hole-in-the-wall bar with Laurel and some of her friends, I was startled to hear the lyrics of 'Marry Me' by Train coming from my purse. At first, I was confused, but then scrambled for my purse while laughing myself silly. The phone went quiet as I dug frantically through gum wrappers, random papers, lipsticks, and other clutter to find my phone. I excused myself and stepped outside to return the call. As soon as the voice on the other end answered, I didn't give him another chance to speak.

"You proposed, again? By ringtone, this time? I'm starting to worry about you, Vance," I said as I leaned back against the rough brick of the building outside.

He laughed softly. "I wanted to be sure you knew it was me calling."

"How do you know I don't have a bunch of other guys proposing to me right now?" I asked coyly.

"I don't, but how many are so clever as to sneak a ringtone into your phone when giving you their contact information?" he teased. "I'm sure by now, they have all called you at least once, and have their own boring ringtones assigned."

I chuckled warmly as I scraped the toe of my boot against the sidewalk. "Yes, of course. You do realize though that all of them waited until they had at least kissed me before popping the question for the first time."

A strangled sound echoed across the line before I heard Vance clear his throat. "Well, there will be no more kissing. Maybe a little more kissing. Okay, a lot more kissing, but not by any of those tools. So... changing the subject now. Did you get settled in at Laurel's?"

"Yes. Her place is a little small, so I think she'll be ready to have me out before the week is through, but for now, she seems happy I'm here. We're down at a small bar near her apartment having a few drinks with some of her friends right now. They're nice and all, but New Yorkers and Angelenos are very different breeds of animal."

"This is your first time in the city? How did we not cover this on the plane?" he asked incredulously.

"We were busy telling each other our life stories, I guess. Yes, this is the first time I've been here. I've met one or two New Yorkers before, but I guess they had acclimated to the west coast by the time they'd crossed my path. I don't quite know how to describe the difference."

"New Yorkers are more intense. To them, everything they do or say is... important. They have places to go, things to do. L.A. style is different. Nothing matters quite as much, we'll be somewhere when we get there, whenever that is."

"Well, that's because nothing is going to happen until we get there, anyway!" I replied haughtily. Sighing, I continued, "They're all right. They're just different. I don't think they think very much of me, but they haven't been rude or anything."

"In that case, they love you. New Yorkers are rude to everyone. Even the people they like." Another huff of laughter drifted over the line between us. I let my head fall back against the building and closed my eyes. I had never met anyone like Vance before. There was just an easiness between us, a playfulness that I hadn't experienced with anyone else. I wanted to hear him laugh all the time. I wanted to be the reason that he laughed. It didn't make any sense. Intellectually, I was aware that I had only known him a handful of hours, but I felt like my life had already changed somehow.

"Tomorrow is Monday," I heard him say. "I have a meeting with our east coast partners in the morning. After that, I'll have a better idea of what my week will look like. I will give you a call in the evening, so we can make plans for dinner. Will that work out for you?"

"Yeah, that'll be fine. Laurel mentioned wanting to do some shopping, which for her means dragging me around all day long, in and out of every store within a five-mile radius. I expect tomorrow night we'll be ordering take out and staying in to recover. I'll look forward to your call."

"Until then, Mimi. Goodnight." He whispered huskily.

"Goodnight, Vance." I breathed back and ended the call.

Laurel found me still standing against the wall five minutes later, staring off into space, and my phone in my hand. She had my purse looped over her shoulder and a knowing look on her face.

"So, I assume that was the hottie from the airport?" she asked, looking at me over her glasses.

I nodded. "The very same. He's going to call tomorrow night, once he knows his schedule for the week, so we can make plans."

She leaned her shoulder against the wall next to me and crossed her arms over her chest. She studied my face for a moment before she spoke. "He's different, isn't he? I know you just met him today, but there's something about the way you look right now. I've known you a long time, and I've never seen this look on your face."

Laurel was one of my oldest friends. We met in the fourth grade after her family moved to my neighborhood when her father got transferred to the Los Angeles office by the production company he worked for. She'd been trying to get back to New York ever since, finally getting there after we graduated high school when she was accepted to NYU. I hadn't seen her but for her trips to see her parents for the holidays over the last six years, so this was the first time we were really going to have the opportunity to spend some quality time together, rather than maintaining our relationship through email, texts, and Skype. She was working as an assistant editor in a large publishing house and had a bright future ahead of her. I knew it wouldn't be long before she was a wild success and our chances for visits like these would be much harder to come by, so I did feel a smidgeon guilty that I'd be stealing a night away to see a guy I'd only just met. But, she was one of the few people who truly knew me. She could read me, my thoughts, my moods, just by looking at my face or studying my body language. Granted, I am a pretty open and expressive person, but she had an eerie knack for being able to pin me down with a mere glance. Like right then.

"I suppose the Dopey Dwarf impersonation gave me away this time?" I snarked at her.

"That and the spot of drool on your chin," she said as she shifted her weight to her other foot while keeping her shoulder against the wall. "So, what's his deal? Does he have chocolate-flavored nipples?"

I laughed at her outrageousness and smacked her on the shoulder. "We were so busy talking on the flight, I wasn't thinking about punching my Mile-High Club Card, Whore-rel, but who knows. Maybe by the end of the week, I'll be able to answer that question." I said, giving her a sideways grin.

She jumped up and down, clapping and shouting, "Now who's the whore?" She grabbed my arm, pulling me away from the wall and handed me my bag. "Let's go back to the apartment, put on our pajamas and you can tell me all about your plan to inspect his nipples."

Vance called again the following night as planned, much to my delight. We arranged to meet

Thursday night, for a late dinner, since his meetings were scheduled to run until eight that night. I worried that he might be too exhausted after such a long day, but he insisted.

He went on to explain a little about the deal he was working on that they were trying to acquire a failing business that had a worldwide presence. Fair Trade laws prevented him from discussing any specifics, but apparently, the business was well-known. There were lots of details to hammer out, and the deal had the ability to make or break his career. I instantly shared my misgivings about meeting him, stressing I would be nothing more than a distraction when he should be completely focused on his work.

"Mimi, I would be more distracted by not being able to see you, thinking about how you are going home in a few days and how I would have to wait another week to before I could spend time with you, than by taking time out and spending one evening in your company. Okay? Now relax and just agree to come with me."

Selfishly, I was easily swayed by his explanation and greedily agreed to the date.

We talked long into the night, the conversation eventually turning to how lonely we were as children. Growing up in single-parent households with little money, we were both apartment dwellers. There weren't many children living in either of our buildings and with no siblings, we didn't have a lot of opportunities to socialize other than our school hours. Things like video games and computers were impossible luxuries in both of our little families, so we both of naturally gravitated to the only cost-effective, available form of entertainment besides television—books. We were both amused to learn that we discovered the Nancy Drew and Hardy Boys mysteries at the library when we were in elementary school. While horribly dated, we both devoured each and every one. We admitted that none of our peers fully appreciated our affinity for reading. He shunned his classmates' love of sports, while I turned away from such girlie activities as shopping, make-up, and sleepovers, which only deepened our feelings of isolation. We agreed that the characters in the stories we read became our friends and companions. As we grew older, our tastes diverged. His love for the classics emerged in high school when he developed an unlikely friendship with his eleventh-grade Literature teacher. I became something of a romance junkie around the same age when I finally developed an interest in the opposite sex. Rather than being interested in the boys in my class, however, I swooned for the tall, brooding hero with broad shoulders, chiseled jaw and haunting secrets that made him feel unworthy of love.

"Are you still looking for the same qualities in a man?" Vance asked. I could plainly hear the curiosity in his voice.

As usual, Vance made me laugh with the question. "I think I have come to realize that a man with haunting secrets is not going to be miraculously healed by the love of a good woman, no matter how great it sounds. Besides, who wants to go through all the angst it takes to get to the happily ever after? I'll save all those complications for my book boyfriends. I like my real-life men to be a little more well-adjusted. I need someone who is emotionally stable, down to earth, and forthright. Most of the men in the books I read don't really fit that bill."

I paused for a moment, screwing up my courage to reverse the question. "What about you? What do you look for in a woman?" I cringed as I not-so-subtly fished for information as to whether or not I might have the potential to be that woman. Sitting there in my pajamas, which consisted of a threadbare t-shirt and a baggy pair of men's boxers, my hair piled on my head in a sloppy top knot, and my face scrubbed of any traces of makeup, I was grateful he couldn't see me. I was sure the picture I made was the furthest image from his mind.

"That's a question I'm still figuring out the answer to. There are so many things about women to discover, and I hear that there are many things I will never understand," he chuckled. "But I do know what I don't like in a woman. I don't like phony. I don't like gossipy. I don't like materialistic and pretentious. I don't like high maintenance although I do like someone who takes some interest in her appearance. Yes, I like someone who bathes. Hopefully shaves her legs, and if I'm really lucky, a few other spots as well."

I giggled. "Do you mean like her upper lip?"

"Most definitely. Unless she has superior grip strength like our dear friend Bertha at the airport. You'll recall I was willing to overlook her surprising amount of facial hair in favor of finding out about her other charms. I'm a flexible man, after all." I can hear his smile through his words as we both grow quiet for a moment.

When he spoke again, his voice was earnest, almost intense.

"In all honesty, Mimi, I like someone who is unafraid of her ghosts. Somebody who can show me who she is openly and honestly and wants to see me the same way. Someone who can throw open the closet and be willing to let me inspect the skeletons will give me the greatest gift of all—her trust. Obviously, you don't get to know someone like that overnight, or even over the course of a few months. That level of intimacy takes time, but I like someone who is fearless enough to want to be that vulnerable with someone, someday.

"I also like a woman with a sense of humor, who understands that no one is getting out of this life alive, so it's best not to take it too seriously. At the same time, she knows when it's time to get serious then devotes all her attention to whatever issue, project or problem requires it.

"I like a woman who has compassion for other people, especially if those people are less advantaged than she is. She knows that not everyone gets a fair shake, no matter how hard they try. Sometimes bad things happen, sometimes you depend on other people and they let you down, who knows. But she knows most people are worthy of a helping hand every now and then and at the very least, she doesn't look down on those people. At best, she is willing to pitch in and help."

"For someone who is still figuring out what he likes, you seem pretty specific," I said quietly.

He laughed softly. "Well, I have figured out a thing or two in the last ten years of dating." I heard him yawn on the other end of the line. "If she doesn't have any of those qualities, I find that can be overlooked if she has a nice enough rack."

"You pig!" I cried as I turned out the light and slid down under the blanket on the sofa. "Here I was all impressed by your speech, only to find out you're just a misogynist after all!"

He cracked up, laughing loud and long. "You know I'm only kidding, Mimi. I'm really an ass man."

"I'm hanging up now Vance before you totally annihilate my good impression of you. You've done enough damage for one night."

The amusement was still in his voice as I heard him murmur. "Goodnight, Mimi. Sweet dreams."

Two days of shopping, sight-seeing, one night of partying and one at the theater, a horde of text messages and a few brief phone conversations stolen between Vance and me later, I begged Laurel to let me rest on Thursday, so I wouldn't look like a haggard slice of death for my date that night.

We were sitting in her living room sipping coffee that morning, while she pouted, insisting I came to see her, not go on unsanctioned dates that she did not arrange for me. I let her get it out of her system, knowing to do otherwise would just perpetuate the frowning and foot stomping for another fifteen minutes. I would have asked her to find a date and join us, but I really, really wanted to have time with Vance all to myself. I just wasn't ready to share his attention with anyone else.

"What happened to "chicks before dicks?" she whined.

"Oh, please. It's not like I'm ditching you last minute or leaving you at some club with only condoms in your purse and five dollars for cab fare. I told you about this as soon as I got off the plane. It's one night out of six. I think you can manage without me," I said exasperatedly before taking a long sip of my coffee.

"I shouldn't have to." Her nasally tone reminded me of when we were younger, and she wanted to swing on the swings when I wanted to play hopscotch.

"Strap on your chaps, sister, because we're going eight seconds in the big girl's rodeo today." I reached over and slapped her knee in mock reprimand. She just rolled her eyes at me.

"Fine. I suppose I can call that cute hipster boy I met Monday night."

Laurel never had a shortage of options to keep her occupied. I saw her exchanging numbers with the guy in question, but she didn't mention it and I never pressed her for details since meeting guys was something she did with regularity. If there were anything noteworthy about him, she'd have said something. Right then, he was just another potential pony for her stable.

Looking at me in defeat, Laurel asked, "So, are you wearing the green dress?"

While we were on our shopping spree, I purchased the cutest little dress for my date with Vance. It was mint green chiffon, with a lightly ruched bodice and flouncy skirt. It had a form-fitted silk lining and underskirt. The shoulder straps were covered in rhinestones that shimmered and twinkled when I moved. It flattered my shoulder length blonde hair and really brought out the green in my hazel eyes, making them sparkle.

"Yes. That's the plan." I said, stretching my legs out in front of me. "I am being such a stupid girl, Laurel. I'm sitting here wondering how he will react when he sees me in it. When did I turn into one of those girls? One who cares more about what a guy thinks than what she thinks herself?"

"If I didn't know you better, I'd be disgusted with you too," she joked. "I think there's that one guy out there for all of us that brings out our inner fourteen-year-old, though. Remember Pete?"

I tried to think back through Laurel's relationships. There hadn't been too many serious ones. At the time, she'd gone on a lot of first and second dates more than anything. I thought Pete may have lasted a couple of weeks though. "Wasn't he the bartender?"

"No, that was Paolo. Pete was a cop. I'm sure he still is." Her face got this kind of wistful look and I could tell she was remembering something.

"Oh yes, I remember you went nuts for the whole uniform thing."

"Exactly. There was a lot more to it—a lot—but he reduced me to a giggling, simpering fool just by being within a ten-foot radius. I swear, all I had to do was get a whiff of that musky cologne of his, and I set the women's agenda back by at least twenty years." She turned to face me and rested her elbow on the back of the sofa, chin in hand. "I ran from him because I thought that was wrong. That he couldn't possibly be good for me if he changed me like that. It's been a year, but I've never met someone like him that made me feel as good as he did, and I have never been able to get him entirely out of my mind. I'll sit across from a new guy in a restaurant, at a bar or wherever, listening to them talk and totally tune out whatever they're saying. They're all so boring. Pete? I hung on his every word. He could read me the penal code and I'd probably pay closer attention than a fanboy at the Marvel presentation at Comic-Con. I realize that I miss him. So, now, I think maybe being a little girly about a boy maybe isn't the worst thing in the world. As long as you're not that way about every boy you meet, it might even be a good thing."

I nodded thoughtfully for a moment, truly taking in everything Laurel had said. It was rare that she got so deep, normally choosing to be upbeat and lighthearted, so I knew what she said wasn't something to be taken lightly. Instead of responding with something equally serious, I broke into a wide grin. "Heh... you said penal."

She grabbed one of the throw pillows and whacked me in the head with it. "Forget everything I said. I do not like fourteen-year-old Mimi." She stood and stretched, lifting her arms high above her head, and wiggling her fingers. She dropped her arms, sighed, and looked at me. "I know you're thinking about it, Mimi. I don't know much of anything about this guy, but I do know you. You're not superficial, or vapid, or a hundred other stupid things women become when a man walks into the picture. There's something different about this guy, and it's up to you to figure out what. Now that I've laid that bit of wisdom on you, I'm going to go take a shower."

"Thanks, Laurel. For everything." I said quietly.

She just nodded at me and headed for the bathroom.

Three

I started getting ready for my date at six that evening. I took a leisurely shower, scrubbing every square inch of my body with Laurel's luxurious lavender and vanilla body wash. I also indulged in her splendid hair products, a rich shampoo and conditioner that promised to tame my curls into a sleek and shiny mane. I shaved all necessary parts, taking care to be meticulous with some areas, just in case. Not that I had any plans of course, but no one wants to be caught in a moment of wild abandon only to be brought back to reality by the thought of unsightly stubble.

I took time carefully applying my makeup with the precision of a cardiac surgeon. I went all-out with dramatic beige and plum eyeshadow, and heavy eyeliner with lots of mascara to play up my eyes. They were an odd hazel, mostly green with amber flecks rather than brown. A hint of blush, and a barely-there nude lipstick and gloss. I blew out and straightened my blonde hair before twisting it up into an elegant style, allowing my bangs and a few wisps to frame my face. I took a long look at my reflection in the mirror. I normally went for a much more natural look, so wearing this much make-up kind of made me feel a bit like a Kabuki Theatre performer, but if I had to say it, I looked much better than one.

Wrapped in just my towel, I left the bathroom and headed into Laurel's bedroom to slip into my dress and shoes. Looking at her bedside clock, I saw that I had been so unhurried in my preparations, I had about ten minutes before Vance was expected to arrive. I quickly stepped into my dress, struggling with the back zipper. Giving up at the halfway point, I rushed to strap on my shoes and transfer all the necessities into the new clutch purse I'd also bought on our shopping adventure.

I dashed out into the living room, hoping to get my dress zipped up the rest of the way by Laurel, only to find Vance standing in there looking absolutely edible in a charcoal gray three-button suit and a muted moss green tie. I had to snicker. Despite there being no possible way to know what I was going to wear, we were color-coordinated.

"What's funny?" He asked, with a lift of his brow.

"You. Me," I said, motioning between us with one of my hands.

"I don't quite follow, Mimi. You're going to have to give me a little more information than that."

"Really? That's surprising because it seems you've developed the ability to read my mind."

"Given my complete confusion at the moment, I can assure you that is entirely untrue."

"Look! We match!" I giggled as I came forward and yanked on his tie.

A shy smile spreads across his face. "Just lucky, I guess. That seems to be happening to me a lot these days."

"Perhaps you should take that luck to Vegas." I murmured.

"Only if she takes me up on one of my wild proposals," he smirked.

I shook my head because it was the only thing I could do in response to his crazy teasing. I suddenly realized I was standing there with my dress practically gaping forward in front of him because it was still partially unzipped in the back. I tried to press my clutch to my chest in a casual gesture and asked, "Where did Laurel go?"

"She let me in, muttered something about having to see a martini about a man, grabbed her purse, and left."

"I knew she had a date but thought she would at least say goodbye before she left." I nibbled nervously on my lower lip. "I guess I'll have to ask you. I need a little help."

"This isn't some kind of woman thing, is it?" he hedged.

I couldn't help myself. I took on a very serious expression and nodded soberly. "Kind of."

He looked only moderately mortified. He took a deep breath and exhaled in a rush. Slapping his hands together, then shaking them out, he said, "Okay, Mimi. Hit me with it. I'm your man. Whatever you need, I can take it."

I slowly turned around and gestured toward my back. "Do you think you can zip me up the rest of the way?"

I heard him take another sharp breath inward, but no exhalation followed. A moment passed before he stepped forward and his hand gently came to rest on my lower back, pulling on the fabric just below the zipper. I felt him take hold of the zip, then slowly drag it upward, taking his time. His hand moved to my bare shoulder after he reached the top and rested there for a moment before pulling me around to face him. He looked deeply into my eyes, then his gaze dropped to my lips. I held my breath as I realized that this was it. That sinful mouth was going to touch mine and I was probably going to combust and burn my pretty new dress to ash. Oh well. At least he got to see it for a few minutes. Of course, the lack of dress thing might move events into an interesting direction, too.

Completely unaware of my inner contemplation, he continued to look at me with those smoldering eyes. My lips parted, and my tongue darted out and over them quickly. He noticed the gesture as he moved in slightly. I tilted my head up to receive him, but at the last second, he pulled away and smiled weakly. What the hell? I thought.

"We need to get moving if we are going to make our reservation," he said hoarsely.

I swallowed the disappointment I felt as the moment fell away from us. I had felt the heat rise between us, so intellectually I knew the chemistry was there and it could happen again when the time was right. I didn't know what happened just then, why he pulled back, but damn, I'd have been lying if I said I wasn't hoping that time was very, very soon.

I took a step back and cleared my throat unnecessarily before speaking. "So where are we going?" I asked, for lack of anything better to say. It really didn't matter to me where we went since I wasn't all that hungry. The butterflies were bouncing around in my stomach full force, especially after that near-kiss, so I wasn't expecting to do much more than push my food around on my plate.

He gently ushered me toward the front door as he explained, "With all that we discussed the other day, I realized we never got around to our food preferences. I searched high and low for a place that has a simple menu."

"I didn't know Chili's takes reservations now," I replied wryly.

"Only in New York," he quipped without missing a beat. "Now come, gorgeous. There's a big onion blossom with your name on it out there."

I swiped the keys from the sideboard table as we walked out and locked the door behind us. Vance took my hand as we made our way down the two flights of stairs to the front walk and strolled casually to the end of the block. I admired his lean body as he stepped from the curb to hail a taxi, his long arm raised over his head. Though it was mostly obscured by the cut of his suit, I could picture the cap of his shoulder bunching as it flexed. What I wouldn't have given to see him shirtless right then. Or pants-less. Preferably both. Yeah, wearing just a pair of tight boxer briefs. Dripping wet. I knew I was being pretty pervy, but I couldn't help being a little worked up after our close encounter back up in the apartment. Every self-respecting, red-blooded woman under the age of sixty-five, make that one hundred and five, would feel the exact same way I was feeling. He was a delicious triple scoop ice cream sundae, and I definitely wanted a bite.

Before I lost control enough to tackle him in the street, a cab pulled up and Vance opened the door for me. I slid in, taking care not to flash him the goods. I may have been thinking slutty thoughts, but I wasn't the type to go all Hollywood party girl on him in a desperate attempt to get what I wanted. He jumped in beside me and gave the driver an address that meant absolutely nothing to me. He could have been taking me across the state border and I wouldn't have known.

The ride was comfortable but quiet. We both seemed a little lost in our thoughts. I couldn't know what he was thinking, but my thoughts were certainly erotica-worthy. After about twenty minutes, we pulled up outside a quaint little bistro. I could see through the antique-looking windows that the low lighting gave the small restaurant a warm and inviting glow. As we exited the vehicle, Vance's hand settled low on my back, guiding me forward, and sending a shiver up my spine. When he opened the door for me and we stepped inside, I was instantly overwhelmed by the delicious aroma of savory meats, garlic, and other spices, as well as baking bread. My stomach rumbled like a hungry truck driver's. Inside, I snorted at my earlier thoughts of pushing my food around my plate. I expected that if the meal smelled as good as the room did, Vance would be running for the door when I dove head first into my plate.

We were greeted by a statuesque brunette, whose her hair was pulled severely back from her forehead and temples, the rest a riot of curls hanging down her back. Her face was flawlessly made up, and her big brown doe eyes skimmed over me as if I were a piece of furniture before they zeroed in on Vance with the subtlety and precision of a laser beam on a sniper's rifle. She gathered herself to her full height as she smiled brightly. I could practically see her mentally adjusting her breasts and plumping her cleavage.

"Can I help you, sir?" she purred through her thick red lips, oozing estrogen all over the podium and reservation book. I rolled my eyes and scooted closer to Vance, just to emphasize that we came together.

"Ashcroft, party of two," Vance responded, as his arm snaked around my waist, pulling me in close to his side. His action was the only outward sign he was even aware that she was trying to catch his eye.

Her eyes flicked back to me for a moment, her smile tightening as she checked her book. Gesturing for us to follow her with a little less enthusiasm, she picked up two menus and led us to a quiet table next to the window.

Vance politely pulled out my chair before settling on his own. The pit viper handed us our menus, telling us our server would be with us momentarily, all the while simpering at Vance. To his credit, he merely nodded courteously and turned his attention to me. I was not quite so well-mannered. I scowled at her the whole time and mad-dogged her as she drifted back to the front of the room, swishing her hips all the way. I supposed she was hoping he was watching her leave. I turned to look back at him and found him watching me watch her with an amused look on his face. I had the decency to flush a little and grabbed my menu for camouflage. Thankfully, he made no comment.

Vance followed suit and opened his own menu, but after scanning it for a moment, he dropped it to the table in front of him and reached for my hand. Bringing it to his lips, he kissed the backs of my fingers softly before saying, "I'm really glad you are here, Mimi. I have been looking forward to this ever since you agreed to have dinner with me."

Just then, the busboy appeared, placing glasses of water on the table before us, along with the obligatory bread basket and a cruet of oil and vinegar. He then disappeared as silently as he came. Before either of us could say a word, the waiter came to take our drink orders. Vance asked if I would like to have wine with our meal, but I automatically scrunched up my nose in distaste. His eyes bulged for a moment, and the waiter looked aghast.

"What, you don't like wine?" Vance whispered urgently.

I shook my head regretfully. "No, I'm afraid I don't. I have tried several times because I know it's a very social thing to drink, but I just can't bring myself around to the flavor. I've tried many varieties, and it all just tastes too sour to me."

The waiter who looked to be in his late fifties, with thinning grayish hair, a long pointy nose with gold-rimmed glasses perched on the end of it, chimed in snootily, "I assure you, madam, you have been sampling inferior wines. You should try the services of a qualified sommelier. I am sure you could find a variety that would please your palate. Wine is for everyone."

"Do you have one on the premises?" I inquired hopefully.

"Well, err... no. We are just a small establishment." He shook his head.

My first instinct was a snarky comment in the face of his snootiness, but I decided to try to make a better impression on Vance after my less than gracious behavior with the hostess, so I just smiled politely and said, "Then I guess I will just have to order a vodka martini tonight and remember your suggestion for another time."

Vance just grinned and ordered a glass of single malt scotch.

Our waiter promised to return for our menu selections and scurried off to the bar, looking slightly chagrined. I reached for my water glass and took a sip as Vance said, "I know I didn't say it before, but you look absolutely breathtaking tonight. When you came walking out into the living room... wow. I knew I had met a beautiful girl at the airport, but the magnificent woman I'm with tonight belongs in a painting in a museum somewhere, not sitting in a booth at Chili's."

I was equally flattered by his compliment and amused by his reference to my earlier joke. I knew Vance was a light-hearted man who didn't like to let an opportunity to slip in some silliness pass him by, so I wasn't surprised his serious compliment had a dash of humor with it. He made me want to giggle with him instead of suddenly making me feel shy or awkward, which is what such an effusive compliment would have done all by itself. Either we were cut from the same cloth, or the guy just 'got me.'

"Thank you, Vance. You look very good, too." I raised my glass to my lips as if to take a drink. "I wanted to climb you like a monkey as soon as I saw you," I mumbled against the rim.

Vance cupped a hand around his ear and leaned forward. "What was that again? I didn't quite hear it. Would you care to repeat it?" he said, his laughter barely disguised by the words.

I shook my head and mouthed the word "No," at him.

He sat back grinning wildly at me. "Shall we look at these menus then, before the waiter gets back? I don't think 'Randolph' will be pleased if we aren't ready to give him our orders. He doesn't seem like a patient fellow."

Relieved, I nodded enthusiastically. "Let's do."

I contemplated the seared tuna, but ultimately decided I did not want to have fish breath and selected the chicken and fresh linguine instead.

Vance made the very manly choice of the seared New York Strip Steak. We declined to order an appetizer, choosing to nibble on the bread from the basket.

As we were waiting for our entrees, Vance studied me from across the table as he sipped his drink. "I probably shouldn't say this," he began, "but you make me want to throw any notion of self-preservation out the window for some odd reason. I know it has only been a few days since we met, but it feels like I have been waiting for this date, for you, for a very long time."

"I know exactly what you mean. On both counts. I've been very excited to see you again and..." I paused for a moment and took a deep breath.

"And?"

"Whenever I'm with you, talking to you on the phone, or hell, even just thinking about you, I feel like I'm standing on the edge of a cliff... and I have the strongest urge to close my eyes and just jump. I can't explain it, but I have this instinctive feeling that you will be at the bottom waiting to catch me." I waved my hand in front of my face and took a sip of my cocktail, blushing slightly. "I know it's silly."

Vance grabbed my hand, looking at me very intently. "Mimi, I promise you, jump or fall, I will always catch you."

My breath stuck in my throat and I didn't know what to do. We were having a very serious moment, and it made my mind spin that we were moving so quickly. I meant what I said. I felt like I was traveling down a road at breakneck speed and had absolutely no desire to put on the brakes. I instinctively felt Vance was someone I could trust, but a tiny voice was whispering to me that it was all too good to be true. However, I'd already learned so much about this man, we'd covered so much ground so quickly. Surely, the hours spent talking on the plane and on the phone, was equal to time we would have spent on several dates any other couple would have done getting to know each other? Yes, our beginning was unconventional, but to me, that didn't make it any less real.

Closing my eyes, I inhaled deeply and made a decision. I leaned forward and looked back into his eyes and whispered, "I choose to jump, Vance."

He squeezed my hand and beamed at me like I'd just made him happier than he had ever been. "Let's grab a couple parachutes and jump together, sweetheart."

"Deal." I squeezed his hand back.

Our entrees came, and we quietly enjoyed our meals, taking turns sampling from each other's plate, as if something momentous had not just occurred between us. The food was divine, but the energy humming between us was phenomenal. After our admissions, the connection between us grew stronger, more intense, the chemistry between us sparking back and forth. The silence, while not awkward at all, was filled with increasingly heated looks and occasional brushes of fingertips over the table. Soon, the temperature in the room began to feel stifling. I would have ordered another cocktail, but I didn't want to be in any way drunk on alcohol. I was intoxicated enough on his magnetism. I wanted to remember every detail of that night, so I could replay it in my head over and over again.

Vance settled the bill quickly once we finished and led me from the restaurant by the hand. We passed the pouting hostess, who I threw a victorious look over my shoulder. No, I hadn't forgotten her; yes, I was that petty, I admit it.

"Would you like to take a walk?" Vance asked. "Your shoes don't look much good for walking, but it is a nice evening. We don't have to go far if your feet start hurting."

"A walk with you sounds great, but I have to admit these are new shoes and my feet are already killing me. Why don't we just go back to Laurel's apartment and relax until you have to get back to the hotel? I'll even let you give me a foot rub." I offered.

"As eager as I am to get my hands on any part of your body I can, your feet were not exactly the first part I had in mind, I have to admit. That said, I am more than willing to massage whatever needs massaging." He said, laying the brow lift on me.

"Just the feet will do for now," I said giving his shoulder a little shove, pushing him in the direction of the street.

He laughed and stepped off the curb to hail a cab. In short order, we were securely ensconced in a taxi and zipping back toward Laurel's house. As soon as we slid into the back seat, Vance pulled me over to his side and tucked me under his arm. I felt very at home snuggled into him. I rested my head on his shoulder, pleasantly full physically and emotionally, so much so I started to feel drowsy.

Vance's voice pulled me back from the sleepy trance I was beginning to drift into. "No falling asleep on me. I might take it personally," he said warmly.

I covered my mouth as I yawned a little. "Sorry, between the meal, how comfortable I am snuggled up to you like this, and the rocking of the car as we drive, I was feeling very relaxed." I sat up and slid away from him a bit, pulling his arm from around me and taking his hand instead.

"Hey, I liked that," he pouted.

"Yeah, me too, but if you want me to stay awake, something's got to give. I promise once we get out of the car, you can put it back."

He grumbled for a minute, but brought our joined hands to his mouth, kissing the back of mine before dropping them both to his thigh and resting them there for the remainder of the trip home. I thanked him for the meal, letting him know that while I was disappointed I didn't get to partake of the onion blossom he promised, the quality of the food we had more than made up for it. He admitted that he was very relieved that it had been as good as it was since he had found the location on the internet and only had the reviews on Yelp to recommend it.

"I guess my recent streak of luck is still holding out," he said with his winning grin firmly in place.

"Since Vegas is off the table, perhaps we should consider other locales. We are remarkably close to Atlantic City, anyway," I offered.

"If you could stay through the weekend, I might be coerced into taking a side trip," he said slowly. "I won't have any meetings this weekend."

I rapidly did some calculating in my head. I had plenty of time of vacation time left at work. In fact, I'd arranged the trip because I had so much time on the books I had to use some up or I would lose it the following year. I knew my bosses would be pleased if I added another day or two to my vacation. The extra expense wasn't an issue either. I could afford a hotel room for a night or two, and I didn't think changing my flight would be too expensive.

My heart started beating faster as I contemplated the idea of taking a spur-of-the-moment trip off my original itinerary. Could I really do it? Could I be so impulsive? I looked at Vance with wide eyes. He was looking at me with a mixture of hopefulness and excitement. He nodded at me encouragingly, like he knew all the thoughts that were running through my mind because they'd just run through his, and he was just waiting for me to reach the inevitable conclusion.

A slow grin spreads across my face. "Let's do it. As soon as we get to Laurel's let's get on the computer and make this happen."

Vance pumped his fist in the air and let out a whoop that echoed loudly in the small confines of the car, causing the driver to jump. The car swerved, and horns honked loudly around us, accompanied by some shouts and vulgar hand gestures thrown our way. We simply laughed, our impetuosity making us giddy, while our driver had a few profane things to say about the crazy fare he picked up.

When we arrived at Laurel's, we raced upstairs, and I pulled out my laptop. I logged into her Wi-Fi and went straight to a trip-planning website since neither of us had been to Atlantic City before. We figured if we were going to gamble, we might as well start from the get-go. After scrolling through the reviews, we picked the hotel with the highest rating. Even though we'd decided to take a risk, there was no need to get crazy and go with something that only had three stars. We navigated to the hotel's site to book a room. We argued for a few minutes over what type of room to get. I was fine with a simple room with no frills, just standard amenities. After all, all we really needed was a bathroom, a bed, and enough room to store our belongings. Vance insisted we absolutely must have a suite with a fifteen hundred square foot bathroom, a multi-media entertainment center, and a deep soaking bath with a shower for two. He was passionate in his position, arguing that Lady Luck was a fickle bitch and must be treated with the utmost delicacy, spoiled beyond belief, coerced into smiling upon us and massaged into submission at any and all costs. I wondered out loud if he was planning on gambling or convincing her to carry his children.

He gave me a curious smirk then grabbed the computer from my lap, pulled out his credit card and made the booking. He navigated next to the car rental website and looked for available sedans. The first site he went to only had economy vehicles available.

Laughing, he looked at me. "It's not a long drive, but there is no way I'm driving a Ford Focus for any reason."

He moved on to another site, and it appeared they had all sorts of vehicles available. Even though it was more room than we needed, he was sold on a Chevy Equinox. He went ahead and reserved it, too.

He pinched his lower lip between his thumb and forefinger, causing it to pooch out a bit, making him look adorable. I twisted to face him, tucking an ankle under my thigh, and resting an elbow on the back of the sofa, to watch him think. I studied the way his hair flopped over his forehead and curled slightly behind his ears. He was probably due for a haircut, but all I wanted to do was run my fingers through the length of it. For as wavy as it was, it looked very soft and silky. I let my eyes wander to his strong profile, over the ridge of his brow and the perfectly straight, strong slope of his nose. There was a dusting of stubble over his cheeks and chin, not a heavy five o'clock shadow, you could definitely tell he shaved that morning, but it was obvious he would have to again the next day if he wanted to maintain that clean-shaven look.

He turned and caught me studying him. "What? I'm thinking," he said, misinterpreting my gaze.

"Don't hurt yourself." I couldn't help teasing him. "Just what are you risking life and limb over?"

He gave me a dirty look. "I'm trying to decide what time I will be finished tomorrow so we can leave. I want to get out of here early, so we have as much time as possible to enjoy ourselves." He reached into his pocket and pulled out his iPhone. Opening his calendar, he scrolled through the events scheduled for the next day. He smiled at me in relief.

"My only meeting is scheduled for ten. I think it will only go through lunch, so we should be able to get out of here around two." He turned back to the laptop and navigated to the American Airlines website, so I could change my flight. "Do you have any special plans with Laurel?"

My stomach dropped a little. I knew she was not going to be happy about the trip at all, given her pouting over the date that morning. I began to feel a little guilty as this trip would qualify as a violation of the "chicks before dicks" code. I looked at Vance, my sudden bout of hesitation written all over my face.

"What is it? Did you forget about something you had going on this weekend?" He looked like it was Halloween, and someone had just stolen all his candy.

"No, we haven't made any special plans. I just think she's going to be upset with me for leaving early. She kind of gave me a hard time just for going out tonight."

"Then invite her along," he offered. "I don't know if she'll be able to get away on such short notice, but she's more than welcome to join us."

I pulled my phone out of my clutch and saw that it was only eleven thirty. I scrolled to Laurel's number and smiled nervously at Vance as I listened to the line ring at the other end.

"Don't tell me your date is already over," Laurel answered without saying hello.

"No. We're done with dinner, but now we are hatching evil plans of world domination and want to know if you want in on them."

"Normally I'd be all over that, but my last attempt didn't go so well and I'm currently on probation. Long story."

"I know how it goes. In the alternative, how would you feel about an impromptu trip to Atlantic City tomorrow? Do the terms of your probation prohibit you from leaving the state?"

"Hell yeah! Great idea!" She exclaimed. I was a little startled when I heard a muffled, "Hey Pete! Do you have to work this weekend? Feel like going on a trip to Atlantic City?"

"Pete?" I mumbled into the receiver.

"Another long story," she replied. "Well, not really that long, but not something I can explain right now."

"I understand, but you are officially on notice that explaining will be done," I warned.

"No chance I could avoid that bit of emotional bonding?" she whined.

"No amount of begging, pleading or offerings from your vast selection of shoes will save you."

"Fuck."

"That about sums up your situation," I said. "We'll finish making the arrangements and I'll give you all the information when you get home."

"Good deal. We'll see you in about half an hour," she sang before ending the call.

Vance was smiling at me as I set the phone down. "So, I guess we have to book another room?"

Four

The following afternoon, we were on the Garden State Parkway heading south to Atlantic City. My iPod was plugged into the onboard docking station and Laurel and I were serenading Vance and Pete from the backseat. We'd decided to let the guys sit up front and bond with each other, but I didn't think they'd been able to do much talking over our renditions of classic eighties hair band anthems. In all honesty, we were in the backseat because I was hoping to have a chance to corner Laurel about what was going on with Pete, but she'd been able to avoid the conversation with her vocal stylings.

We arrived in Atlantic City around six that evening after struggling with some weekend traffic on the Expressway. We checked in at the hotel and agreed to meet up at eight for dinner, so we'd have some time to rest and clean up from our trip. As we were riding up in the elevator, I felt the butterflies begin to rise in my stomach again. I was going to be alone with Vance. In a hotel room. In close proximity to a bed. Hell, in the same bed, at some point. I hadn't actually thought about this part when we made these plans. How had I overlooked this? Had he? I tried to look over at him out of the corner of my eye. He was lounging against the side of the elevator and laughing with Pete and Laurel about something Laurel just said. I had no idea what since I was having my own mini-Fukushima over in my corner of the elevator. He seemed relaxed and not the slightest bit perturbed or even excited. There was no evidence of elevated pulse, nor telltale sheen of perspiration on his brow. I began to feel insulted. Shouldn't he have at least been marginally excited about having this time alone with me? Did he think I was a sure thing? I huffed indignantly. If that's what he was thinking, he could just go ahead and think again. I crossed my arms and thrust out a hip. I'd show him easy.

Somewhere in the deeper recesses of my mind, I realized that I was being irrational, and this was probably the result of my sudden case of nerves, but the psycho that had taken up residence in my frontal lobe was in control and she was taking no prisoners.

Pete and Laurel exited on a lower floor than ours since they had one of the regular rooms. The elevator was then empty except for me and Vance, who smiled at me guilelessly. Of course, in my state of mind, I interpreted it as a leer and moved to the other side of the small cab and glared at him. His face fell into a look of confusion.

"Is something wrong, Mimi?" he asked.

"No. Why would you think anything is wrong?" I responded airily.

"Um, maybe because you scurried to the other side of the elevator like I had some kind of communicable disease and are looking at me like I just farted in a room full of your relatives?"

My lips twisted despite my fit of madness. I tried to hold onto it, keeping my arms tightly crossed in front of me and back pressed to the wall, but my temper crumbled in the face of his furrowed brow and the look of genuine concern on his face.

I sighed. "I was just thinking about our sleeping arrangements."

"And the idea of sharing a bed with me makes you think violent thoughts if your body language is any indication," he surmised as the doors opened to our floor.

We made our way to our room silently. He opened the door for me and I strolled in unencumbered as Vance was carrying both our bags. I looked around at the elegantly appointed suite, before turning back to him, feeling sheepish. I knew my behavior wasn't making any sense, and I was beginning to feel embarrassed, but I didn't know how to explain my temporary break with reality.

Vance dropped our bags by the door and moved to the sofa. He fell into it, spreading his arms across the back.

"Why don't you sit down and explain to me what is going on, Mimi?"

I sat down in the chair across from him and folded my hands in my lap. I unclasped them, then clasped them again. I ran a hand over my hair before resting an elbow in my lap and covering my mouth with my hand. He looked at me expectantly but didn't rush me as if we had all the time in the world for me to spit out whatever was screwing with my head.

"I'm sorry. I just had a bit of a freak-out moment. I'm not sure why. It just dawned on me that I never really considered the implications of us sharing a room, and there only being one bed and all, and...," I realized I'd started to ramble, and paused, taking a deep breath.

"And you started thinking I had made certain assumptions about where our relationship was headed," he offered.

"Well, yes. I suppose so. It kind of offended me," I admitted.

"I see." He nodded, considering my words carefully as he crossed his arms behind his head.

"I know I was being silly. You've been nothing but great. I don't know what got into me," I began to stammer. I stopped, blowing out a big breath. I decided 'Screw it,' and to be completely open with him. The worst thing that could happen would be that he thought I was totally mental, which probably wouldn't be too much of a distance from where we already were. I didn't think I had too much to lose.

"I got nervous. I really like you, more than anyone I've ever met in my life. The more we are together, the more I feel this connection between us, and it is so powerful. I feel like it should scare me, or I should feel threatened by it, or something, but I don't feel any of that. I want it to grow so big that it consumes me. Sometimes, I just want to get lost in you.

"In the elevator, I realized that I never even paused to consider our sleeping arrangements even once. I don't have a time frame for how much time is required before I sleep with someone, but I'm also not known for sleeping around. I wait until I feel comfortable, but at least I stop and take a mental inventory to be sure I am comfortable. I didn't even give it a thought with you. It was as if we had been together for years and had slept together a million times, it was such a natural thing.

"That was what did my head in. I had a moment of insecurity. I looked over at you and you looked so at ease. In the back of my mind, I wondered if you were having any of the same surreal thoughts I was, or if you were just more comfortable with the intensity between us, or if I was totally misreading the situation and this was just something far more casual for you. Unfortunately, this translated to a much more psychotic thought process in the front of my brain and I attributed it all to you just wanting to get in my pants because that was much easier to confront than everything else."

He smiled broadly. "That's what I've been looking for, right there."

"Uh, what?" I said, now more confused than before.

"That kind of unguarded honesty. You just put it all out there, showing me all that was inside you. Not just your head, but your heart as well." He leaned forward, resting his forearms on his knees, and clasping his hands between them. "This is what draws me to you, Mimi. Your ability to take those kinds of risks with your emotions rather than wrapping yourself up in some kind of armor and hiding away. Most people are afraid to be vulnerable, but you aren't. You let people see you, really see you, and that's beautiful. Your exterior is very attractive, don't get me wrong. I think you are very sexy and I imagined having my hands all over you before I ever even spoke to you, but now that I know you, now that I have seen inside you, I crave your heart more than your body could ever satisfy."

I couldn't stop the tears that filled the corners of my eyes. If I'd had any doubts about him feeling the weight of the connection between us, they'd just been obliterated. He didn't say he loved me, but he might as well have. He'd said he wanted—no craved—my heart. What he didn't know at the time was he had already won it. I may have offered a little of myself just then, but Vance had always been the one completely unguarded, giving himself in large amounts, holding nothing back when we shared ourselves, our lives, our pasts with each other. Vance was the one who lived fearlessly. If I were to be perfectly honest, it was me who was doing the craving of hearts. How silly was I in the elevator? Vance and I had never even shared so much as a kiss. We had that near kiss before dinner the night before, but in the excitement of planning the trip, the opportunity never rose again. The night ended with just a warm hug at the door with Laurel and Pete in the living room watching us say goodbye. I was overcome with the urge to rectify that situation immediately. He had just given a very touching speech about how he wanted me emotionally far more than he was interested in me on a physical level, but what better way to express those feelings than by rubbing up against him like a cat marking its territory? It didn't make a whole lot of sense to me either, but I was still going for it.

I launched myself across the space between us and he caught me with a look of surprise as I straddled his lap. My lips crashed down on his as I wound my arms around his neck and tangled my fingers in his hair. The texture was as thick and silky as I imagined, but his lips—oh his lips!—were softer than any man's had a right to be. I had this stray thought that he must go through Chapstick like a fiend, but the thought was chased away as I heard him moan softly. His arms wrapped around my back, pressing me into him even as his mouth softened against mine, slowing down our kiss to something gentler, something we could savor.

He took his time, only giving me the softest of kisses on my lips, my cheeks, and my chin. He reached up and brushed my bangs from my forehead before cupping my face in both hands and looking deep into my eyes. He seemed to take in every detail before he moved in again, touching his mouth to mine, his tongue slipping out this time to swipe over my lower lip. I gasped softly against his lips as he dipped in again for a long slow caress against my tongue before exploring the recess of my mouth. He was very languid in his discovery as if he was totally unconcerned with anything but unlocking the secret to my passion. His hands joined the gentle rhythm of his tongue, sliding over my back, tracing the curve of my spine, and finally settling on the swell of my ass. He softly squeezed the firm flesh, gripping it with his fingers just enough to inspire me to move against him. My hips slid forward over his thighs as he pressed me against his body, my knees squeezing tight against his trim hips as our bodies connected in the space where our need was most evident. His thick shaft strained against his zipper as it pressed against my soft core through my shorts, and the sensation only made me want more. More of his mouth, more of his hands, more of him. I slid my hands down his chest and began to undo the top button of his shirt, nuzzling and placing soft kisses along the length of his neck.

I traced my tongue along the curve of muscle the gap in the material exposed before he pulled my hands away. I leaned back and look at him questioningly, unsure as to why he stopped me since I was rather certain we were both enjoying the moment.

"As much as I like where you were headed, Mimi, we need to get cleaned up and ready for dinner," he said.

"You can actually think of something like dinner right now? I must not be very good at this if you have anything on your mind besides—"

"Trust me," he cut in before I could say anything further, "it is taking a fantastic amount of self-control to not circumvent our plans for the evening. However, from the little I know of Laurel so far, I do not expect that she would allow us to stand them up without harassing us endlessly. This I can't allow, because when I take you to bed, Mimi, I won't let you out until the sun comes up—a day or two later—and I won't tolerate any interruptions."

I think my insides liquefied from the heat in his gaze and in his words as he said the last part. He was right about one thing, if I hadn't needed to after our drive here, I surely needed to clean up after that little interlude. I leaned forward and gave him a lingering kiss, one full of promise and hope for the future. We'd come to some important understandings in that last hour and shared some amazing moments of intimacy. I realized there was so much more to look forward to and I was eager to experience it all with Vance.

Regretfully, I slid off his lap as he stood. He grabbed my hand and brought it to his lips, his eyes promising me everything I never knew I was missing, but now desperately wanted. I didn't know how to move on from that moment. It seemed wrong somehow, to just go about something as mundane as getting ready to go out to dinner when something so wondrous had occurred between us. I didn't know what I thought should happen next but getting ready to meet Laurel and Pete wasn't it.

Vance retrieved our bags from the door before leading me into the bedroom. He handed me mine and waved toward the door on the other side of the room. "Why don't you take the first shower while I unpack? It will only take me a few minutes to shower and get ready."

The bathroom was gorgeous, with marble floors and countertops and a huge soaking bathtub in the center of the room. I wished I had time to luxuriate in it, but I had just enough to take a quick shower and speed through my hair and make-up if I was going to leave Vance enough to shower. Putting my toiletries in the stall, I turned on the spray which the website touted as a shower "for two." At the time, I had wicked images of Vance and I enjoying some sexy fun time in it, but after our conversation, I didn't think this trip would to allow for any sexy fun time at all, since he said when we finally got to something like that we'd be alone for an extended period of time without interruptions. We weren't likely to have any time like that this trip if I knew Laurel, which I totally did. I wasn't quite sure how I felt about that. On one hand, I was disappointed that I'd have to wait until we were both back in Los Angeles, which wasn't for another week. On the other hand, well... Yay! He did say a day or two in bed with no interruptions. Couldn't really be disappointed by that. Unless he was really bad at it, but judging by his kissing, I didn't think that I'd find myself a prisoner to some horrible sex.

As the steam from the warm shower began to fill the room, I hurriedly undressed and jumped in. The spray across my skin felt heavenly, heating my muscles, and loosening them from the long car drive from the city. I rushed through shampooing and conditioning my hair, soaping up my body and doing a quick shave of all my pertinent body parts again. You know, that just in case thing again.

Turning off the water, I wrapped my hair in one of the amazing towels hanging on the rack and my body in one of the luxurious fluffy bathrobes courteously provided by the hotel. It was too steamy in the bathroom for me to dress in there. I'd never get dry, and I had lotions and creams to apply before I got dressed. I didn't want to be a sticky mess when I attempted to put on the little black dress I'd brought to impress Vance.

I grabbed my bag and walked back into the bedroom. Vance was sitting on the bed, leaning back against the headboard with his legs outstretched in front of him, shoes off, television remote in hand as he flicked through the TV stations. He was the picture of a guy kicking back. All he needed was a beer in his other hand.

"It's all yours." My voice cracked a little on the words. "At least until I need it again."

He looked over at me with a small laugh. "You sure? I can wait until you're totally done. It really won't take me long at all."

"I'm sure. Besides, I need this room to do part of my routine. I can't do some of it in the bathroom while it's still humid in there." I informed him.

"I'm sure it's some secret lady ritual, so I won't even bother to ask," he responded as he stood and picked up his bag. He pointed over his shoulder toward the bathroom. "You know where to find me if you need me."

"I'm sure I'll be just fine but do me a favor and knock before you leave the bathroom just in case I'm not done with my regimen."

"You mean in case you're naked." He wiggled his eyebrows at me as he leaned against the door jamb.

I shot him an evil glare and hefted the bottle of lotion I'd pulled out of my bag as if testing its weight to pitch at him. He held his hands up in surrender and straightened up from the doorway. "Point taken. No need for violence. I'll knock." He shut the door behind him with a soft click.

Thirty minutes later, we were in the elevator riding down to meet Pete and Laurel in the lobby. After a brief discussion, we decided to head over to the boardwalk to find a restaurant and do some gambling afterward. We eventually ended up at a steakhouse at Caesar's. We had a great time, with the conversation flowing easily. Pete was cracking jokes and pretty much keeping us entertained with interesting stories from his job. We particularly enjoyed the story about the stop he made of a conspicuously drunk woman, who just happened to be model beautiful. She threw herself at him, offering him all sorts of sexual favors and baring certain parts of her anatomy if he would just let her go with a warning. Unfortunately for her, Pete arrested her anyway. At her court hearing, she was much more subdued and far less friendly towards him. No body parts were exposed.

I was also very pleased to see Laurel and Vance hitting it off well. They chatted and teased each other as if they had known each other for years. It made me happy that Vance fit in since it only solidified in my mind how right we were for each other.

Rather than linger over a few cocktails after our meal, we were all itching to hit the casinos. We decided to stay at Caesar's for a while to see if Lady Luck was in residence.

"That bit—" Vance began. I reached up and pressed my fingers to his lips with a cautioning glare. "I mean that beautiful lady..." he started again, looking to me for approval. I nodded, and he continued, "--is traveling with us, so it doesn't matter where Mimi and I go to gamble. You and Laurel are on your own, Pete," he said with a chuckle.

Pete gave him a wry grin. "We'll just see about that, buddy. I'll wager with you right now. It's ten o'clock. We'll meet you back here in the lobby at two, and we'll compare winnings. We'll just see who Lady Luck is with tonight."

"Oh, this is a bet I can't lose," Vance said, slinging an arm over my shoulders and sticking his other hand out to shake. "This woman is luck personified, sucker."

Pete tossed his arm around Laurel and pulled her in close. "Heh, that's only because she's been spending time with this one." He kissed her cheek before shaking Vance's hand firmly. Laurel and I simply rolled our eyes and mouthed the word "Boys" to each other. Pete steered her away from us and they wandered off to parts unknown, presumably to win a fortune and then rub our noses in it.

Vance and I strolled past numerous gaming tables, blackjack, roulette, and craps. We stood for a while watching each game, enjoying the energy of the players as their excitement of playing the odds infected those around them. Every now and then, Vance would look at me questioningly to see if I wanted to play, but I'd just shake my head and we'd move on. I was too intimidated by the tables. I was much more the kind of person to park myself in front of a poker machine with a cocktail and feed bills into it all night long. I didn't like the pressure of playing with other people. Even though blackjack is arguably still a solitary game between you and the dealer, you can piss off the guy next to you if you hit when he thinks you should have stayed and you take the card that would have made his hand. I'd seen it before and it's not pretty. So, I was content to stick with a machine that was happy to take my money and never judged my choices. It was a beautiful relationship, really.

I shared my preferences with Vance, so he led me to the slot machines. We found an area with twenty-five cent machines, which was just about my speed. I chose one on the end of the row, explaining that seat placement was everything.

"Sitting in the middle of the row is unlucky," I informed him. "Everyone likes the end seats, so these are the machines that are more highly played, thus making them bloated with money and just waiting to pay off."

Vance asked, "Doesn't it also stand to reason that they may have paid off recently before we came over? There's no way to know."

I stroked my machine, cooing softly to it. "You wouldn't do that to me, would you baby? You have been sitting here waiting for me all this time, haven't you, your big jackpot belly just waiting to spew its guts into my waiting hands?" I looked at Vance with a raised eyebrow as if daring him to challenge my statement. He looked simultaneously amused and disturbed by my display with the machine.

I shrugged and fed a twenty into the machine, hitting the "Bet Max" button. I was dealt a natural straight. I looked over at Vance with a smug look on my face. Pushing all the hold buttons, I collected my winning credits and pressed "Deal." We spent an hour playing and ordering free cocktails from the roving waitress as my credit tally slowly climbed higher. I heard Vance alternately curse and cheer from the seat next to me. At the end of the hour, we turned to each other and compared our balances. Vance was up a whopping ten dollars, while I had collected an additional one hundred and fifty, over our initial investment of twenty dollars. I figured that wasn't too bad considering it was easy to keep feeding money into the machine and lose track of where you started altogether.

Vance let me know he needed a few minutes to get up and stretch but admitted what he really wanted was to hit the craps table. I figured I should quit while I was ahead, at least for the night. I wanted to do my part to help Vance win his bet with Pete, and any more time in front of the machines might undo all the progress I'd made. I'd spent enough time in front of them to know how your luck can turn on a dime and your credit balance can be depleted in a matter of minutes.

We headed over to the tables, and Vance stopped at one that seemed particularly lively. I had no idea what was going on, all I knew was some guy at one end of the table would roll some dice, people would shout and everybody either cheered or groaned when the dice stopped. Chips would go back and forth, and then the process started all over again. I didn't get it, but everyone seemed to be really enjoying themselves.

Vance pulled out a few bills out of his wallet and put them on the table. This confused me since everyone else seemed to be playing with chips, but I watched in silence. A waitress came by asking for drink orders, so I took advantage and ordered a dirty martini for me and a glass of scotch for Vance. I turned back, and Vance mysteriously had a tray of chips in front of him. I watched as dice were rolled, more people cheered, a guy with a stick thingy moved chips around on the table which I assumed meant people lost when he scraped them toward himself.

Our drinks eventually arrived, and I was grateful because by this time I was getting fidgety from boredom. The table had calmed down from the raucous tone it had when we first walked up.

Vance thanked me for his scotch, studying me briefly as he took a sip. "You're bored out of your mind, aren't you?" he asked.

I sighed unhappily. "I'm sorry, but yes. I don't understand a thing that's going on, and everyone seems to have lost their enthusiasm for the game, so it's not even entertaining to watch anymore. I'm sorry if I'm spoiling it for you."

"You could never spoil anything for me. Let me see if I can try to make some sense of this for you. That guy with the dice at the end of the table? He's the 'shooter.' He has to roll a seven or eleven on his first roll. If he rolls a two, three or twelve, he's 'crapped out.' If he hits any other number that becomes 'the point.' If the shooter rolls the point number, that's a win, but if he rolls a seven, he loses. Meanwhile, everyone else at the table, like you and me, can place bets on whether he is going to roll the point or another number. There is a little more to it, but that's the basic gist." He looked at me closely, and I was sure my eyes were glazed over because even with that short and sweet summary, I still didn't really understand it and to be perfectly honest, I didn't much care.

"You still don't understand, do you?" he asked.

"I think I have a mental block when it comes to with anything that has the word 'crap' in its title," I said dryly. "Would you be upset if I went over to those slots just over there and amused myself while you play here?" I asked, pointing to a bank of machines just beyond the tables with big wheels overhead, garish flashing neon and a progressive jackpot sign rapidly racking up figures as we looked on.

Vance smiled sympathetically and shook his head. "Not if you give me a kiss for good luck before you go."

"Place your bet and pucker up, hot stuff, because you're about to get very, very lucky." I purred, giving him a scorching look.

He pulled me close and whispered in my ear, "Careful now, precious. There's only so much luck a man can take in a public place."

I laughed out loud before taking his face in both my hands and pulling him toward me. I exhaled softly, letting my breath fan over his lips before gently rubbing my lower lip against his. I nuzzled against him once, twice before trailing my tongue along the seam of his mouth, requesting entry. His lips slowly parted, allowing me in, and I licked delicately against his tongue, moving in a tender dance of sweet promise. I didn't linger too long, only enough time to leave him wanting, before pulling away. I gave him my best beguiling smile and whispered, "Win big, Daddy. Baby needs new shoes."

He laughed as he reached into his coat pocket for his wallet. "Crazy dame. Do you need any money?" He asked, pulling out a few bills and stuffing them into the neckline of my dress even as I shook my head no. He just grinned, turned me in the direction of the slot machines and patted me on the ass.

About half an hour later, I was sitting at one of the dollar machines, (Vance had stuffed five hundred dollars in my bra; I figured it was his money, why not go big?), and sipping my fourth dirty martini. It was a neat little machine, one where if you got the symbol of a wheel anywhere in the reel, you got a free spin of the big wheel at the top of the machine. If you got that spin, it was an instant win, whatever dollar figure you landed on the big wheel. If you landed on the progressive line, then you won the jackpot.

I wasn't paying too much attention, because, hey, fourth martini when the wheel symbol popped up in my pay line. I pushed the bonus spin button and took another sip of my drink, looking around the machine to see if I could get a glimpse of Vance at the craps table. I could just barely make out the top of his head, as the table seemed to have gotten very lively again, with lots of cheers and waving arms obscuring my view of him.

A shrill ringing and a flash of lights, followed by a scream from the woman next to me, caused me to jump and spill my drink all over the front of my dress. I turned back to my machine to see what all the fuss was about when the lady grabbed my arm and yelled directly into my ear.

"Ohmigod, girl! You just won the jackpot!" I blinked twice at her as I stuck my finger in my ear in an attempt to restore my hearing. Looking forward, I realized that, yep, that was indeed my machine that was about to cause someone an epileptic seizure. My eyes immediately looked to the progressive jackpot screen which appeared to be frozen. Did it say what I thought it said? Ten thousand, two hundred thirty-two dollars and fifty-three cents. How the hell did one get fifty-three cents on a dollar machine?

I turned to the very nice, forty-something lady next to me again. She fit every stereotype I had ever heard about Jersey women. She had black hair sprayed up-to-there, a ton of makeup on, red fingernails so long they could be described as talons and a skirt so short, it could probably have doubled as a belt. When she spoke, however, there was no trace of an accent. She was probably from Boise.

I asked, "What do I do now? I don't think these machines hold that much money."

She grinned at me wildly, her eyes glittering with excitement. You'd think she was the one who'd hit the jackpot. "Just sit tight, sweetheart. A casino employee will be along in a jiffy. I'll stay here with you until they get here. You don't want to be alone and have some asshole try to take advantage of you, or worse."

"What do you mean? Like someone would try to jack me for my machine? Don't they have security cameras and stuff around here to prevent that?" I gasped, practically throwing myself in front of my machine. Perhaps the alcohol in my system made me a touch over-dramatic.

She patted my knee. "People are just crazy, honey. Money and desperation, both of which are in ample supply here, do strange things to people. I didn't mean to scare you. I've got your back. Don't worry, nothing is going to happen."

I looked at her a little dubiously but decided to go with it.

Just then, a cashier, in the company of a rather large security officer and a man in a suit, walked up to us. The cashier had a set of keys and brushed me aside to open my machine. I had no idea what she was doing but guessed the contraption had to be taken out of play for a while.

I presumed the guy in the suit was some sort of hotel official. My suspicion was proved correct when he stuck out his hand. "Congratulations. I am Mr. DeAngelo, the casino supervisor for the evening. Your name is...?"

I stood and shook his hand. "Um, Mimi Bishop." I swayed a little on my feet, partially from the alcohol, partially because I was dazed by the surreal quality of the moment. Had I really just won more than ten thousand dollars? American money?

My new friend patted me on the shoulder and whispered, "Congratulations, honey. I hope your good luck rubs off on me." Then she disappeared into the crowd that had begun to form around us.

The security guard moved in a little closer to me as Mr. DeAngelo placed his hand on my elbow, gently guiding me away from the machine. "If you would come with me, Ms. Bishop, we have some paperwork for you to complete before we can distribute your winnings."

"Sure," I said, as a stray thought popped into my head. "Is that where I get to take the picture with the big check?" Stupid martinis.

He chuckled in reply. "Yes, Ms. Bishop. That's where you take the picture with the big check."

Five

An hour, a mountain of paperwork, one photo and cashier's check later, I was wandering around the casino looking for Vance. He wasn't at the craps table where I left him earlier, and he was nowhere in its vicinity, either. My warm glow had long since worn off and was beginning to be replaced with concern. I dug into my purse for my phone, only to find I'd left it in the room at our hotel.

As I wandered about, I happened by a small ladies clothing store just off the casino floor when inspiration stuck, temporarily putting my concerns on a shelf. Looking at the mannequin in the window, I grinned to myself and slipped inside. I strolled out about 20 minutes later with a devilish gleam in my eye and light package in my hand.

I returned to my search, hoping I would eventually happen upon him, but had no luck. Then I remembered we were supposed to meet Laurel and Pete back in the lobby at two. Of course, being a casino, there were no damned clocks anywhere. I stopped a passing couple and asked for the time, pleased to learn I had ten minutes before we were supposed to meet.

I made my way to the lobby, but no one else was there yet. I spied a grouping of chairs and tiredly dropped into one to wait. Promptly at two, a very loud and obviously "happy" couple came tripping into the lobby. Pete and Laurel staggered over to me with big Kool-Aid smiles plastered on their faces.   They each flopped into an empty chair, giggling like fools.

"It looks like you both had a good time," I said appraisingly.

"I'll say we did!"   Laurel exclaimed, far too exuberantly, in my opinion.

"Oh yeah," Pete chimed in. "Your man, Vance, better be prepared to pay up!"

"Is that so?" I murmured quietly. They were both looking very smug despite, or maybe because of, their obvious intoxication.   I wondered how much they won. Unless Vance managed to lose his ass at the craps table, I didn't think Pete and Laurel would top my winnings.

"Where is Vance anyway?" Laurel's brows drew down in a frown. "Don't tell me he's ashamed to show his face." The thought obviously amused them both because they erupted in another fit of giggles.

"Actually, I don't know," I said. "We split up at one point tonight, and I lost track of him. I was wandering around looking for him before I finally came here, thinking this is where he would be at two. I would have called him, but I forgot my phone in our room back at the hotel."

Pete pulled his cell phone out of his pocket. "Let me just give the man a call. He gave me his number earlier, in case we split up and needed to regroup." He scrolled through his contacts, then put the phone to his ear.

"What's up, loser?" he practically shouted into the phone. "We're all here in the lobby waiting for

84

you. What? Why?" He paused for a long time, obviously listening as Vance talked. "I see. Well don't worry, she's here with us. I'll find out what happened and get back to you as soon as I can, buddy. Hang tight."

Pete ended the call and looked at me curiously. "What happened earlier tonight, after you left Vance, Mimi?"

"What? I played slots for an hour. Why?" I said hesitantly, not wanting to give away my secret.

"Did anything unusual happen while you were playing slots?" he asked suspiciously.

He clearly knew something was up, but I wasn't going to admit to anything without some hard evidence against me. "Why would you think that?"

"Well, it seems our boy, Vance, saw you being led through the casino by a security officer and a Mafioso-looking type. He went to find out what was going on, but he needed to cash out his winnings. By the time he did that, you were nowhere to be seen. Consequently, our friend made something of a spectacle of himself."

I covered my mouth, a half-gasp, half-giggle. "Oh, no."

"Oh, yes. In his words, he, and I quote, 'went ape-shit.' So, I ask you again, Mimi. Did something happen?"

"Yes, but it wasn't anything bad. Where is Vance now?" I asked, trying to steer the conversation onto the more pressing issue.

"They're holding him at security. They're under the impression he might be some kind of threat to you. He tried to explain that he is here with you, but they've basically put him in a room and left him there. They haven't really given him much of a chance to sort things out."

I jumped to my feet in a panic. "We have to go help him right now! I'll talk to the security officers and explain we're here together, so they realize this is all a big misunderstanding."

Pete and Laurel followed me through the casino back to the security offices. In the small reception-like area that I so recently walked out of in a much different mood, there was a female officer working on what appeared to be some paperwork. She had a very no-nonsense look about her. I marched forward, intent on resolving matters as quickly and efficiently as possible.

"Excuse me, ma'am. I'm here about a gentleman who was brought in about forty-five minutes to an hour ago. His name is Vance Ashcroft. There has been a big misunderstanding that I'd like to help clear up."

She gave me a look that told me she was going to be less than helpful.

"There is no misunderstanding. Mr. Ashcroft is considered a threat to one of our guests and will remain detained until the authorities arrive to take him into custody."

"That is completely unnecessary. If only I could explain to someone in charge—"

"As far as you're concerned lady, I'm in charge. You can bond your friend out once he's been charged and his bail has been set."

"Jail? Bond? Bail!!!" I sputtered. "This is absolutely ridiculous. This is really all one colossal mistake."

"Mr. Ashcroft was attempting to follow one of our jackpot winners. He admitted it himself. There is no mistake, Miss..." I finally reached the end of my patience with this aggravating woman. "Bishop! My name is Mimi Bishop! I am that jackpot winner! Mr. Ashcroft is my boyfriend!"

I heard Pete and Laurel mumble "Jackpot winner?" behind me. I turned and shushed them with an exasperated look.

The security officer snorted. "Sure, you are. Like I said, you can help your friend once he's down at the police station. Now, please leave."

"There would be a problem with that since Mr. Ashcroft is our ride! Please call Mr. DeAngelo. I'm sure he will be happy to help sort this matter out. He will definitely confirm my identity for you." I motioned to the telephone on her desk with my hand. "Go on, call. I'll wait."

She rolled her eyes at me. "Fine," she said tersely.

I turned my back to her and joined Pete and Laurel as we waited for Mr. DeAngelo to show up. I gave Pete my best stink-eye.

"You could have stepped in at any time, Mr. Police Officer. Couldn't you have thrown some weight around or something? Used some of your connections to spring my boyfriend?"

"We're not downtown yet, Mimi. Once the police show up, I might be able to do something, but with these guys, I don't think my badge would get us very far. Besides, you just marched right up there like a little tyrant and started making your own demands. You seemed to be doing just fine."

"Hmph. I think Suzie Security would have been far more impressed with you than you think. She obviously wasn't with me. Still isn't. I think she's expecting DeAngelo, the casino supervisor who helped me earlier, to throw me out of here."

"So, you won a jackpot?" Laurel did her best to interject casually.

"Not now, Laurel." I gave her my best withering stare. She raised her hands in submission.

"Fine, fine. You can't blame me for being curious."

The door opened, and Mr. DeAngelo walked in looking just as fresh as he did earlier. It was amazing to me that anyone could look so polished at nearly two-thirty in the morning.

"Miss Bishop! What a surprise to see you again so soon. I hope you haven't had any issues in our casino since you left the office. I heard about the unfortunate event with the gentleman who was attempting to follow you. You can rest easy knowing he was easily subdued and detained." Mr. DeAngelo did his best to look concerned and reassuring at the same time.

"Yes, about that. There has been a terrible misunderstanding. The man that has been detained is my boyfriend, Vance Ashcroft."

He frowned heavily, his brows drawing together, causing deep grooves in his forehead. "No, that can't be possible."

"I assure you, not only is it possible, it's what happened. He was only following me because he saw you and the security officer leading me away through the casino. He thought I was in trouble and was concerned. Surely you can understand his distress when he was refused information and not allowed to come to my aid in a situation when he feared I needed assistance," I explained in my most reasonable voice.

Mr. DeAngelo's shoulders sagged, and he looked a lot less polished than he did when he walked in. He pinched the bridge of his nose between his thumb and forefinger and called out in a slightly strangled voice, "Karen?"

"Yes, Mr. DeAngelo?" Suzy Security responded in a much more pleasant tone than she used with me.

"By any chance did anyone happen to speak to Mr. Ashcroft about why he was attempting to follow Miss Bishop? I mean, in detail, after he was brought to security?"

"Yes, as far as I know. However, it was determined that his story wasn't credible and the decision to call the authorities was made."

Mr. DeAngelo tilted his head back, looking at the ceiling. "Did anyone attempt to contact Miss Bishop to confirm the veracity of his story before deciding to call the police?"

"Well, no." Suzy—Karen—replied somewhat chagrined.

"Please escort Mr. Ashcroft out here immediately, Karen." He said with a long-suffering sigh.

She jumped up from her place behind the desk and scurried through the door just to the right of it. Mr. DeAngelo looked at me with an apologetic smile but didn't say anything. I knew I should feel grateful that they were looking out for my well-being, even if they were a little overzealous. If it were a stranger sitting in the other room rather than Vance, I would have had a much different mindset. Unfortunately, it was Vance and I was frustrated at the gymnastics I had to go through just to try to explain what happened.

Before long, the door opened again, and Karen walked in with Vance, who looked harassed. When he saw me, the stress melted from his face. He quickly walked over and took me in his arms.

"I was so worried about you," he began. "These ass-clowns wouldn't tell me anything, so I tried a little too hard to 'persuade' them, I guess. They weren't very receptive to my tactics."

I laughed quietly. "I'm sorry about the whole mess. I should have looked for you before they brought me back here to let you know what happened, but I was in such a daze, I just blindly followed them."

"What did happen, Mimi? Why were you detained?"

"You mean they didn't tell you?"

"No, they only accused me of being some sort of threat to one of their guests and stuffed me in that backroom and left me there. They never talked to me again," he explained.

"I wasn't detained. I won the progressive jackpot on the machines I was playing, and they brought me back to the casino supervisor's office to complete their paperwork and give me the winnings."

Mr. DeAngelo mumbled quietly, but with a very amused sounding voice, "And to take the picture with the big check."

Vance glared at him, but still wrapped in his embrace as I was, I rubbed his chest soothingly.

"Yes, to take the picture with the big check. That was very important to me at the time." I reached into my purse and pulled out the Polaroid they gave me and showed it to Vance.

He studied it for a moment, smiling, then his eyes bulged, and he whispered to me, "You won ten thousand dollars?"

"Ten thousand, two hundred thirty-two dollars and fifty-three cents." I nodded rather smugly while whispering back, "I think we're a shoe-in to win the bet against Pete and Laurel."

He leaned closer and breathed into my ear, "I do too, considering I won eight thousand playing craps."

I leaned back and gave him a wide smile. "It's too bad you never settled on the terms of this wager."

His face screwed up as he realized they did, indeed, forget to actually bet anything.

At that moment, Mr. DeAngelo broke in, offering his olive branch. "On behalf of Caesar's management, I'd like to offer our sincerest apologies to you and your friends, Mr. Ashcroft. In our haste to ensure Miss Bishop's safety, we were less than courteous, less than objective and reasonable with you. We would like to rectify this error in judgment and make amends if possible. We value your patronage and do not want this ugly incident to entirely spoil your experience at our casino. Can I offer you all vouchers for a complimentary stay at our hotel and free meals while you are here, perhaps?"

I opened my mouth to tell him we live in Los Angeles and it was not likely we would ever come back to this crappy town, much less his crappier hotel, but Vance cut me off.

"Your offer is very generous, Mr. DeAngelo, and we will happily accept. I have no hard feelings. As you said, you were looking out for someone precious to me, so I can hardly be upset about that." Once again, I realized Vance was a much more gracious person than I was.

Mr. DeAngelo looked relieved and excused himself to retrieve said vouchers. I was about to launch into a frustrated lecture at Vance, who cut me off before I could begin.

"I know what you're going to say. I have no intentions of coming back either, but Pete and Laurel live close by, so maybe they can make use of the vouchers. If nothing else, they can give them to their friends, who can use them. At least that way, someone will benefit from this shitty situation."

I smiled at Vance's logic. He was thinking a few steps ahead of the situation whereas I only saw what was in front of me. I could learn a thing or two from him.

Mr. DeAngelo returned with two vouchers for three-night stays for each of us. We offered thanks all around and finally left the security offices once and for all. We breathed a collective sigh of relief as we reached the casino floor and made our way to the hotel's exit. We were all eager to leave the premises.

Everyone was quiet as we walked to the car. Once comfortably settled inside and on the road back to the hotel, Vance cleared his throat and looked in the rear-view at Pete. "So, brother. What was your total for the evening?"

"Well," Pete—who suddenly seemed far less confident than he did when he and Laurel came stumbling into Caesar's—said, "we initially lost six hundred between the two of us, but our luck changed at the blackjack tables and we walked away fifty-five hundred in the black." By the time he finished, some of his confidence had returned and he sat back in his seat with his arms folded across his chest. Laurel leaned against his side, giggling softly.

I shook my head a little and looked over at Vance knowingly. He was nodding as he responded. "Wow, that's really good. Congratulations. I lost a thousand initially at the craps table, but Mimi won one hundred and fifty at the draw poker machines."

Laurel cackled from the backseat and Pete clapped his hands together and whooped. "I knew we'd have you beat! Now you have to pay up!"

"Only two small problems with that, buddy. One, I'm not finished. Our luck changed once we split up. After Mimi left to go play slots, I started winning at the craps table. My net winnings were seven thousand one hundred. Then, Mimi hit the progressive jackpot on her slot machine and she won ten thousand, two hundred dollars."

"Ten thousand two hundred thirty-two dollars and fifty-three cents, to be exact," I chimed in happily.

"Yes, Mimi. Ten thousand, two hundred thirty-two dollars and fifty-three cents. So that brings our total to seventeen thousand three hundred dollars." He looked at me. "I'm rounding down, babe. I know there's two hundred thirty-two dollars and fifty-three cents to add to that total."

I nodded enthusiastically.

He continued, looking back at Pete in the rearview again "So it would appear, my friend, that we smoked you."

Pete sighed heavily from the backseat. "And what would the second problem be?"

I turned and grinned wildly at him. "In your haste to measure dicks against each other, you two bright-barts failed to determine what you were wagering for. Nobody won anything except bragging rights. So, for now, Pete, Vance's dick is bigger than yours. Eleven thousand, eight hundred inches bigger." I looked at Vance and stage-whispered, "That's a lot of dick."

He just grinned and nodded.

Pete and Laurel just groaned from the backseat. They huddled together trying to console each other while Vance patted my knee and murmured, "Well done, babe."

Once we got back to our hotel, Pete pulled Vance aside as we were walking towards the elevators. Vance waved us on, so Laurel and I continued to the bank of lifts.

"I wonder what that's all about," Laurel speculated. "Pete has been a little weird since about halfway into the trip home."

"Weird, how?" I questioned.

"I don't know. Kind of quiet and fidgety, I guess."

"I'd say maybe he wants to borrow money, but since you guys won a grip, I doubt that's it," I said.

"Yeah. I have no idea, but I intend to find out." She said with a determined look on her face. I had no doubt that she'd squeeze the information out of Pete at some point.

We watched from afar as Pete and Vance stood with their heads together, talking quietly. Finally, Vance pulled away with a grin on his face. He nodded at Pete, and with a fist bump, they headed our way. I reached over and pushed the elevator call button, giving Vance a look as he threw his arm over me. He just shook his head and muttered, "Guy stuff, babe."

We were all quiet as the elevator came and we rode to our respective floors. We said goodbye to Pete and Laurel when we reached theirs, and Laurel promised to call me the next morning. Vance gave Pete a look, and Pete just nodded back knowingly.

I looked sideways at Vance as I crossed my arms over my chest and shrugged his arm off my shoulders as the doors closed. "Guy stuff, huh?"

"Yep. Kind of like when you're out with two or more girls somewhere and you all disappear to the restroom for half an hour or more. We don't question what happens when you're gone. Same thing here. To speak of it would violate the bro code."

"The ladies' restroom is like our church. You have your man caves; we have the ladies' room. That's how it works. You do not get to hold your version of Tile Talk in the middle of a hotel lobby. It violates the rules of sanctified conversation."

"Tile Talk?" he asked.

"That's what it's called. What do you guys call it?"

"Um... shooting the shit?" he offered.

"Of course," I muttered.

The doors opened, and we walked to our room. I was still huffy. I didn't like secrets unless I was the one keeping them. He and Pete barely knew each other—how could they have bonded so deeply that it would trump the connection that he and I had? I felt like Vance was betraying me in some

96

tiny way. Okay, that was bullshit. I was feeling very nosy and it was driving me crazy that he wouldn't tell me. I made a mental note to get even.

Once inside the room, we headed directly for the bedroom. I immediately retrieved my overnight kit. He grabbed the remote and flicked on the television.

"I'm just going to get ready for bed. It's been a long day and I am ready to crash. Do you need to use the bathroom before I take it over for the next few minutes?" I asked.

"Nah. I'm good. Go conquer civilization, or whatever it is you intend to do in there," he teased.

My purchase while searching for Vance was a short, black lacy chemise, in anticipation of sexy fun time. Even though that was supposedly off the table, I intended to give it my best shot to turn that around. After the way he ignited my fire with his kisses earlier in the evening, I thought the sisterhood would revoke my membership card if I didn't at least try to coerce him into sampling the goods.

I scrubbed my face and reapplied my makeup once I discovered the excitement of the evening had left me looking somewhere between a jilted prom date and roadkill. I brushed my hair until it shone, then put on my sex-kitten attire. It was actually sexy despite being a simple bit of lingerie. It was all lace, with the good parts obscured successfully but plenty of skin showing through, too. It had spaghetti straps, a plunging neckline that revealed the totality of my cleavage and a hem that hit just below the curve of my ass—which meant the front got the imagination going, but just barely. One wrong move and all one's questions were answered. Fortunately, I'd also brought along a black lace thong, so I could keep the suspension of disbelief alive a few minutes longer.

Once I was satisfied that I looked as enticing as I was ever going to look, I opened the door and did my best sexy slink into the room.

Vance was still glued to the television, reclined against the headboard, a pillow stuffed behind his back. His shirt was pulled out of his pants and totally unbuttoned, giving me my first glimpse of his smooth chest. From what I could see between the front panels of the material, his skin was smooth and virtually hairless, with a warm golden glow that begged to have my hands skimming every square inch. I could partially see the curvature of the muscles of his chest and abdomen, but not enough to satisfy my hungry imagination. It was just enough to make my mouth water, this tempting piece of hard candy, but I wanted more.

I cleared my throat softly to get his attention. His eyes flicked away from the screen before turning back to whatever sports commentary show was on. I stomped my foot and tried again. He looked again, this time really looked, then quickly sat up, swinging his legs over the side of the bed.

"Mimi..." he choked out hoarsely as if his throat had suddenly gone dry.

I sauntered over, stopping in front of him and wedging my knee between both of his. I gently spread them apart and stood between them as I placed my hands on his shoulders. His hands immediately went to my hips and squeezed gently.

"Remember down in the casino," I began, "just before I left you at the craps table? When I said you were about to get very, very lucky?"

He swallowed hard and nodded his head roughly. "I do," he replied.

I lowered my face to his, slowly, an inch at a time as I whispered, "I think it's time for me to follow through on that statement, don't you?" Our lips were only millimeters apart as I finished my sentence and I could feel the warmth of his breath whispering across my lips.

His hands tightened on my hips as he pulled me closer and tilted his head to bring his lips the rest of the way to meet mine. They landed lightly, ghosting over my mouth with a barely-there brush. He teased me rather than deepening the kiss and solidifying the connection. He was a master at dragging out the anticipation and making me ache for him, with only a few innocent touches of his lips. The stubble from his upper lip and chin scratching at the soft skin around my mouth awakened those nerve endings, causing a chain reaction through my whole body.

My need surged out of my control, so wrapping my hands around his shoulders, I climbed into his lap and straddled his hips. I tried to deepen our kiss, but he slid his hands up to my ribcage and held me back just a little. I wanted to devour him, to strike the match and set fire to all this passion inside me, but he was having none of it. He lifted his mouth from mine and looked me in the eye tenderly.

"There's no hurry, Mimi. We have the rest of the weekend to make love to each other, and I intend to spend every second discovering every inch of you. How you react when I touch you here..." He glided a finger down the side of my neck. "How you respond when I kiss you there..." He pressed the fingertips of his other hand to soft spot behind my ankle. "And when I kiss and touch and lick all points in between." He leaned in and breathed against my ear. "I'm going to make you mine, Mimi. Every last bit of you, and I won't let you rush me through it. No matter how hard your passion rides you, no matter how desperately you want it. You're going to be aching and begging by the time I am ready to bring this to completion, but I promise you, it will be worth it."

I didn't know whether to choke him out and demand that he satisfy me right then and there, or to expire on the spot. His words aroused me more than I ever thought possible, but I had to admit I was a bit intimidated too. It was obvious he intended to control every bit of our lovemaking, and I wasn't used to that. In that past, I'd been used to an exchange of control, of it bouncing back and forth between me and my partner in a spirited encounter for a half an hour or so. What Vance had described sounded vastly different from anything in my experience, and I was out of my comfort zone. I wanted him though, more than I'd wanted anything in my entire life, so I was totally on board with the plan.

I cupped one of his cheeks in my palm and nodded slowly. "You'll have to bear with me. I think you're different from anyone I've ever been with—not that there have been all that many, but enough—anyway, I'm not quite sure what you want from me. What should I do? I think I might need some, um, guidance, you know? Oh, hell. Can we just pretend I'm a virgin or something?"

Vance leaned his head against mine and began to laugh softly. "You're overthinking this, Mimi. Just relax." He picked me up off his lap and laid me in the center of the bed. Standing, he pulled his shirt off his shoulders and let it drop to the floor. While he dealt with his belt, I admired the hard planes of his chest. The nervous flutters in my belly subsided and were replaced with a slow burning fire that threatened to rage out of control.

He toed off his shoes and slid his pants from his narrow hips, leaving himself before me in just a pair of black boxer briefs. His body was even more marvelous than I expected. His chest was perfectly sculpted, the pectoral muscles carved in broad swipes just below well-muscled shoulders. Nothing about his torso was overly bulgy, just perfectly lean and sinewy, powerful without being overpowering. His abdomen was ridged in a tight six-pack, with his obliques doing that wonderful V-shape thing leading down into the waistband of his underwear. There was a fine dusting of dark brown hair over his lower abdomen, but not enough that it suggested he was a candidate for serious manscaping down there.

He crawled into bed next to me and took me into his arms. He kissed me more firmly that time, more than his usual soft, teasing brushes of lips. He sucked my bottom lip between his teeth and bit down gently before rubbing his tongue across it. I couldn't just lay there and be completely passive, so I sneaked my tongue out to tangle with his. I managed to hold back from trying to take possession of his mouth since I'd learned that would cause him to withdraw. I wanted him to keep kissing me, so I tested this small liberty and he allowed it. We lay there for a long time, our tongues caressing the other. Vance stroked my hair as his kisses moved from my mouth to my cheek and neck. I lay back, allowing him to move over me. He bit down on my earlobe gently as his hand traced down from my hair to my neck to my shoulder and down to my chest. He skimmed the outside swell of my breast with his fingertips before cupping the weight of it in his hand. I moaned softly as his deft fingers found my nipple and plucked it into a hard peak as his tongue traced around the outer shell of my ear. I shivered at the dual sensations, amazed that he could produce such a strong response from my body with these simple actions.

I ran my hands over his back, feeling his smooth skin beneath my palms, my heart picking up the pace. His lips wandered down to my cleavage, inching closer to the hand that was continuing to torment my aching nipple. Somehow, he managed to capture the strap of my chemise between his teeth and slowly dragged it down and off my shoulder, exposing me to him. His other hand moved to the corresponding strap and gently slid it off that shoulder, pulling the entire top down to my waist. Sighing, he nuzzled his cheek along my breastbone.

"You are so beautiful, Mimi. Your skin here is like silk beneath my lips," he whispered, his breath a specter dancing over my flesh, raising goosebumps as it traveled the length of my torso. My nipples tightened into little beads of need, begging for the touch of his mouth. Amazingly, he didn't make me wait, as his hand cupped the soft flesh of one breast, plumping it up. His lips closed around the tip with a swirl of his tongue. I couldn't help myself as the need rose inside me. My traveling hands wandered more frantically, kneading and squeezing the muscles of his back, as he took a deep pull of the tiny bud in his mouth. My body writhed beneath him, hips grinding against his involuntarily, seeking to fan the flame between us.

Vance pulled back, making a tsking sound. He took hold of my wrists and pinned them to the bed next to my head. He gave a little shake of his head and said, "You need to be a good girl, Mimi. I'm taking my time with you, and you are going to soak up every ounce of pleasure I give you. Now, behave."

I closed my eyes and tried to still my mind to let him take control over my body. It was hard. I wanted to touch and squeeze and feel him, but I realized at that moment, I wanted to do it on my terms, not his. He intended to spoon feed himself to me, in tiny doses, and I had to appreciate every morsel I was given. With that realization, I relaxed and resolved to give myself over to the moment and all that Vance was offering.

He resumed his attention to my breast, licking around the nipple, and down the underside of it, tracing its shape as if committing its contour to memory. He returned to its center and took the whole areola into his mouth and sucking deeply on it as his hand came around, squeezing more firmly that time. His other hand let go of my wrist, fingertips trailing down the length of my arm, before settling on my neglected breast, palm down. He pressed down with his fingertips and began caressing the flesh in a circular motion, all around the circumference of my breast, everywhere but the center. My skin was fabulously sensitized, the peak straining upward, yearning for the relief of his touch. His index and middle finger scissored around it and pinched ever so slightly sending a bolt of electricity straight to my swollen clit. I couldn't help it, my hips bucked up against his and I moaned in response. He dragged his mouth across my chest and sucked deeply on that nipple once before licking his way down and over my ribs to my abdomen.

I cracked open my eyelids and watched as Vance drew my nightie down my body, instructing me to lift my hips so he could remove it from me altogether. I watched as he caressed the skin of my belly as if he had never seen one before. He stroked and petted it, pausing to plant sweet kisses along my hip bones. His hands glided down over my hips to my upper thighs, caressing and squeezing the flesh. His lips and tongue followed the path his hands had made, teeth scraping and nipping little spots as he went along. My skin was so alive it was tingling everywhere, and I was so wet with need, I could barely stand it. My teeth were on edge from want.

I felt his fingers trail back up the insides of my thighs and although I did my best to stay still, I couldn't stop myself from squirming slightly under his touch. If he didn't continue his path upward, I would go mad with the desire he built in me. At last, I felt his gentle touch on the top of my mound, before lightly tracing the dampened fabric between my legs. Gradually, he added more pressure, parting me beneath the material, until his fingers were right up against my pleasure center. I cried out loudly when he connected with the swollen nub, partially in pleasure, partially in relief, and my hips pushed back against him of their own accord. His hand moved back and forth, just rubbing against my clit in a lazy rhythm. Enough to ease the ache a little, but nowhere near enough to quench the fire that was burning me up.

"Shhhhh...," he hushed softly, as his fingers wrapped around the sides of my underwear and slid them down my legs. With surprising swiftness for Vance, since before now, it seemed like the man didn't know how to do anything quickly, his fingers returned to my throbbing pussy and resumed their leisurely caress against that bundle of nerves. I looked down to find him staring at me again, not my face but my body. He seemed fascinated by the sight of his hand touching me there, the glistening moisture coating his fingertips, the sound of his slow strokes against my wetness. He bent closer to watch more intently I think, but then his tongue darted out and licked long and slow, from my entrance all the way to my clit, in one big swipe. It took everything I had not to clamp my legs around his head and grind my pelvis against his mouth, I was so yearning for satisfaction, but instead, I forced myself to open my body wider to him. I pushed my legs as far apart as they would go, pulling my thighs toward my chest at the same time. Vance looked up at my face for a moment and smiled broadly before returning his mouth to me and giving another very thorough lick.

I should have known Vance would do this differently than all the other men I'd been with, just as he'd done with everything else. He didn't go straight for my clit and suck on it like there was no tomorrow. No, instead, Vance licked every part of me as softly as a butterfly's wings, paying attention to every single part. He circled my clit with his tongue, danced over it, occasionally, I'd feel a very light scrape of his teeth over it, but never once did he suck on it, or bite it or anything anyone else had ever done, or even that I'd read about in books. It drove me absolutely wild. I couldn't thrash about on the bed like I wanted to because that would

106

break our connection and stop him from propelling me to heaven. I whimpered and moaned uncontrollably, as he continued to torment me until suddenly a burst of pleasure rushed upon me in an unexpected gust of feeling so strong, I was completely overwhelmed by it. I screamed his name as my consciousness flew through space, and I was blinded by a rush of color speeding past my vision. Vance's hands gripped my hips and he finally pulled my clit into his mouth, sucking ever so gently, sending a new round of spasms through my body. The pleasure was so sublime, I didn't realize that I'd twisted my fingers into Vance's hair and was clutching the strands for dear life. As I came back down, my body suffused with an all-encompassing feeling of bliss, I slowly unclenched each of my muscles and took a shuddering breath. I had never had an orgasm so intense, so powerful, and so sudden, rush over me like that. Normally, it was a slow building experience, like a spring coiling tighter and tighter inside me until it could no longer withstand the tension and broke free, unleashing its force in a shockwave through my body. This... this was like a freight train I couldn't see coming, barreling down on me, knocking me over and running me into the ground. Holy hell, if more of this was what I had to look forward to, I didn't think I'd survive.

Vance kissed and nibbled his way back up my body, resting his hips in the cradle of my quivering thighs. I tasted myself on his tongue as he kissed me deeply, searching my mouth with a hunger he had denied himself until now. It was obvious his previous iron control on his passion was beginning to thin as his hands traveled over my flesh with less finesse and more urgency. We became a tangle of frenzied body parts, frantic hands, writhing torsos, twisting legs. His hands gripped the hair at the side of my head as his lips continued to eat at my mouth, devouring me. I dragged my fingernails down the length of his back as I caressed his legs with the soles of my feet, before bringing them up to hook my toes in the waistband of his boxer briefs, pulling them down over his hips. He immediately moved to assist me, raising his body off mine, and pushing them the rest of the way off. His body was coated in a fine sheen of perspiration and the soft lighting in the room made his skin glisten. My gaze wandered over his form, down his toned chest and abdomen until it finally rested on the magnificence of his heavy cock jutting up between us. Instinctively, I reached for it, wrapping both hands around him and squeezing gently. I watched in fascination as a pearly drop of pre-cum beaded at the head before slowly dripping down onto my fingers. Sliding my thumb across the tip, I smoothed the remaining fluid over the crown, swirling it around and around. Vance threw his head back onto his shoulders, taking slow, deep breaths as I began to slide my hands up and down the thick length of him. Tearing my eyes away from the beautiful sight of his hard cock in my hands, I looked up to watch his face as I touched him. His eyes were pressed tightly together, and the muscle in his jaw flexed as he gritted his teeth. I increased my pace just a little faster, determined to test the boundaries of his control. He tortured me endlessly, wasn't it fair that I played just a little?

Vance's hips began to work in tandem with the pace of my hands, thrusting sharply forward with each down stroke. He groaned loudly as I squeezed harder, his voice coming out slightly choked.

"God, Mimi. I wanted to go so very slow with you this first time, but I can't wait any longer. I need to feel you."

He pulled out of my grasp and dropped down on me, kissing me with an abandon he had not previously permitted himself. His hands roved over my body and hooked around my thighs, spreading them wide beneath him. He placed himself against my center and I barely had enough time to gasp out, "Vance, condom."

"Right, right. Sorry," he muttered. He jumped off the bed, grabbed his wallet from his pants and pulled a foil packet out, papers and bills spilling from its folds as he did. He dropped it to the ground carelessly as he returned to the bed, tearing the packet open with his teeth at the same time. He knelt between my spread legs and rolled the latex on his rigid length, which appeared to have doubled in size since I last looked at it. Once it was safely in place, he covered my body with his again, sliding his hands beneath my hips, angling them towards him. He placed the head of his cock at my slippery entrance before meeting my eyes. Despite the urgency we both felt before, the brief interruption slowed things down a bit, and Vance was back in control. As we gazed at each other, he slowly slid into me inch by inch. It was slow, it was intimate, and it was a moment I would never forget as long as I lived. For the first time in my life, I knew what they meant when they said you became one with someone. Every part of me was fused to Vance as our bodies joined together. Nothing had ever felt more natural or more right. It was as if my body, my soul, my heart was a home for his.

He seated himself fully inside me and held there, both of us treasuring the moment when he filled me completely. It didn't take long, however, before baser instincts won out and our bodies were forced to move with each other, thrusting and withdrawing, giving and taking, clawing and writhing.

Vance moved his hands from under me to brace himself on his forearms as I wrapped my legs around his waist. I clutched his shoulders desperately as he moved his body against mine. He didn't simply pound his hips into mine. Vance made love with his whole body. His chest slipped up and over me, a smooth caress of his skin against my sensitized nipples, the hard ridges of his abdomen massaging the flesh of my belly, his pubic bone pressing and grinding against my clit in the most delicious way, as his phenomenal cock filled me again and again and again.

"Mimi, your pussy is heaven." He breathed into my ear. "I didn't think anything could be better than tasting you, but fucking your sweet little cunt is like magic."

His dirty words set my blood boiling that much higher, my passion soaring into the stratosphere. I couldn't help twisting beneath him, aiding him in reaching that spot deep inside me so his cock stroked it repeatedly.

"Oh, Mimi. Is that it, right there?" he asked as the head of his cock kept passing over that sensitive spot. I nodded in response, biting my lip, as he did it again and again. Without warning, he punched his hips forward, hitting directly into the nerves clustered there, and I instantly fell apart in his arms.

Just like last time, this orgasm bore down on me in stealth. No steady build up, no climb to the peak, just a sudden shove off the cliff into a sea of ecstasy and I was instantly drowning. I was vaguely aware of my own cries echoing off the walls of the room, but I was far too lost for any conscious reasoning. In my bliss, I devoured any inch of Vance's skin that was within reaching distance of my mouth. My lips, tongue, and teeth traveled the terrain of his face, neck and chest, kissing, licking, sucking, and biting. I became particularly fascinated with one of his nipples, and when I bit down, Vance thrust hard between my legs and cried out in a long groan. I felt him pulse within me, emptying himself in hot spurts. He collapsed on me, breathing harshly against my neck.

After his breathing slowed, he raised his head and looked down at me. He smoothed the hair from my sweaty face and smiled softly. "Wow." He mouthed at me with wide eyes. I couldn't help but giggle.

"Yeah," I whispered back. "Wow."

He rolled off me with a dramatic sigh and we both stared at the ceiling quietly for a time, allowing our heart rates to return to normal. The silence was comfortable, but I couldn't resist breaking it after a little while.

"So, we're going to be doing that again, right?" I asked.

"A lot," he agreed with a quick nod. "Just as soon as I'm sure you didn't break my dick with your magic pussy."

I burst out laughing. "I don't think you have anything to worry about. I, on the other hand, should be more concerned about my pussy, what with the ninja orgasms and all."

He lazily rolled his head to the side to look at me. "Ninja orgasms?"

"Oh, don't look so innocent. You know exactly what I'm talking about."

"I haven't got the slightest clue, precious." He said rolling onto his side to face me.

I rose onto my elbows, so I could look him in the eye. "You know, the orgasms that just came out of nowhere? Twice, I was laying there, enjoying myself immeasurably mind you, but with no signs of orgasm on the horizon, when WHAM! I'm suddenly set upon by stealth orgasms. A sneak attack if you will. You have crazy, mad, ninja orgasm skills," I said flopping back down onto the bed.

He chuckled and rolled over onto me, trapping me beneath him once again. He kissed me deeply before pulling back and smiling down at me. "Do these crazy, mad, ninja orgasms satisfy you?"

I raised my hand and shook it in a little see-saw motion, all the while grinning like a loon.

He kissed my forehead and flopped back down. "Good enough for me," he said.

I burst out laughing again.

Six

Vance made good on his word and did not let me out of bed for the entire following day. It wasn't until eight that night when we were ordering our third meal from room service, I realized we hadn't heard a peep from Laurel all day. I made note of this after Vance placed our orders. He gave me a mischievous smile.

"What is it?" I asked suspiciously.

"Do you remember last night, when you got all twisted up because I wouldn't tell you what Pete and I were talking about?"

I huffed. "Oh, yeah. I forgot I was mad at you about that. What does that have to do with this?"

"Well, he was telling me he had the exact same plans for her today as I did for you. We were basically agreeing to keep you two away from your phones today," he admitted.

My jaw dropped in shock. I didn't know whether to laugh or to be ticked off at being manipulated. If I had really stopped to think about it, I would freely admit to myself that I was exactly where I wanted to be, and quite likely so was Laurel, otherwise nothing would have stopped us from calling each other.

"Maybe I should call her now and make sure everything is okay," I said, feeling guilty when I realized I hadn't thought about her once all day.

"She's fine. If she weren't, she would have called. Pete wouldn't have stopped her if there were something wrong or if she were unhappy, no matter what we agreed upon," Vance reassured me. "Now, come over here." He said from his place on the bed, his arms open wide.

I happily climbed on and snuggled into his embrace. We were both wrapped up in the robes provided by the hotel following a nice, long, shared bath in the soaking tub. Our muscles were pleasantly warm and relaxed although some parts that shall remain nameless were sore. I expected those areas would require rest and time to recover. Although if I had anything to say about it, there would be no rest in the near future. My flight back to Los Angeles was a little over a day away, and we were to spend part of the next day driving back to the city. Then, I wouldn't see Vance for another week, at least. No, rest was not on the immediate agenda at that time.

Vance nudged me a little with his shoulder. "What are you thinking about, Mimi? You seem far away suddenly."

I sighed softly. "Rest," I said, turning slightly so I could look at his face.

His eyebrows rose. "Rest? Have I worn you out?" he teased.

I laughed and pushed his shoulder playfully. "No. I was thinking how I wasn't going to let you get any between now and Monday morning when I leave."

His look immediately sobered. "Our time is ticking away, isn't it?"

I inhaled deeply and blew it out in a huff. "Yes. Whenever I think of it, I just feel so... bummed."

"I don't like thinking about it, either, but maybe it's something we should talk about," he said. "We haven't discussed it at all. Do you even want to see me when we get back home?"

I looked at him like he just asked me if I wanted to have a third breast implanted. "Of all the ridiculous questions I have ever been asked... try to keep me away from you! I hate to inform you, buddy, but you are stuck with my ass." Rolling my eyes, I muttered, "Do I want to see you when we get back home..."

He laughed, raising both hands in surrender. "It was a fair question. We only planned that one dinner date, and then this spontaneous trip. I didn't want to be presumptuous."

"News flash, genius. The minute I went to bed with you was a pretty good indicator." I crossed my arms and just looked at him. "What about all that other stuff we talked about? That wasn't a great big clue, either?"

Vance suddenly looked like a little boy, very young and unsure. "Sometimes guys need to be reassured too, Mimi," he said quietly.

I hurried to curl in close to him and wrap my arm around his waist. I hadn't expected to hear such a serious and vulnerable response. I wanted to assure him of my feelings as honestly as I could.

"I want to see you again and again and again, Vance. As often as I can," I whispered. "I don't know how I'm going to last a week without you."

I looked up into his face hopefully. "Is your car parked at the airport or do you need a ride?"

"I took a car service to the airport. If you are hinting at your services as a chauffeur, I would be grateful for a ride," he said.

"Yay! Just text me your flight information and I will be waiting for you at baggage claim."

"Then I'll take you out to dinner again," he offered.

"I was more in the market for an invite to your place."

"Well, depending on what time I get in, we may be able to do both." He grinned at me. "In the meantime, I will call and text you every day."

"You'd better, or I will blow up your phone and embarrass you in front of all the 'big boys,'" I warned him teasingly as I relaxed back into his chest.

After a filling meal of roasted chicken, new potatoes, and asparagus, we discussed our plans for the evening. The idea of staying in and spending the night the way we spent the day was very tempting. However, it was our last night in Atlantic City and we both felt like we should experience more of the city than just Caesar's casino and security offices. We decided to head back over to the boardwalk and just stroll until we found some place that interested us.

We took our time getting ready and it was nearly eleven when we left our room. Vance looked edible in his simple outfit of a gray button-down shirt with the sleeves rolled up his forearms, black pressed dress slacks and black leather belt and shoes. He was wearing his signature cologne that always made me want to do my best impression of a gold medalist for the pommel horse and vault onto him. I was wearing a short red dress, fairly plain with its scoop neckline and tank straps, but covered in a short fringe. I had bought it a few months earlier with no idea where I would wear it but thought it was too hot to pass up. My look was completed by a pair of red, modest heeled shoes, with a strap running across my ankle. Very retro.

There were plenty of people out along the boardwalk. Clearly, the party was just getting started. We strolled with our arms wrapped around each other and simply took in the sights around us. The fresh sea air was peppered with the pungent scents of food wafting from each of the restaurants. A cacophony of voices, sounds from slot machines and music drifted from many of the doors as they opened and closed as we walked by.

In the distance, I could hear the throbbing of a lively beat. My heart picked up its cadence and I felt a wild hum begin to buzz in my veins. I knew that sound. As we drew closer, I could pick out the pulsing rhythm of Latin music, which was by far my favorite kind of music to dance to. Ever since I was a little girl, I found the sound to be infectious, the drums, the horns, the guitars calling me to move my body. I looked at Vance excitedly. He was looking at me with a wide grin on his face as well.

At the same time, we both blurted out, "Do you know how to salsa?"

Nodding in unison, we both rushed to the door of the club where the music was coming from like a couple of kids with a handful of cash heading to the candy store. We stumbled through the door and into nineteen-fifties Cuba. It was amazing. We headed toward the bar to warm up a little and survey the crowd. The music was loud and the crowd a little heavy, but not so thick that you couldn't move, and we could still hear ourselves speak.

We both ordered mojitos as we watched the dancers dip, whirl, and twirl around the dance floor. They seemed to be of all skill levels, which was a relief. While I was a passable dancer, I certainly didn't do it often enough possess any fancy skills. I needed a strong partner with a good lead to feel certain I wasn't making a total ass of myself on the dance floor, but either way, every time I danced, I had a blast. Being swung, spun, and twirled around, reminded me of pretending to be a princess when I was a little girl when I would go out into our yard in a fancy dress and spin around to watch my skirt billow around me. I got that same carefree, beautiful feeling from dancing salsa.

Once we finished our drinks, Vance took my glass and set it on the bar along with his. He grabbed me by the hand and led me to the edge of the floor. We stood and watched a little closer for a few minutes before he leaned closer and asked in my ear "What is your skill level?"

"I would say that I'm above a beginner, but just below an intermediate dancer. I don't go often enough to really practice my skills, but I've mastered the basics and know a few intermediate steps. I can't really do anything fancy though."

"How long has it been since you last danced?" he asked.

"It's probably been at least eight months," I admitted.

"Do you trust me enough to lead you through a few steps that you may not have tried before? I will help you through them. If you're not embarrassed, I'll walk you through them first," he offered.

"I don't know, I don't want to look like such a newbie in front of everyone else. I mean I know I will if I just stick to very basic moves, but no one will be paying attention to me. If I stop and walk through something, it might attract attention."

"So what? I'm sure it'll happen more than once tonight. If it increases your enjoyment of the evening that's all that really matters. We'll stay here over at the corner where we're out of the way of the more advanced dancers, and no one will mind," he said, doing his best to convince me. It worked. The man could talk me into anything.

"Alright. I'll give it a shot," I said with a giddy grin. The fact was that I totally trusted Vance with my body. I knew instinctively he would guide me easily and keep me from crashing into anybody. I felt very safe putting myself in his arms.

He took my hand again and led me the rest of the way onto the floor. Turning, he placed his other hand on my hip while I rested my left hand on his shoulder. He guided me into the basic step on the downbeat, for the first three counts of eight, giving me a chance to warm up and shake the rust off.

Next, he moved me into a right turn, then back to a basic step, then to a side step and another turn, back to basic, a hammerlock, and so on. He led me expertly through all the beginning steps, letting me familiarize myself with them again before we moved on to more complicated movements. Before long, I was comfortable and nodded while smiling at him to let him know I was ready to conquer more elaborate steps. The next thing I knew, Vance had me performing intricate sequences that I'd never dreamed I could do. Our eyes were locked on the other's the entire time, and the hum of electricity between us began to throb along with the music. The touch of his hands as he spun me around or caressed me as he brought me close into him, intoxicated me. My pulse began to pound, and the fringe on my dress flew wildly with every shake and shimmy of my body.

The thin sheen of perspiration that began to slick my body only heightened my awareness of the seductiveness of the evening. It was like making love all over again in a way. We were touching, our bodies sliding against each other, moving apart, coming back together again. We were connected physically, mentally, and emotionally. Our breathing was labored and heavy; and though we were clothed this time, we were still creating a kind of magic together. One that made sparks fly and hearts swell. Though different from making love with Vance for obvious reasons, it was just as exhilarating, and I couldn't stop smiling and laughing the entire time.

We danced for over an hour before we decided to refresh with more mojitos. There was a seat available at the bar, so Vance lifted me up on it and moved to stand in the space between my knees. I rested the cold glass against my forehead to help cool me down. Strands of my hair were plastered to my sweaty neck, and I figured I must look like wet death after all that physical exertion.

"You are an excellent lead, Vance. You should teach classes," I said.

"I used to, actually, when I was in college," he responded. "I told you I grew up in the East Valley?" I nodded. "Well, it's a predominantly Latino area. My friends taught me how to dance when I was in high school, and I got 'salsa fever' as they say. I got pretty good, and it was a natural progression that I should teach. I didn't make a ton of money, but it was enough to cover my textbooks each semester and I had a blast doing it. It always made me feel good to take someone who knew nothing and give them skills to do something that brought them joy."

"I hope that I can learn more from you. Apart from this weekend I spent with you, nothing else has ever made me feel so alive," I said with a blush.

Vance's cheeks colored slightly as well, and he got the humblest look on his face. "Mimi that is the most... wonderful thing anyone has ever said to me."

I leaned in close to his ear, so he could hear me better as I whispered the most heartfelt words I had ever spoken to that point. "It's true, Vance. Nobody has ever affected me the way you do. This feeling I have when I'm with you? I want to feel it forever."

He looked me deep in the eyes and said just one word, shaking his head in amazement. "Fearless."

He wrapped his arms around my shoulders and pulling me in close to his chest, he squeezed me tightly.

We spent the rest of the night dancing and drinking mojitos until the bar closed, simply enjoying the time we had together being young and free and feeling the beginnings of love growing between us.

The following day, Vance and I were moving a little slow even though we slept right up until a half an hour before checking out. We had gotten back to the hotel a little after four and made love until six. It was no less satisfying than any of the times during our marathon the day before. We were both exhausted from the exertion and the effects of the alcohol we had consumed though. So, it had been slow and lazy, which suited me just fine. I was learning that Vance's approach to sex was mostly slow. He was the kind of man who liked to draw things out, to make the most of every touch and kiss, to play my body like a violin, rather than pounding it into submission. I supposed that's where his ninja orgasm skills came into play. I didn't know, wasn't going to complain, nor was I going to examine it too closely. The technique obviously worked for the man, and I was its beneficiary. Best not to look a gift horse in the mouth, and all that. I didn't want the stealth orgasms to go away. They were far too good.

Pete and Laurel met us at the truck, both looking about as good as we felt. We exchanged grunts instead of greetings and loaded our gear into the back. Rather than trying to corner Laurel to squeeze information out of her, I opted to sit up front with Vance for the return trip for the simple reason I wanted to hold his hand. I wanted to extend any time we had together for as long as I could. We spent most of the ride in comfortable silence, whether we were nursing our respective hangovers, me snoozing, or lost in thought over our weekends, it was hard to say. I did a bit of all three. I felt no need to talk, other than murmuring here and there to Vance about the music, or the odd thing I noticed about the scenery going by. He seemed just as content to hold my hand and to sneak little happy looks at my profile.

We arrived in the city around three-thirty in the afternoon. Pete and Laurel said goodbye on the stoop as Vance helped me upstairs with my bag. He left it by the front door and joined me on the sofa to chat for a bit.

"Thank you so much for this trip, Vance. I really had a wonderful time." I said on an exhale. I had a tightness in my chest as I knew this was the last conversation we would have in person for several days. I hated that I wouldn't get to see him whenever I wanted to. He had become as important to me as air even though it was crazy. I'd known him exactly a week, and I felt like he was essential to my survival.

"You're welcome, Mimi. It was definitely the time of my life. Even if I did almost get arrested." We both laughed.

"I need to get back to my hotel and take a nap if I'm going to call you tonight, which I absolutely have to do. I don't know if I will have time to call you in the morning before you leave. I have a seven o'clock breakfast meeting."

"I hate to see you leave. I would suggest we nap together, but this sofa isn't exactly built for two, and if I accompany you back to your hotel, not only will we not nap, I won't leave, and I won't make my flight tomorrow."

"I wouldn't care if you missed your flight tomorrow," he gave me a teasing wink, "but I'd miss my meeting and that would be very bad for my career. If I lose my job, I can't support you after we're married."

I groaned. "Are you proposing again? You've been so good. You almost went all weekend without doing it."

"No, Mimi. I promise you. I will propose to you at least once a week until you agree to be my wife. Consider yourself warned." He stood and placed a soft kiss on my forehead.

"I'm going to leave now. Get comfortable and take your nap. I'll call you as soon as I wake up." He brushed the back of his knuckles across my cheek before turning for the door.

"Until then," I whispered.

After he left, I set the alarm on my phone for two hours later and snuggled down into the sofa, instantly falling into a very comfortable sleep.

I woke to my alarm going off and the growling of my stomach just after six in the evening. I wandered through the apartment, looking for Laurel, to find her sprawled across her bed, drooling all over her pillow. I tried to rouse her to see if she wanted to go grab something to eat, but she just mumbled incoherently about Pete and an octopus, so I left her to her dreams and headed back to the kitchen to see if there was anything in the refrigerator to make a meal out of.

The fridge was near empty, and the only promising thing in the pantry was a jar of peanut butter and a loaf of bread. I could have braved the New York streets by myself and found something with more flavor, but I still felt hung-over despite my very restful nap. So, I made a sandwich, then settled down on the sofa and turned on some mindless TV.

I kept looking at the time on my phone, in anticipation of Vance calling. When nine o'clock rolled around, my uneasiness started to grow. Though he didn't give me any sort of time frame as to when he'd call, I had expected he'd call much earlier. He had said he'd call when he woke up. He couldn't possibly still be asleep, could he? Maybe it had taken him a while to get to sleep. I wondered if I should call him. I didn't want to wake him if he was still resting. I waited for another hour, then decided to call after all, because I had to get up at four the following morning to catch my six-thirty flight. I placed the call and it rang until it went to voicemail.

"Hey, Vance, it's Mimi. I'm really sorry I missed you, but I will give you a call when I land tomorrow. Hopefully, I will get to hear your voice then. I hope your day goes well tomorrow. Bye," I said before hanging up.

I was sure there was a very good explanation as to why he didn't call, but I was so disappointed. I felt like we missed an important opportunity even though that was silly. It was just one phone call.

I got up and packed all the stuff I didn't need for the morning, set out an outfit to wear and grabbed my nightclothes. I went through my nightly routine then settled back onto the sofa, all the while with this nagging feeling in the pit of my stomach.

As I turned out the light, I realized that Laurel had slept straight through the afternoon and evening. Maybe that's what Vance had done too. His disappearing act didn't mean anything. Nothing at all. I set my alarm for four a.m. and rolled over to sleep.

The following morning was a whirlwind of activity. I overslept by half an hour and was missing a shoe. I'd thought I had everything together the night before but apparently, neglected to make sure my shoes were accounted for. In the end, I had to unpack another pair and write my favorite pair of flats off as a loss. They weren't anything special or expensive, or even all that attractive, they were just super comfortable. Finally, I was ready to go, and Laurel walked me down to the cab waiting in front of the building. We exchanged quick hugs goodbye and promised to Skype that evening because she still owed me an explanation about Pete.

The cab made its way through the dark streets, the lights shining down onto puddles formed from sidewalks that had been hosed off in preparation for the day's business ahead. I leaned my head against the window, still feeling a bit like a kid who was denied a day at Disneyland. I tried to shake it off and pull on my big girl boots. It wasn't as though it was my last chance to speak to him. I knew I'd talk to him that afternoon when my plane landed. At least, I hoped I would.

I didn't have much time to think about it again once I got to the airport as I had just enough time to get through security and make a mad dash for the gate. I got to my seat just as they were closing the doors to the plane. I accepted a pillow and blanket from the flight attendant and despite the extra sleep I got the day before, I was able to drift off for most of the flight home.

Once awake, I tried to concentrate on a romance novel I'd stuffed in my purse before leaving Los

Angeles. Unfortunately, my mind kept turning back to Vance and the fact he didn't call. I knew I was being obsessive, but I couldn't help it. We had just connected in such a way, I couldn't understand why he wouldn't be as eager to talk to me as I was to him. Which of course made me then worry something was wrong. Semi-disgusted with myself, I crammed the book back into my purse and leaned back into the seat. I closed my eyes and did my best to distract myself by remembering everything that had happened over my entire trip, from start to finish, until the plane was making its descent at LAX.

Once we reached the gate, I waited until everyone disembarked before grabbing my stuff from the overhead compartment and making my own way off the airplane. I wasn't in any particular hurry. It was about ten a.m. in Los Angeles, and I had nowhere special to be, no one anxiously awaiting my arrival home. I'd check in with my bosses, a few friends, and my mom, but those calls could wait until later in the afternoon. The only call I wanted to make was to Vance, but suddenly, I felt hesitant. I knew I was unsure because his not calling last night was unexpected and I didn't know if it meant anything or not. I felt surprisingly vulnerable.

I slowly moved toward the baggage claim, procrastinating over turning on my phone, knowing I should just do it and get it over with, but scared of doing it and finding no messages waiting.

"It's Vance," I told myself quietly. "Nothing has changed between the time he dropped you off at Laurel's and now." A tiny voice whispered in my head, "Except, he didn't call…"

While I was waiting for my suitcase to come around on the carousel, I reached into my purse and grabbed my phone. While it powered on, I located my luggage and pulled it down. As I wheeled it out to the curb, my phone started pinging with alerts for both voicemail and text messages. I queued up in the taxi line and stared at the phone in my hand. I had eight text messages and three voicemails.

I listened to the voicemails first. The first one was from Laurel at five-thirty that morning, letting me know she found my shoe and wanting to know if she should send the pair to me in L.A.

The second was left at five forty-eight and was from Vance. He simply apologized for not calling the night before and asked me to call him before my flight left.

The third was also from Vance and time stamped at seven a.m. It was much longer than his last one.

"Mimi, it's Vance again. I had hoped you would call before you left, but your flight should be in the air by now. If you are upset with me for not calling, I don't blame you, but I didn't willfully not call. I had a terrible migraine headache when I got back to the hotel after dropping you off. I took some pain medication and it knocked me out. I slept straight through to this morning. I never even heard my phone ring when you called. I'm sorry. You have no idea how disappointed I was when I woke up this morning. I hate the fact that you left, and I didn't get to hear your voice again. I feel like I got robbed or something. I keep telling myself to stop being a pussy, it's just one phone call, but the truth is after this weekend, I want you with me all the time. If I miss an opportunity to see you, to hear you, to share something with you, then I've lost something important to me. I don't want to lose any moments with you, no matter what they are. Please call me when you land even if you're mad. I'd rather hear you tell me off than hear nothing from you at all."

I decided to read the text messages later and call him back once I was in the cab on the way home. He picked up before the first ring ended. "Hi, Mimi. Hang on just a second. Don't go anywhere." I heard talking in the background, but it was muffled as if he had his hand over the receiver. I heard a door shut and then he was back, his voice coming through the line, as crisp and clear as if he were sitting next to me.

"Sorry, I was in a meeting and had to excuse myself. I am so relieved that you called."

"Vance, if you're in a meeting, I can call back at a more convenient time," I told him.

"No way. Now that I have you, I'm not letting you go. I didn't get to speak to you last night, so I'm getting my time with you now," he said adamantly.

"Vance, seriously. You have work to do. I will be home all day and evening. I have no plans at all."

"Good. You can talk to me now and later," he insisted.

I sighed and settled back into the seat. "Fine. You win." In a much softer tone, I asked, "How's your head?"

"Much better now. Good as new, in fact." He sounded chipper although I didn't know if it was because he felt good physically or because he got his way.

"Does that happen a lot?" I asked. "I mean, headaches. Do you get them often?"

"Not really. I'll get them when I'm working on a big deal, you know from the stress, I think. But occasionally, I'll get a migraine. When I do, I take this medication my GP gave me, and it puts me right out. It sucks because I'm out for hours, but at least I don't have to feel the blinding pain. I should have called you before I took the pills, but I figured you had already gone to sleep and honestly the only thing I could think of was going to sleep myself."

"It's all right. I wasn't mad. I was just concerned when you didn't call. I would have called you this morning, but I overslept and left Laurel's late. I was in a rush and barely made my flight. I didn't get your messages until just now."

"Did you get my text messages?" He asked.

"I did, but I haven't looked at them yet. I checked my voicemail first and called as soon as I heard yours."

"Oh," he chuckled. "Well, by all means, feel free to delete them without reading them. I won't mind."

"That bad, huh?" I laughed.

"Probably more pathetic than anything. You'll really think I'm a pussy when you're done reading them."

"Sounds like excellent blackmail material for when I meet your friends," I threatened.

"Oh, sweetheart. You are never meeting my friends. Not because of this, but because they are all a bunch of degenerate bastards. I wouldn't want to ruin your good impression of me by exposing you to them."

I laughed harder. "Now I absolutely have to meet them. I'm sure I would love them all."

"I know they will love you. Another reason to keep you far away from them." He sighed. "I'm afraid I do have to go back in with all the big boys before they think I'm a slacker." He lowered his voice to a husky whisper. "I'm so glad you called though, and that you aren't mad. I really was worried."

"I think it would take an awful lot to make me mad at you, Vance Ashcroft," I said quietly.

"Here's to you never finding out, Mimi. I'll give you a call when I get done here. I promise."

"I'll be waiting," I said before ending the call.

Seven

Later that afternoon, Laurel and I connected on a video Skype call. After confirming I had arrived safely without meeting any other tall, dark, and model-like men, and that I did not need her to send me my shoes, we got down to the business of discussing how Pete re-entered her life.

"So, young Laurel... please, tell me everything. Thursday morning, we were in your apartment and you were telling me all about 'the one who got away.' Friday afternoon, he's on the Garden State with us on the way to Atlantic City. It seems there's a whole chunk of information that I'm missing here," I said.

I watched through the computer screen as she rested her chin in her hand and twirled a strand of hair around a finger on her other hand. "Well, there's not a lot to tell. After you and I talked, I thought about everything I told you. The more I thought about it, the more of a hypocrite I felt. How could I say all those things to you if I wasn't willing to go after what I wanted? Obviously, from everything I confessed to you, I wanted Pete. He is the only guy that has mattered to me in like... ever. So, even though I treated him badly by pushing him away without really giving him any explanation, I swallowed my pride and gave him a call.

"I got really lucky, Mimi. He was actually glad to hear from me. I told him I wanted to meet for a drink after work and talk, and he was on board with that.

"When he arrived, I didn't waste a second, or I would have lost my nerve. I hadn't even had anything to drink for liquid courage, I just spilled my guts out onto the table for him. Told him everything I told you."

I just sat there listening quietly. This was huge for Laurel. She was never really the relationship type, always preferring to be on her own and doing her own thing, beholden to no one. While she had admitted to deep feelings for this guy the other day to me, admitting them to him had a whole host of other implications. I wondered how she intended to reconcile those feelings with her intrinsic need for independence.

Laurel went on. "He told me he had been confused when I pushed him away because he'd thought we were starting something pretty special, too. Turns out he was just as into me as I was him. Fortunately, being a little bit older, and apparently a little bit wiser than yours truly, he decided to give me my space and see what happened."

"So, what does that mean for the two of you now?" I asked. "Are you an official couple?"

"Well, in the sense that we've agreed that we're not going to date anyone else, yes. However, we've decided to let things develop at whatever pace they do. He knows I'm fiercely independent and have issues with typical relationship kinds of things."

"Like calling and letting someone know where you are, or if you're going to be late, or if you're still alive, and things like that?" I said, laughing.

"Shut up. I'm not that bad," she said, sticking her tongue out at me.

"No, but almost."

"We'll figure it out as we go along, I guess. I know I have a big learning curve to deal with here, but he said he's willing to be patient with me. For some unknown reason, the guy seems to think I'm worth it. Hopefully, I can keep him fooled for a little while longer," she said.

"You are worth it, and you know it. I really hope it works out for you. I liked him a lot, and he and Vance sure seemed to hit it off."

"Oh please. It was almost a full-on bromance. What was up with that deal they made?" she said, rolling her eyes.

"As if you're actually complaining," I said, tossing a pencil at the computer screen.

"I know, right?" She winked.

We gossiped for a little while longer, mostly trading secrets about the day we each spent sequestered with our men in Atlantic City. By the time we logged out, I was already missing her company. I wondered when we would have a chance for another in-person visit again.

As promised, Vance called that night and every other night before he returned to Los Angeles. He did his best to call during the day too, but he was so wrapped up in the deal they were working on, this didn't happen very often.

Our evening conversations brought us closer, helping to maintain and nurture our connection while we were apart. I also learned that Vance was quite skilled at the fun sexy times even when three thousand miles away. Armed with a very creative imagination and a sultry voice, the man could make my toes curl with a husky whisper, a well-placed dirty word, and a few helpful suggestions.

Once he returned to Los Angeles, we were swept away on our own wave of new love, romance, and passion. Weeks flew by and Vance made good on his word to propose to me at some point during each and every one. In actuality, he managed to propose to me every day, often multiple times a day, whenever he called my cell phone and his ringtone played. However, he came up with other ways to ask me. Sometimes it was as simple and cliché as sending me a bouquet of roses to my office with a card that simply read "Marry Me?" Another time it was an email with an internet meme of a naked baby in a top hat with a big belly and a funny look on its face. It said, "Marry Me" at the top, with "And All This Can Be Yours," at the bottom. Another time, it was a post-it note stuck to the mirror on my car's visor. It read "You're beautiful. Now marry me." I saved them all in my jewelry box, even going so far as to print out the email with the baby, too.

We spent every possible moment together. Vance's job was demanding, and he worked long hours, so we had exchanged keys to each other's apartments for convenience's sake early on. Often, I let myself into his place after I got off work to begin making dinner for him, so he'd have something ready when he got home. If he was going to be especially late, he'd come to my place after I was already in bed.

One such night, about six weeks after he returned from New York, I woke to the sound of him staggering into my apartment, crashing into furniture as he tried to make his way toward the bed. I was startled, thinking he must be drunk. I couldn't understand why he would be coming home shit-faced at eleven p.m. on a Wednesday night, but I brushed the thought aside. I had to get him into bed before he hurt himself or broke all the furniture in the room.

I turned on the bedside light and was about to hurry to his side, but he croaked out,

"Please, no light. Turn it off. It hurts my eyes."

He didn't sound drunk, but rather in pain. I turned the light out quickly and rushed to him, grabbing his arm and leading him to the side of the bed. In the dim light from the window, I could see his eyes were squeezed tightly shut and his face looked pinched. I undid his tie and unbuttoned his shirt most of the way. I slid his jacket off his shoulders and removed his belt. I guided him down into a reclining position and took off his shoes. I put a hand to his forehead and his skin was clammy and sticky, cool to the touch.

"What is it, Vance? What's going on? Are you hurt?" I whispered worriedly.

"I just have a terrible headache, Mimi. I'll be fine. I just need to sleep," he mumbled.

"This seems like more than just a headache. Do you have any of those pills you took in New York?" I asked.

"No, no. It's not that bad." He assured me, even though he hadn't opened his eyes once and I could see that he was perspiring heavily. "If you have a nighttime formula of ibuprofen, though, that would be good."

I hurried from the room to grab him a couple capsules and a bottle of water from the refrigerator. He cracked open his eyes when he sat up to take the pills, and I held the bottle of water to his lips, but he immediately laid back down with a huge sigh as soon as he was done. I moved to help him out of his slacks, but he waved me away.

"Please, Mimi. I'll be fine like this, I promise. Sleep is all I need."

Silently, I returned to my side of the bed and climbed in next to him. I was relieved to note that his breathing evened out quickly, and he was asleep within the hour. I kept an eye open all night long, watching him, concerned that there was more going on than a simple headache.

The following morning, Vance was fine. There were slight circles under his eyes, but if you weren't looking at him closely, you'd never notice. We were sharing a light breakfast of bagels and cream cheese, with coffee and juice, when I approached the topic of his headache. He was very nonchalant about it.

"It was just a tense day at work. I woke with a small pain in my head in the morning that got progressively worse as the day went on. By the time I left for the day, I could hardly see. It took everything I had to drive over here. I would have gone home, but I wanted to be with you even if I wasn't much in the way of company."

"Last night you said it wasn't as bad as the migraine you had in New York. It looked pretty fucking bad, Vance. You could hardly walk."

"Please don't overreact, sweetheart. I know how it must have appeared, but honestly, it doesn't happen very often. Don't worry." He placed his hands on my shoulders and pulled me toward his chest.

"But I am worried. Pain like that is not normal. I really think you should see a doctor, Vance." I slid my hands around his waist.

He kissed my forehead and looked into my eyes. "I have seen a doctor, Mimi. Remember? That's where I got the pills. Trust me, everything is fine."

I frowned at him but didn't say anything more. If he'd already had the issue checked out, maybe I was overreacting. I didn't know anything about migraines, but I'd had friends who got them. They'd never acted like they were any big deal, so maybe I should just relax.

Several more weeks flew by, and with them came the end of the summer. Vance's best friend,

Griffin Bennett, decided to throw a dinner party one Friday evening so he and all their other friends could meet me. According to Vance, they'd gotten tired of him being the absent party in their group and weren't going to let it slide any longer. In other words, they wanted to check me out.

We were at Vance's house, and I was putting the finishing touches on my hair in front of the bathroom mirror as he leaned against the door jamb watching me. He was giving me a thumbnail sketch of his friends' personalities, which he assured me was absolutely necessary. To be forewarned was to be forearmed, and all that.

"Griffin is cool. You don't really have to worry about him too much. He's a level-headed guy. He's an investment banker, has his act together for the most part. Although he is a big practical joker. He tends to go lightly on women, so don't worry. Unless you're dating him, in which case you're in big trouble. But you're not, so you're reasonably safe. His current girlfriend, Casey, will be there. She seems like a nice girl, but I don't know her very well. They haven't been dating very long.

"Then there's Bryant Lewis. He is the guy who is always getting his heart broken by some girl, so he will latch himself to your side to tell you all about the latest one to get your sympathy. Which is just a ploy to get into your pants. He works in insurance. I can never remember exactly what he does, he's explained it many times, but it's so boring I end up tuning out. He's a weenie, he's always been a weenie, but he's our weenie.

"Last, there's Justin Sever. He's the real degenerate in our group. Leather wearing, tattooed, Jack Daniels drinking, Harley Davidson driving stereotype, but the most loyal guy of us all and definitely the guy you want at your back in a bar fight. He's a graphic artist by day, badass biker by night. He's mostly quiet, but if you get him talking, chances are you've made a friend for life.

"I've known these guys since the fourth grade, they're like my brothers. They may give me a hard time, they might tease you a little, but they already know that you're special to me. They may say they want to check you out, but trust me, they won't be anything but one hundred percent on their best behavior with you."

I finished with my hair and smiled at him. "I'm not really all that nervous, Vance. Of course, I want them to like me and everything, but mostly I'm excited to meet them. I want to be part of your world and meeting your friends and getting to know them is a big deal. I feel like I'm really becoming a permanent part of your life."

He pulled me into his arms and pressed his nose to the top of my head and breathed deep, inhaling the floral scent of my shampoo. "You've been a permanent part of my life from the moment I met you. Only neither one of us knew it at the time."

"Not until you proposed, anyway," I said lightly.

He laughed. "What can I say? I catch on pretty quickly."

He released me and took me by the hand. "You ready? We should get going if we don't want to be late."

I turned off the light in the bathroom and walked out with him. "Let's go have some dinner. I have some men to bewitch."

"Over my dead body, Mimi..."

Dinner went smoothly, with no hiccups or disasters of any kind. His friends were perfect gentlemen to me though it was just the three of them and us. Apparently, Griffin and his girlfriend, Casey, had something of a falling out and their status was questionable. Being the only woman in a roomful of men at a dinner party was somewhat surreal. I half expected a charred meal in the kitchen and bucket of fried chicken on the table, but it turned out that Griffin was an accomplished cook. It wasn't anything elaborate, we had simply grilled salmon steaks with lemon, whipped sweet potatoes, and spicy yellow squash, but it was very tasty.

Vance's descriptions of his friends were remarkably on point. Griffin was a very put-together, well-groomed, blond man, with green eyes, deeply tanned skin, and a dazzling smile. He sat at the head of the table during dinner, and I sat to his left, across from Vance. He was dressed casually in a dark blue dress shirt with the sleeves rolled up and khaki trousers, with a brown belt and matching loafers. Well-spoken and intelligent, he was the perfect host and I immediately felt at ease with him. He didn't play any tricks on me, but I could see why he would be successful at pulling them off. His demeanor was such that you would never see it coming unless you had been warned beforehand and were already on guard. Needless to say, I didn't turn my back on him once.

On my left was Justin, but he was quiet throughout the whole meal. He spoke to me only to say hello when we were introduced. Otherwise, he just listened to everything everyone had to say. He didn't contribute much to any of the conversations, only speaking when someone directly asked him a question. He was an enigma.

Nevertheless, the meal was pleasant, and I could plainly see that these men had been friends for a very long time. There was a lot of teasing going on between them, and I enjoyed just sitting back and watching their interaction. They made sure to include me, asking me questions about myself, or telling me stories about Vance as a kid, or about the trouble they all got into as boys. I enjoyed every minute.

After dinner, we moved out to the backyard and sat around Griffin's fire pit, drinking beer, listening to music, and just chatting. Bryant cornered me and engaged me in a one-on-one conversation. He was actually a very sweet guy. He had boyish good looks, sad eyes, and the countenance of an adorable little puppy dog that you just wanted to pick up and cuddle. True to Vance's description, after some initial small talk, he started in about Tammy, a stripper he fell in love with two weeks ago when he came into her club, and who apparently dumped him last weekend for a girl she met at a party. He was positively shattered and was convinced that only the love of a sweet, girl next door type would heal the broken pieces of his heart. I listened sympathetically for a time but started looking for a way out of the conversation after about half an hour.

Salvation came, surprisingly, in the form of a tall, dark, tattooed man, straight out of an MC romance novel. He was at least six foot three, had a shaved head, soulful, brooding brown eyes, a nose that looked like it had been broken at least once and a goatee surrounding full lips that were meant to be kissed. His body was big and broad, with lots of muscles, and unlike Vance's swimmer's body, this guy looked like he was used to hard work. It was hard to believe he had a daytime desk job. I'd have sooner believed he cut down trees for a living.

"Alright, Bryant. You've accosted Mimi enough for one night. She's Vance's. She's not going home with you tonight to give you a pity fuck. Go call one of your regular go-to girls who fall for your broken heart routine."

"You'll never understand, Sever. You've never been shattered by a woman because they all fall at your feet. Mark my words, one day a woman will come along, she will own you and then she will leave you. You will be a broken man and then you will come to me and apologize before you look for comfort anywhere you can find it." Bryant took a long a sip of his beer before standing and walking over to where Vance and Griffin had been sitting talking shop since we came out here.

Justin sat down next to me chuckling. I heard him mutter under his breath, "That'll be the day."

"What? You don't think you'll ever have your heart broken?" I asked.

"No, I'm quite sure that's possible. I'll just never apologize to that fucker," he said affectionately and we both laughed.

"I hope he didn't chew your ear off too much with his desperate attempt to gain your sympathy. He gets his heart broken at least twice a month. We're all used to it. If there's a female in residence, he immediately seeks her out and looks to get on her good side using his current tale of woe. It's his angle. He's always seeking an "in" with the next chick he meets. He's really the biggest dog of us all. A player in a weenie's disguise."

I laughed and waved a hand as if dismissing the apology. "Don't worry. Vance warned me all about him before we got here. I was well prepared for all of you."

He grinned. "Good man, that Vance. You got yourself the best of the bunch. I know he and Griffin are the closest of all of us, they lived next door to each other growing up. I'd lay down my life for any of these guys. But Vance... Vance, I'd do time for him if he was in trouble."

I looked at him quizzically, knowing there was a story there, but also knowing instinctively it wasn't one Justin would share. Somehow, I didn't think Vance would, either. I was content to let this secret be theirs even though I have already mentioned how I felt about secrets.

"So, how did you two meet?" Justin asked. I had the feeling that I was at last being truly checked for worthiness by Justin. It was more a joke from the other guys, the premise for this dinner party. They just wanted to see their friend and knew chances were slim they weren't going to be able to peel him from my side, so they just invited us as a package deal. Justin however, really wanted to make sure I was worthy of his buddy's affection.

I explained the whole story of how we met, going so far as to explain our trip to Atlantic City and our mishap with security. He was howling by the time I'd finished.

"I'd have given money to see Vance being ushered off by hotel security. I don't think he's been in that kind of trouble a day in his life." He laughed, shaking his head.

He asked some more questions, about my life, my job, and my friends. I asked some about him too, and he was surprisingly open. He'd always liked to draw as a kid and had a real talent for it, but when he became a teenager, he'd become fascinated by computers. It was only natural that he combined his two passions and became a graphic artist. He worked freelance because it afforded him the opportunity to make his own hours, which he really enjoyed. He liked to travel, so it gave him the opportunity to schedule himself enough time off to ride off to parts unknown whenever he felt like it.

We spent what felt like hours talking. We were eventually interrupted by Vance, who came over to

148

join us, sitting on my other side and pulling me close into the curve of his arm.

"You trying to move in on my woman, Sever?" Vance teased.

"Well initially I saved her from Lewis, but after sitting here talking to her for a while, I might just kidnap her when we get to Vegas and marry her," he joked.

"What is it with you guys wanting to marry me? Wait, what do you mean when we get to Vegas?" I sputtered.

Vance just laughed. "One, you're just too good to not want to keep forever. Two, the guys all want to make a weekend of it and hit the road. What better destination than Vegas?" He and Justin shared a look that struck me as odd, but I pushed the thought away.

"Haven't we learned our lesson with impromptu trips to gambling towns?" I asked with one raised brow.

Vance laughed, "But baby, we came home eighteen thousand dollars richer! Besides, I thought we'd keep a lower profile this time. You know, eat some good food, and see some shows. The guys and I plan to do some golfing tomorrow morning. I thought you could spend time at the spa."

Justin snorted softly next to us, and I shot him a look, but he just raised his hands, palms out, as if to say he was innocent.

"Alright. No good reason not to go, I guess. A day at the spa does sound good. But you're paying," I said pointing my finger at his chest.

Vance clapped and rubbed his hands together eagerly. "Great! Let's go home and pack. Griffin is taking care of the arrangements."

Justin gave me a slow, but very sincere smile. I smiled back feeling as if what Vance said before we left was true. I had just made a friend for life.

Eight

We arrived in Las Vegas late that night, near midnight. We all checked into our rooms at the MGM Grand and planned to meet for breakfast the following morning at seven. It was far too early by my standards, given the time we rolled in, but the boys wanted to get on the green as soon as possible. I would get to go back to bed as Griffin booked me for an appointment at the spa at ten. I would spend most of the day there, not getting back to the room until about five, since I was getting the works: an hour and a half massage, a facial, a full body scrub and a manicure and pedicure. I was even having my hair trimmed and styled.

After a decent night's sleep (even if it was a little short) and a hearty breakfast for us all, we each went our separate ways. I never made it back to bed. I opted for a carafe of coffee from room service and simply lounged in the room watching a movie until it was time to head to the spa. I added a full waxing service to my treatment in lieu of the body scrub. My skin seemed soft enough to me, but I was due for a little attention in the body hair department, and by now, it was obvious how I felt about that little issue. I decided to be daring and go for a Brazilian wax to surprise Vance. He'd never said one way or another whether he liked bare skin down there or not, but all the romance book heroes seemed to go nuts for it, so I figured I'd give it a try. It'd always grow back (much to my continued consternation) if he preferred the little strip I normally had.

My day of pampering went by at a leisurely pace and except for an eye-opening and painful waxing session, the day was an exercise in bliss. I floated back to the room on a cloud of relaxation to find Vance already showered and dressed for the evening.

"Hey sweetheart," he said. "Did you enjoy your day?"

"Mmhmm." I could barely form words I was so relaxed. "I did. How was golf?"

"I had a great game, but as usual, Griffin won. He always does. He plays for business almost every weekend, so he gets more practice in than the rest of us. Justin almost never plays. He just comes along to drink beer and drive the golf cart."

"I'm with him," I said. "To me, that's the only part of the game that sounds fun. Say, aren't you dressed to go out a little early?"

"I got tickets to see Cirque du Soleil at eight, so I thought we could have dinner early. I thought with you being at the spa all day, you either had a very light lunch or none at all."

He was right, I'd only had a garden salad, so it was probably for the best that we ate early, or I would be gnawing on his arm by the time the show was over.

"Just let me get dressed and put some make-up on and I'll be ready to go."

Vance took me to a restaurant at the top of one of the casinos for dinner. We were seated at a table next to one of the windows, and the view was breathtaking. We ordered a seven-course tasting menu, and all of it was like a mini-orgasm on a plate. I was moaning over the chocolate soufflé at the end of the meal when Vance ordered a bottle of champagne. I thought it odd that he would order a bottle just then when our meal was practically over. I wasn't any kind of expert, but I thought that was something that was normally ordered at the beginning of a meal. I shrugged it off. The man could order whatever he liked as long as he didn't come between me and that little ramekin of chocolate nirvana.

I was contemplating graphic oral ministrations with the remnants of the dessert on my spoon when the champagne arrived. The waiter made to open the bottle, but Vance waved him away. Puzzled by Vance's odd behavior, I quickly forgot the spoon and I looked at him closely as he pulled out his phone. Was he calling the boys to come join us? I was even more confused when "Marry Me" started playing from my clutch purse on the table. I looked at my purse, then at him. He had a very serious, but slightly unsure look on his face. I looked at my purse again, just as the music stopped. Vance swiped his finger across the screen of his phone, and the music began to play again. Finally, I understood. My eyes went wide as I reached into my purse with a shaking hand. I didn't say anything, I just tapped the answer call button and held the phone to my ear, my gaze riveted to Vance's.

For a moment, Vance didn't say anything, either. Then, he cleared his throat and whispered huskily, "Will you, Mimi? Will you jump off that cliff again? Because I already have and I'm waiting here at the bottom to catch you."

Tears filled my eyes because I knew this time, it was not one of his playful proposals. It wasn't one of his little jokes meant to make me smile. This time he was deadly serious. He really wanted to me to be his wife. Here, in this gorgeous restaurant, after a marvelous meal, he didn't get down on one knee or hide a ring inside my dessert (which was a good thing because, with the way I devoured that soufflé, I probably wouldn't have noticed). No, Vance asked me in a way that made perfect sense to us. Somewhat silly, but very sweet. Just like every day I had spent with him. Just like I knew our life together would be, forever. Maybe we had only been together a short time in the grand scheme of things, but I was never more certain of anything than I was of the fact that we were made for each other.

I tried to respond, but the tears that threated earlier were dripping down my face and my throat had closed. All I could do was simply nod and give him a trembling smile. His face lit up and he whispered "Epic," into the phone before ending the call and placing his phone back into his pants pocket.

I half sobbed, half laughed as he reached into his jacket pocket, pulling out a ring box and rounded the table to kneel beside me.   He went the traditional route after all.

"Thank you, Mimi. I have one more question to ask. Will you marry me here? This weekend? I don't want to wait a minute longer than I have I to without you as my wife."

I giggled. "This was your real reason for coming here this weekend, wasn't it? It wasn't the guys' idea at all."

Vance winced slightly. "Well, I might have been the one to introduce the idea..."

"You were that sure I'd say yes?"   I asked skeptically.

He shook his head vigorously.   "Not in the slightest. I was hoping really hard, but if you'd said no, I thought there was a better-than-average chance that we'd still find a way to have a good time in a great city. Now, I don't want to be a complainer or anything, since I'm still very grateful you said yes, but would you mind looking at the ring and maybe putting it on?   This is not the most comfortable position to be in."

I clapped a hand over my mouth to stifle the laugh that bubbled up from my throat. "Oh, I'm so sorry." I took the ring and handed it to him. He slipped it onto my finger with the most amazing smile I had ever seen on his face. I tore my gaze away from the sight, to admire the ring. It was a gorgeous princess cut diamond, probably about a carat and a half, flanked by little round diamonds and set in platinum. It was exactly what I would have chosen for myself. I put my hands on his shoulders pulled him towards me for a long sweet kiss. I heard the faint sound of clapping around us, startling me from the little bubble that had formed around us ever since my phone had started ringing.

I pulled back, slightly embarrassed and whispered, "I suppose I should let you off your knees now."

"I would be ever so grateful," he returned.

Vance stood and grinned at the patrons who were enjoying our show, wiped his brow and then fist pumped at them. There were a few titters of laughter, some hoots and whistles and a couple of "way to go, bro's" before everyone turned back to their meals. Vance sat and finally uncorked the champagne. Just as we were getting ready to toast our engagement, I looked at him seriously.

"One thing. If we are seriously going to do this, there's something you're going to have to do for me."

Vance looked surprised at first but looked back at me just as soberly and said, "Of course, Mimi. What do you need?"

"You really have to retire the fist pump thing," I said.

"Wha- wait, what?"

"Seriously. You look like such a dork when you do it." I shook my head slightly.

"But I thought you liked that I was dorky," he sputtered.

"I did. Well, I do, but we're going to be married. It's time to present a much more adult image to the world. We're not children anymore."

Vance responded by throwing his napkin in my face while I giggled.

Later, as we were walking down the strip, arms wrapped around each other, looking at the lights and generally enjoying the giddiness of the moment, Vance pinched my side as he cleared his throat. "You never did answer me, you know. Will you marry me this weekend?"

"I'll marry you tonight, if you want," I said.

"Do you really mean that? I thought you'd want to look for a dress, get your hair done, call your girls and see if they can make a last-minute road trip or something. Your mom?"

"Nope. The dress I'm wearing is just fine. I had my hair done at the spa today. We can have a party with everyone when we get back to celebrate. We haven't even met each other's mother yet. They can wait a little while longer. For the ceremony, I want it to be just you and me. Is that okay with you?"

"That is absolutely one hundred percent fine with me." His dazzling smile returned. "What are we waiting for?"

I looked up at him with a high wattage smile of my own. "I guess Cirque du Soleil will have to wait for another night."

Fortunately, the county clerk's office in Las Vegas was open almost all hours. We had no difficulty getting our marriage license. Deciding where to have the nuptials performed was a little more challenging. The hotel wedding chapels were booked well in advance, so we spent a good portion of the early night driving to various places on the strip to see if anyone could accommodate us. We finally ended up at a tiny little chapel at the end of the strip around ten p.m. They just happened to have a time slot available at one fifteen in the morning, so we grabbed it. With some spare time on our hands, I insisted we go find a ring for Vance. There was no way I was letting him get married without one.

Fortunately, in a city like Vegas, it wasn't hard to find a jewelry store that was open at such a late hour. In fact, it wasn't hard to find about twenty of them. We entered the first and walked right back out. It was a gothic themed store, and everything was a little too... gothic. The next store had a better selection, but we just didn't find anything we liked. It went the same way at the next two. At the fifth store, we found a platinum band with a vine-like pattern hand-carved through the center. It was unique and suited Vance's style perfectly. It was three thousand dollars, which Vance made a fuss about paying for, but I refused to let him pay for his own ring. After several minutes of bickering, I threatened not to consummate the marriage that night and for the foreseeable future, to which he grumblingly but smartly conceded.

We arrived at the chapel just ahead of the appointed time and I purchased a small bouquet of red roses from the chapel florist. I was wearing a short, baby pink dress with spaghetti straps and matching slingback pumps. It was a very simple look, and my hair was long and straight, laying loose on my shoulders. I had diamond studs in my ears, but other than my new engagement ring, I had no other jewelry to speak of. One could probably say I looked elegant more than anything if not a little plain.

Vance looked handsome in the same suit he wore on our first date, although he was wearing a charcoal patterned tie, with tiny red threads running through it. Fortunately, we didn't clash too badly.

The entire ceremony took about ten minutes. It seemed odd to me that you could bind your life to someone else's for eternity, in a short span of time, but in a town like Vegas, where fortunes turn in an instant, I supposed I really shouldn't be too surprised. Even as the odd notion occurred to me, I was deliriously happy to be joined to this amazing man. I didn't know how we would go about blending our lives when we'd never seriously discussed doing this. In fact, I realized with a start, we'd never even told each other that we loved each other. I guess we just took it as fact by the way we always treated each other, and in all the many other things we said to each other.

We were walking back down the aisle arm in arm as the realization dawned on me. I was about to bring him to a stop but thought better of it. I wanted to find the perfect time to tell him like he did with my proposal. If he were to tell me first, I wouldn't be able to hold back from saying it to him, but I hoped I could find a romantic and memorable way to tell him.

Outside in the car, Vance turned to me looking like a little kid. "Do you mind if I call the guys now? They're going to be pissed that I didn't tell them beforehand, but I can't wait to tell them the good news now. They'll be even more pissed if we don't let them celebrate with us, at least for a little while."

"You mean to tell me you don't immediately want to whisk me away to bed?" I said, slightly disappointed. I thought we'd immediately get down to the X-rated portion of the festivities.

He immediately looked torn. I could see the gears turning in his mind. On one hand, he really did want to share his happiness with the people who were as close to him as brothers. On the other hand, well... fun, married, sexy times.

I decided to help him out. "Let's look at this rationally. At any time, did having a celebratory drink with the guys ever ended up with you getting a blowjob or other carnal pleasures?"

"Not from them," he replied with a pointed look.

"Bad example. Let me rephrase. Did having a drink with the guys ever ended up with you getting a blowjob or other carnal pleasures that made your toes curl, your hair stands on end and want to slap your mother, from me?"

"They can wait until tomorrow." He turned the key in the ignition and left skid marks as he tore out of the parking lot on the way back to the hotel.

Once we were back in the room, I excused myself to the bathroom and cursed my lack of forethought. I should have taken the opportunity to do a little shopping for some essentials instead of our leisurely stroll up and down the strip. I had no sexy lingerie to seduce him with after leaving this room. No candles to light to set the mood. I had only me. I thought about that for a minute and decided that maybe, just maybe, that was enough.

I took a few minutes to brush my hair until it shone and touched up my makeup. I took off all my clothes and freshened my perfume. With a last look in the mirror, I took a deep breath and opened the door.

Vance was standing by the bed with his back to me. As he turned and looked over his shoulder, his eyes widened, and his jaw went a bit slack. I stood there as bare as can be. No sexy pose against the door frame, no beguiling look. I was completely vulnerable. I didn't fidget awkwardly or feel unsure. I was just me, giving myself to him wholly and completely, standing there waiting for him to accept me just like I was.

Before he could turn fully around, or say anything, I began. "I don't have anything to offer you to set a scene of romance or to make tonight extra sexy. I don't have any tricks or anything like that. All I have is me and my heart, and as you know, both are completely and totally yours. They always have been. I love you, Vance. I haven't said that out loud before, but I've been saying it in my head from almost the day we met."

161

Vance turned and unbuttoned his shirt. He removed it slowly, letting it fall on the floor next to him. He removed his shoes, belt, pants, and briefs next, until he was completely naked, his proud cock jutting out before him. He came to stand before me.

"Now I am as bare as you are. I don't have any special gimmicks to offer you either that other couples probably use to make their wedding night more adventurous. I don't know about you, but I don't want or need that. I only need this. You and me, with nothing between us. This is what is real and special. Everything we do together is romantic and memorable to me Mimi because you are there. There isn't a memory I have of you..." he smiled boyishly, "few as they may be right now, that isn't colored by my love for you. Even the ones of you brushing your teeth or putting on your shoes. That's romantic to me. The little things that happen in the course of a day or a lifetime with someone. Not how many candles were lit on a certain night, or how many seductive glances were shared over a glass of wine. This memory, however, the memory of you coming to me completely exposed, body and soul, telling me that you love me? That transcends romance. There isn't even a word for it."

He reached for my hand and led me over and onto the bed. He followed me, guiding me down as he touched his lips to mine. He kissed me with his usual delicate touch, but he didn't tease like he normally did. That night, Vance's passion flared high and hot and before I knew it, he was kissing me with a fever I have never felt from him before.

His tongue was an invader in my mouth, plunging and conquering its recesses, only to retreat before thrusting forth again. I took advantage of the situation and allowed myself to explore the curves and planes of his body. Every dip, every crease, every ripple of his muscles, was traveled thoroughly by my searching hands.

Vance's hands were not passive either. He groped and squeezed every available inch of skin, plumping and kneading as he made his way down my body. He licked my neck, down between my breasts, my belly, dipping into my navel. His tongue circled over my hipbones, making me giggle involuntarily as he continued down my thighs to the backs of my knees. He turned me over and began working his way back up until he reached the back of my neck and bit down hard.

He pulled back and began running his hands over my back, making circles over the muscles, not massaging exactly, more like tantalizing the skin, sensitizing it to his touch. He worked his way down until he was circling the fleshy part of my buttocks. His touch grew firmer as he growled out, "Have I ever told you how much I love your ass, Mimi? It is so round and perfect. Always begging me to take a bite out of it." Just then I felt him bend forward and sink his teeth into my skin. Not too hard, nothing that would've drawn blood of course, but certainly enough to grab my attention. He soothed the sting with his tongue and sat back with a little chuckle.

"That will probably leave a bit of a mark tomorrow."

I started to make a smart comment back but thought better of it. Vance was in some kind of passion zone, and I wasn't about to disrupt the flow. While I loved Vance's normal languid approach, I was really into his wild and uninhibited side.

Vance trailed his fingers down between my thighs and traced the seam of my outer lips. He coated his fingers with the moisture that had collected there before bringing them to my mouth and rubbing them over my bottom lip.

"Taste what I do to you, Mimi. The sweetness your body makes just for me." He whispered huskily.

His words reduced me to a puddle of need as my tongue flicked out over my lip involuntarily. I whimpered softly as I tasted the heady flavor of my arousal on my own skin. His hand returned to the soft flesh between my legs and slowly eased it apart, his fingers softly pressing against the little knot of nerves aching for his touch. Slowly, he began to draw little circles over it, before sliding two fingers from his other hand inside me. I lifted my hips to allow him better access and squirmed against his touch. He thrust deep, pumping his hand back and forth while I worked myself in time with his rhythm.

"That's it, Mimi. Fuck that pretty little pussy on my hand. You look so beautiful when you are like this. So open and ready. Looking for your pleasure with me. God, I love to watch you."

I loved it when he talked dirty to me. He made me feel like some kind of sex goddess. Like no matter what I did, it was the most erotic thing he'd ever seen, and it inspired me to just abandon any notion of embarrassment or shame, or whatever might hold me back. I rose to my hands and knees and pushed back hard onto him, rocking faster and faster, feeling my breasts swing back and forth and my temperature rise higher and higher. I tossed my head back on my shoulders, panting as I felt myself getting close when Vance withdrew his hand and came to his knees behind me.

He ran his hand over my ass, squeezing gently. "I'm going to take you like this, Mimi. I'm going to watch myself work this hot little cunt, see my dick wet with your juices as it moves in and out of you. Finally, there's not going to be anything between us. You're completely mine now. There will never be anything between us again." He said as he slid into me, right to the hilt.

I gasped as he filled me, the angle of this position allowing him to reach depths he hadn't touched before. Ever since the first time we made love, we'd always take a moment to enjoy the initial connection of our joining. It wasn't solely for me to adjust to his size or anything like that. It was more to appreciate that second when we became one when our bodies melded along with our hearts and the satisfaction that came with it. It would only last a moment as the need to move always won out. On our wedding night, it overtook us sooner, the height of our passion being what it was.

Vance gripped my hips and set up a hard rhythm right away. I moved against him, pushing back as he thrust forward, my fingers digging into the mattress beneath me. We were both panting and grunting as our bodies slapped together, the sounds echoing through the room. We were slamming into each other, driving harder, faster, as if we could finally become one body through sheer force.

He wound his hands into my hair, pulling my head back and stilling my body as he pounded harder into me, his cock angling over that cluster of nerves inside me that pushed me toward oblivion.

"Take me, Mimi. Take all of me. Every single solid inch... it's yours." He gasped out as I felt him begin to swell impossibly larger inside me.

"When I come, you'll take every ounce, every drop, and along with it, you'll take my soul, too." His voice broke on the last few words and I felt the rush wash over me, beginning at the soles of my feet, burning through my body like a wildfire, up my legs, to my core, then radiating through the rest of me, incinerating me from the inside out. Vance thrust into me deeply, yelling out his release with pure abandon, before collapsing onto my back, taking us both down to the bed. We lay there like that for long minutes, both of us struggling to piece our minds back together after such shattering pleasure. Finally, he rolled off me, gathering me in his arms, my back to his front, and held me as we both attempted to regulate our breathing.

Finally, he spoke to me in a hushed tone. "I'm sorry, Mimi. I don't know what came over me. I wanted to make love to you slowly. To show you how much I cherish you, how much I treasure you. Instead, I was like a wild animal."

I turned in his arms and put a hand on his cheek. "No, Vance. Don't you dare apologize. I love it when you take your time with me, you know I do, but that was unbridled passion. That was you raw, and uncontrolled and safe with me. That was you at your most vulnerable, just the way we both wanted tonight to be. Don't ruin it with regret. I'm not some china doll that you have to wear white cotton gloves to admire." I grinned a little cheekily. "You know, it's okay to get me a little dirty from time to time."

"God, Mimi. You are so perfect." He said, kissing the top of my head. "I can't wait to grow old with you."

"Let's not be in too much of a hurry to grow old, okay there, buddy? I'm looking forward to many years of admiring your gorgeous body. I don't want to rush through that part too fast." I teased.

"If Jack LaLanne can stay fit into his nineties, then I can do the same for you. As long as you keep looking at me the way you do now," he said.

"Who's Jack LaLanne?" I asked, completely confused.

I think our mutual plan had been to sleep late into the afternoon the next day because we made love two more times, not falling asleep until well after dawn. This was not to be when Vance's phone started ringing around ten the following morning. We both ignored it and the call went to voicemail, along with the one that came immediately after it. When it rang for the third time, Vance groaned and rolled over, answering it with a very pleasant, "What do you want, fuckwit?"

He was quiet for a few beats, then grumbled, "No, we need sleep. We got married last night and have been up all-night consummating said marriage. Have breakfast by yourselves." He hung up, tossing the phone back on the nightstand and pulling the covers over his head.

"Three, two, one…," I counted down.

On cue, Vance's phone started ringing again and I could swear the sound was shriller than it was before as if it could convey the urgency of the caller's intent through its electronic tones.

"Griffin, right?" I asked.

Vance mumbled something that sounded like yes from his place under the covers.

"You realize that, after what you said, if you don't answer the phone, he will be up here pounding on the door next, right?"

Vance shot up in bed and answered the phone just as it began its next round of ringing.

"Yeah?" He answered in a much more agreeable tone. He laughed a little. "Yeah, you heard right. She told me she'd marry me right away after I asked her last night, so I didn't give her a chance to change her mind."

He was quiet for a few minutes while Griffin talked. "Sure, give us some time to get dressed, then we'll meet you in the lobby. See you in a few." He touched the screen to end the call and tossed it back on the nightstand. "Looks like we're having breakfast with the guys. We're going to be called on the carpet for not allowing them to come with us."

"I'd better hurry through a shower then. I love you, but I'm not showing up to a meal with your friends smelling like this." I said, giving myself a good sniff.

"And just what, exactly, do you smell like?" Vance asked with a goofy grin.

"Like a groupie with a pass to an Aerosmith concert after party," I said as I walked naked to the bathroom.

I closed the door on Vance's howling laughter.

The guys forgave us quickly. They even went so far as insisting they throw our wedding celebration party when we returned home. We objected because we wanted to have something formal, much more like an actual wedding reception, but the guys had their own plans. They felt it should be much less stuffy and more beer bash-y. I presumed this was to pay me back for depriving them of a bachelor party for Vance.

"I can't believe you actually got married, Mimi!" Laurel exclaimed during one of our regular Skype calls after I got back from Vegas.

"I know, it's pretty wild, but he's just the one. I can't imagine my life without him," I said.

"Yeah, yeah. I know all about it. He's all you've talked about for months." She rolled her eyes. Then she grinned widely at me. "Seriously though, I'm super thrilled for you both. I wish you all the love and happiness in the world. Well maybe not all, I'd like to keep some for myself, but all the rest of it—you guys can have that."

"Thanks, that's very sweet of you, Laur. Do you think you and Pete will be able to make it out here for our reception slash frat party?"

"I'll be there no matter what, but Pete is still trying to get the time off to go. Whose bright idea was it to throw you a kegger to celebrate your wedding? Vance's? How is your mother taking that?"

"No, it wasn't Vance," I laughed, "Although he's not overly upset by the idea. It's the brainchild of his group of friends. You'll meet them, and it will all make sense. I decided it was easier to just go with the flow. Our little ceremony in Vegas was enough for me. My mom, well... she's resigned to the idea. She's just happy that I'm happy."

"Well, that works for me, too. At least this way I don't have to put on some ugly dress that I'll never wear again."

"That can still be arranged, you know," I warned teasingly.

We joked around for a few more minutes before ending the call and logging out. It was hard to believe it had only been a few short months since I had visited her in New York, so much had happened since then. This time, I'd be seeing her as Mimi Ashcroft.

Our "reception" ended up being fantastic. Everyone was relaxed and happy, there was no pressure that people feel on "The Big Day" so we were free to just be in love and share our happiness with our friends. My mom did insist on a formal wedding cake and a photographer, and later I was grateful for her foresight. She and Vance's mom, although both unhappy with us at first for leaving them out of such a special occasion, were more than happy to make each other's acquaintance. We had introduced them at a private lunch with just the four of us and they hit it off immediately. At the party, they spent most of it together walking around laughing at everyone's antics and taking random snapshots, presumably for blackmail material later.

I was pleased that Laurel and Pete were both able to make it to the party and we spent some time talking and laughing with them, reminiscing about Vance's time in the security offices at Caesar's.

My coworkers and good friends from the firm, Grace, Liz, and Jessica came to the party too. While I wasn't as close to them as I was to Laurel, they were my best girlfriends in Los Angeles, and prior to meeting Vance, I had spent a lot of my free time with them. Vance and I had been so wrapped up in each other since our respective returns from New York, they hadn't even met him yet. Unfortunately, there was so much going on, other than a brief introduction and a few hugs and cheek kisses and promises to get together soon, I didn't see much of them that evening. I did notice, however, that they somehow found Griffin, Bryant, and Justin and had them cornered at one point.

171

The music poured from the speakers all night long and the alcohol flowed freely. There was plenty of finger food, people danced and fortunately, despite the college-party vibe to the occasion, everyone kept their clothes on and there were no embarrassing incidents. The party wound down around three in the morning and we all called it a success.

We spent the next year in a state of newlywed bliss. We both did well at our jobs though Vance continued to work long hours. We spent our weekends either with our friends out on the town—interestingly, Grace and Bryant, Liz and Griffin and Jessica and Justin began dating after the reception party—redecorating Vance's home to reflect our new blended life or occasionally taking time for a romantic getaway. Our lives were simple and uncomplicated. We were young and in love and had everything we needed in each other.

The only thing marring our happiness, at least from my perspective, was Vance's continued headaches. He didn't have them all the time, maybe once a month, maybe less frequently, but when he did have them, they were debilitating. He missed work on a couple of occasions because they were so bad. I spoke with a co-worker of mine who took medication for migraines, and she told me that she had them somewhat regularly, too. She didn't have them quite as often as Vance did, but she assured me they were not serious, and I had nothing to worry about. Some people just got them.

Whenever I tried to talk to Vance about my concerns, he was touched, but he firmly reminded that he had already received medical attention and there was no need for me to worry. Finally, I just came to accept it as normal and life went on. I had never been happier in my entire life.

Nine

The weekend of our first anniversary coincided with a fund-raiser for a charity supported heavily by Vance's law firm. We had initially planned to take a long romantic weekend at a bed-and-breakfast in Carmel, but since this event was in support of breast cancer research, a cause that was dear to one of the partners of his firm who had lost his wife to the disease several years ago, Vance didn't feel comfortable skipping out on it. So, the night before our anniversary, we were in our bedroom, preparing to attend a formal gala when the two of us would much rather be secluded in a hotel room feeding each other oysters from a room service delivery cart.

Something about Vance had seemed "off" all day, but I couldn't quite figure out what. I'd asked him if something was wrong at various times, but he just brushed me off, even seeming annoyed by the question. I chalked it up to me being a little too mother hen-ish, but it bothered me because Vance was never short tempered with me. In fact, I'd never seen him be short-tempered with anyone. I ultimately shrugged it off, figuring I'd only make matters worse if I continued to nag him about it.

After putting my earrings in, I turned to Vance to see if he was ready to leave. As he fastened his last cufflink, he looked at me expectantly, as if waiting for me to say something.

"I was only wondering if you were ready to go," I said hesitantly, unsure of his mood.

He nodded, grabbing his wallet and putting it in his inside breast pocket. "I'm as ready as I'll ever be." He extended his arm toward the door, indicating I should exit before him.

My indigo gown made a swishing noise as I walked down the hall ahead of him. It was a very pretty dress, strapless with a wrapped bodice and full skirt. It was my usual simple taste, nothing elaborate or flashy, just understated and elegant. My hair was rolled tight in a twist at the back of my head, with wisps falling in the front framing my face. I wore tiny pearl earrings and a matching necklace. My only other jewelry were my wedding rings. Normally Vance would have made several comments about my appearance, but he hadn't said a single word. In fact, he hadn't said much of anything at all.

When we walked out to the car, Vance went straight around to his side, got in and started it up. I didn't want to be a spoiled brat or anything, I was more than capable of opening my own door, it was just that he was acting so out of character, I stood there for a moment staring blankly into space. The window on my side of the car rolled down, and Vance leaned over the seat to look at me.

"Are you going to get in, or are we going to sit in the driveway all night?" He asked sarcastically.

I blinked a couple times but nodded in response before opening the door and climbing inside. I adjusted my skirt, shut the door quietly and fastened my seat belt. I remained quiet all the way to the gala venue. For his part, Vance didn't say a word, either.

Once we arrived, I put on my happy face, made pleasant small talk with his superiors at the firm, and did my best to be the charming wife. Vance was more communicative than he had been but remained somewhat aloof. I tried to make up for his standoffishness by being even more gregarious with anyone who crossed our path.

Blessedly, dinner was eventually served, giving us a reprieve from socializing. My stomach was a mess of nerves from all the uneasiness I was feeling over Vance's uncharacteristic behavior, so I just pushed my food around my plate. A glance in his direction revealed him doing the same although he was taking healthy gulps of the scotch he had gotten from the bar before we sat down. Halfway through the meal, he excused himself and was gone a long while. I had assumed he went to the restroom, or to make a call. He eventually returned with another scotch. By the smell of him, he'd had at least one other while he was away.

After dinner was cleared and dessert was served, some tables were moved away and the floor was opened for dancing. A lively band was playing all different genres of music. I enjoyed watching the couples turn and twist around the floor, and it brought to mind the night in Atlantic City when Vance and I danced salsa at the little club on the boardwalk. I turned to him to remind him of the fun we had, only to see him glowering at me as if I had done something wrong.

"Vance?" I started. "What is it, sweetheart?"

"Nothing." He said, taking the last gulp of his drink. "Are you ready to get out of here?"

"I... I was just thinking it might be nice to have a dance. Wouldn't you like to dance at least once before we go? I mean, we're all dressed up and everything. It's not every day I get you into a tux." I smiled weakly at him.

"No, I would not like to fucking dance. I would like to get the hell out of here." He stood and walked to my chair. Thinking he was going to help me up, I put out my hand, but he reached into his pocket, pulled out his keys and dropped them into my extended palm.

"You're going to have to drive. I had too much scotch." He said, before turning his back and walking toward the door.

The ride home was as silent as the ride there although waves of hostility poured off Vance. I spent the time trying to figure out what had gotten into him. I ran through the evening in my head repeatedly, but nothing seemed out of place. I would have written it off to a bad drunk, but one, even though Vance wasn't safe enough to drive, he didn't seem all that intoxicated. Two, he had been in some kind of mood before he ever got near the scotch.

Once we arrived home, I went straight to the bedroom to change out of my dress. I was so anxious, I was ready to jump out of my skin. I was out of sorts, unsure what to make of his behavior, didn't know what I should do. Talking to him was out of the question. It was clear he could barely tolerate my presence. With that thought, I looked at the clock on the bedside table. It wasn't even nine yet. I put on a pair of jeans and a t-shirt and decided to just go for a drive. I couldn't take another minute of the tension and he most definitely didn't want me around, so the best thing to do was to take a little time out.

After I'd brushed out my hair, I grabbed my phone and keys and left the house on silent feet. I didn't know where Vance had disappeared to, but he was somewhere in the house since his Mercedes was still parked in the driveway. I hopped into my Lexus and backed slowly out of the driveway, without turning on my headlights. I don't know why I felt like I needed to sneak away, but I didn't want to attract any more attention to myself than I already had that night. Once in the street, I turned the lights on, but still accelerated slowly away.

I drove around for a while, unsure of where to go or what to do, until finally deciding to head to a quiet little bar I'd been to with Vance and his friends a few times. A quiet and comfortable hole-in-the-wall sort of place where I knew no one would bother me.

I entered the dimly lit room and went straight to the bar. I ordered my favorite dirty martini and took it to a booth near the center of the room. I just sat there, sipping my drink, unable to think of anything but Vance's odd behavior. No matter how

I looked at it, there was no explanation for it. It seemed like everything irritated him, but as if I bothered him most of all. I couldn't think of what I had done to piss him off, and honestly, my feelings were more than a little hurt. I thought I should be angry back at him for being such a dick, but I couldn't get past the fact that our anniversary was the next day. Maybe being in love had made me overly sentimental, but all I could think was we should be making love and congratulating ourselves for being so happy together. Instead, here I was in some shithole nursing a drink by myself.

While I sat there lost in thought, I didn't notice that a presence was looming over me, taking in my distracted state. It was a good thing that this person knew me and meant me no harm because I was so completely unaware that I nearly jumped three feet when Justin sat down across from me with a beer in his hand.

"Hello there, Peaches." He said, taking a deep drink from his bottle of Bud. "Why on earth are you in a place like this alone? Where is your other half?"

"Jesus Christ, Justin! You scared the fuck out of me." I cried out, clutching my chest. "Don't you know better than to sneak up on a girl like that, unless you want to get maced?"

"If you have mace in that purse, it wouldn't have done you much good tonight as out of it as you were. I would have had you down the street before you even thought of trying to get to it." He observed. "What's going on? You don't look so good."

I sighed unhappily. "It's just been a weird night. Well, the whole day has been weird, really."

"What's weird is seeing you without Vance attached to your hip. I'm assuming this has something to do with him."

I nodded. "Yeah. He has been acting strange all-day long. Very distant, irritated. We went to this charity function tonight, and he was practically hostile towards me. I don't get it. I don't understand what I did to upset him. Whenever I asked what was bothering him, he denied anything was wrong, but he seemed annoyed that I was even asking. I've been running the day through my head, trying to think of something—anything—that could have set him off, but there's nothing."

Justin considered what I said. "That's pretty unusual for Vance. He's the most even-tempered person I've ever met. Everyone has their bad days though. Maybe he just woke up on the wrong side of the bed."

"I know. I mean I haven't known him as long as you guys, obviously, but I do live with the guy, and he's never acted like this before.

"Tomorrow is our anniversary. I've been looking forward to it so much. Our trip away already had to be canceled, so I would hate for it to be spoiled further by something like this. Maybe it's silly to be sentimental, but it's kind of important to me."

"It's not silly to celebrate your anniversary. It should be a happy occasion. I hope he gets over whatever is up his ass and doesn't let you down. If it helps you feel any better, I know him, and I know how he feels about you, so I just don't see that happening," he said sincerely.

I smiled gratefully. "Thanks, Justin. I have to admit, I don't have a lot of experience in this area."

"What do you mean?" He looked at me with a confused expression.

"You may find this pretty funny, but Vance was my first real boyfriend. I mean, I dated a lot; I wasn't a virgin or anything when I met him. I just never really got into a serious relationship with anyone. I certainly never fell in love. The guys I saw were just nice men whose company I enjoyed. Some I liked better than others, some I was even infatuated with for a little while, but nobody lasted longer than a month and that was just fine with me. I enjoyed being single and unencumbered, free to meet new people and do whatever I wanted to do when I wanted to do it. Then I met Vance and he changed all that for me. Suddenly, nothing made sense without him."

Justin looked at me in surprise. "How old are you again?" he asked.

"I just turned twenty-five last month," I said.

"I suppose that's not too young to never have been in love, but most people have thought they were by that age and have had at least one serious relationship."

"I know. It puts me at a bit of a disadvantage, because I'm pretty much feeling my way through this, and I'm married. There's a little more on the line. It's not like I can just throw up my hands if it's not working and consider it one of life's experiences and walk away. Not that I'm thinking about that now or have ever thought about it before. Things so far have been surprisingly easy. Vance is remarkably easy to please, so much so I feel like I hit the jackpot with him. I'm spoiled by him, I admit it. I guess that's the problem tonight. I've had it too easy and I don't have the skills to know how to deal with what happened today. So here I am trying to figure it out. I'd be home talking about it with him, but it was obvious I was the last person he wanted near him. I felt it was best I give him some breathing room and go somewhere to think."

"You probably made the right decision. I wish I could give you some advice on how to deal with this, but like I said, I've never seen or heard of Vance acting this way before. It's very interesting, to say the least. However, if he keeps acting this way, hurting your feelings and all, and you want me to have a talk with him, I'd be more than happy to tell him to pull his head out of his ass for you," he offered. "You're my friend now, too. I look out for my friends."

I smiled gratefully. "Vance told me that about you."

Justin took a long sip of his beer. "He knows me well."

"There's something special between the two of you, isn't there? I sensed it when you spoke to me that first night at Griffin's house when you grilled me to see if I was good enough for Vance. You know, the night before we got married. Huh…" I stopped and thought for a second. "I guess that was a year ago tonight."

He thought for a moment, too. "You're right. Anyway, aside from Vance and I going way back, I owe Vance a lot. It may be hard to believe, but when we were just kids, Vance was my protector."

"You?" I gave his big, muscled frame an obvious once-over. "You're right, I find it very hard to believe."

"Yep." He motioned to himself with his hand. "I was not always the proud owner of this fine, Zeus-like physique.' He smirked. "I was actually a scrawny kid, shorter than everyone else. Didn't hit my growth spurt until the end of high school. Vance caught a bunch of kids circling me and threatening me one day in elementary school and chased them all off. He befriended me and pretty much kept everyone off me until I could hold my own. He was the one who got me into working out and building myself up. Once my hormones finally kicked in, it became surprisingly easy to pack on the muscle and I got a lot bigger than everyone else but by then, everyone already knew not to mess with me because Vance would be there to take care of it. He may be a laid-back guy, but if he does get mad, he's pretty scary. Fortunately, I've only ever seen him get that way when something he cares deeply about is threatened."

I nodded, feeling extremely proud knowing my husband was such an honorable guy that he would stick up for the underdog, even when he was just a boy.

I checked the time on my phone and learned it was almost midnight. I hoped Vance had already gone to bed and I would be able to sneak in and go to sleep myself, waking up with tomorrow being a better day. As if reading my mind, Justin spoke up.

"It's getting late, Peaches. You should probably go home and get some beauty sleep. No matter what tomorrow brings, it's still a big day. I know you, and you'll want to take pictures. You won't want dark circles under your eyes for those."

We both stood from the table to leave. I gave Justin a big hug, grateful for the conversation and insight he provided that night. He provided a much-needed distraction from my miserable confusion and just his company made me feel better about the whole situation. I was convinced more than ever that Vance had just had a bad day and there was nothing major going on.

Justin walked me out to my car, and as I saw him swing a leg over his motorcycle just as I turned out of the parking lot and drove away, I said a small prayer that he would always be safe on that contraption because he was just too good a soul to lose.

When I pulled up to the house, there were no lights shining through the windows. It was completely dark, not even the porch light was on. I walked carefully to the door in the pitch black, cursing when I stubbed my toe against a large potted plant near the end of the walk. I tripped up the steps and finally made it to the front door, with my key at the ready. Surprisingly, it was unlocked. I stepped in quietly, closing the door behind me with a soft click. I made my way through the house partially by memory, partially by touch, to the bedroom. Vance lay sprawled across the bed, still in his unbuttoned tuxedo shirt and pants. Rather than wake him to coax him over to his side, I decided to leave him be. I changed into my pajamas silently and made myself comfortable in the guest room. It was a nice room, but we had never really gotten around to doing much with it. It was spartan, containing only a bed and a dresser, and the most boring of linens and a comforter. Nevertheless, I snuggled down under the covers and closed my eyes. After my conversation with Justin, my mind was much less troubled, and I had little difficulty falling asleep.

The following morning, I awoke earlier than I expected. Sleeping in the guest room was okay, but the bed was far less comfortable than the one in our bedroom. I felt a little stiff and not as rested, so I guessed this had something to do with my waking up sooner than usual.

I decided to go ahead and proceed as planned as if the day before had never happened. The house was quiet, so after making the bed, I moved around the house as quietly as possible. I didn't want to disturb Vance if he was still asleep. When I peeked into the bedroom, he seemed to be in the same position I found him in last night, only now he had an arm thrown over his eyes. I gathered my clothes for the day and took them with me, so I could get ready in the guest bathroom.

Once I was ready, I prepared a semi-elaborate breakfast of eggs benedict, fresh fruit and cream, coffee, and juice. Just before everything was ready, I heard the shower turn on in our bathroom. I was relieved he was up on his own as I really hadn't wanted to wake him myself. As I waited for him to come out, I felt my anxiety grow over what his mood might be. I began pouring the coffee and juice when I heard the shower turn off and was just plating the food when he walked into the room. Putting on my best smile, I turned to him and greeted him warmly.

"Good morning, Vance. Happy anniversary!"

"Wow, sweetheart. Happy anniversary. This looks wonderful. You didn't have to do all this." He said with his trademark smile. He seemed to be completely himself. I inwardly breathed a sigh of relief.

We sat down and dug in. Our conversation was light and pleasant, with no mention of the day before. In fact, it was almost as if he had no memory of it whatsoever. Not wanting to spoil any part of what I wanted to be a very happy day, I vowed not to bring it up at all. Whatever lingering feelings I may have had, I buried them deep inside to be dealt with at another time, if ever.

After breakfast, we took a drive up the coast to spend the day in Santa Barbara. The weather was gorgeous, the kind you only find in Southern California in late summer. I remember wishing we had rented a convertible, so I could feel the sun on my face and the wind rushing through my hair. I wanted that feeling of being young and carefree and alive, the way I always felt with Vance. He was back to normal mostly although he did seem a little quieter than usual. I pushed any concerns I had to the side and kept up a constant stream of chatter, while he just smiled and nodded, seemingly entertained by my enthusiasm for the day ahead of us.

We spent our time at Stearns Wharf, shopping, visiting the Sea Center, and even doing a little fishing at the edge of the wharf. We didn't catch anything, but we had a good time trying. It was nice just being out in the fresh sea air, in a beautiful and peaceful setting, enjoying our time together. When the sun set, we drove downtown to a beautiful Mexican restaurant. It was gorgeous inside, with antiqued beige walls, old world woodworking, wrought iron railings surrounding the second floor, terra-cotta colored curtain panels with golden sheers, and these charming star-lights dangling from the ceiling. We chose to sit at their raw bar, sampling their fresh ceviche, fish, and oysters and enjoying margaritas with premium tequila. We exchanged gifts; Vance gave me a beautiful necklace with a teardrop diamond pendant while I gave him a TAG Heuer watch I had seen him eyeballing online. It wasn't an elaborate celebration of our anniversary by any stretch of the imagination, but it was very much like our wedding. Quiet and intimate, romantic and loving. It was a relaxing time spent together, just enjoying each other's company.

As we were leaving the restaurant, hand in hand, I suggested we prolong the evening just a little more by taking a short walk down the block enjoying the warm night air. Vance smiled indulgently at me and led me toward the sidewalk. Just before we reached it, he seemed to stumble over something. It was dark, and the streetlights didn't shine well at the corner of the building where we were walking so I couldn't see what tripped him. All I knew was we were walking one moment and then next he was tumbling forward. He let go of my hand when he started to go down, but he didn't have time to get his own fully under him before he hit the ground. While his right hand helped break the fall and kept his face from hitting the ground, his left hand was twisted somewhat awkwardly beneath him.

I rushed to his side and helped him roll over into a sitting position. He immediately cradled his left wrist in his right palm, confirming my fears that he had injured it, but looked up at me rather sheepishly. "Well... there goes any hope I had for impressing my lady tonight."

Not really in the joking mood, I said. "Hush. This lady's been impressed with you for ages. What happened? Was there something on the walkway? Should I go move it so no one else trips? They really need better lighting out here. Once we get you on your feet, I'm going to go have a chat with the manager."

He struggled to get up with me doing very little in the way of helping him by holding onto his elbow. "Relax, Mimi. You don't have to chew anyone out. I just tripped over my own two feet."

"You what?" I asked incredulously. "Is your shoe untied?"

He looked down, checking to be sure. "Nope, both appear to be tied tight. It seems my big feet have become a drawback for once," he joked.

I smacked him in the arm out of habit, forgetting about his injured wrist, and he winced.

"Oh! Sorry! Sorry!" I exclaimed. "I totally forgot, what with your witty bone still intact and all. Is it very bad?"

"I think I'm going to need an x-ray, actually. I can't move it at all. I've been trying to test it while we've been standing here, but I just can't. It also hurts like hell."

"Okay, okay. Where are your keys? I'll get us to the closest hospital."

After fishing the keys out of his right pocket, I got us to the car and found the nearest hospital on my phone. After programming the address into the car's GPS system, I got us there in no time flat. I may or may not have broken a few traffic laws in the process.

"Jesus, Mimi." Vance griped as I help him out of the car. "I have what might be a broken wrist. My water didn't break. You didn't have to run that red light or drive sixty-five miles an hour in a thirty-five mile an hour zone."

"Forgive me if I don't want you to be in pain any longer than you have to be," I snapped. "Now quit complaining like a little girl while I try to find you a wheelchair."

I felt his good hand on my arm pulling me back as I started to walk ahead of him and heard his soft laughter. "Will you listen to yourself? Mimi, I injured my wrist. My legs are fine. My back is fine. I didn't hit my head. I'm quite sure it's okay if I walk into the emergency room under my own power. You're awfully close to panicking for someone who forgot I was injured only a little while ago." He looked at me with amusement.

I huffed out a breath and scrubbed a hand over my face. "Alright. So maybe I feel a little guilty as well as concerned. Fine, Conan. Let's get you inside and see what kind of damage you've done."

After a few x-rays, several hours of waiting and one visit from the doctor later, Vance was fitted with a cast because he fractured his wrist. He was given some pain medication and told to follow up with an orthopedist the following week. He also got a copy of his x-rays on a handy CD to provide to his doctor.

It was very late by the time we made it home. I helped Vance get out of his clothes and after feeding him some of his pain meds, we snuggled up to go to sleep. Just as I was about to drift off, I heard Vance whisper to me, "Happy anniversary, Mimi. Despite its crappy ending, I was still wouldn't change a thing about our day."

I snuggled even closer to him, resting my head in the crook between his shoulder and neck, relieved that although the night had ended in a not-so-stellar way, everything seemed to be back to normal and our day was, indeed, lovely.

Ten

Vance's wrist healed fairly quickly since it wasn't his dominant arm that was injured. Our daily routines went on as usual for the most part although Vance began coming home from work later and later. He seemed distracted all the time but blamed a new deal at work taking up a lot of his time and attention. He explained he had been given a greater role in this particular case than he normally played, and he felt it was a good sign for his future with the firm. I did my best to be excited for him and supportive of his new duties, but the truth was I missed him. It was no fun spending so much time alone, so I used the time to reach out to Grace, Liz, and Jessica since I had neglected them for the better part of the last year.

One Friday night in December, I made plans to meet the girls after work for happy hour at a local chain restaurant. I sent Vance a text message, letting him know I'd be home around nine, in case he got home before I did.

Everyone was seated around a high table on stools in the bar area when I arrived. As I took a seat and shrugged out of my coat, Liz remarked, "It's great to see you, Mimi. I haven't seen you since your reception last year. You look fantastic."

Jessica nodded. "It's probably been about the same amount of time for me, too."

"I know. It's been crazy, trying to get settled in at Vance's place, getting used to living with another person—"

"All the fantastic sex. We know, we know." Grace interjected, rolling her eyes. She was always the outspoken one in our group. We constantly teased her about having no filters, whatever came up, came out. Any time spent in her company was enlightening of the inner workings of Grace's mind, as well as highly entertaining.

The waitress came by to take my drink order. Remembering my anniversary dinner, I ordered a margarita instead of my usual dirty martini, while the girls ordered another round of their respective drinks. After she left, the girls descended upon me.

"So, you know that's why we were excited you finally wanted to get together. We've just been waiting for you to come up for air to tell us all about Vance's skills in the bedroom," Grace said.

I looked at the three eager faces staring expectantly at me, rabid she-devils wrapped in cashmere sweaters. You'd think I'd married a well-known porn star or something.

"How heartwarming to know feeding your dirty minds takes precedence over rekindling our long-term friendships. Here I thought you might have missed me as much as I missed you three gossipy tarts."

"Yeah, yeah, we missed you too," Jessica said, waving her hand back and forth. Then without warning, she slammed it down on the surface of the table, making the empty glasses jump. "Now give us the goods!" Jessica was almost as bad as Grace although she was a little more diplomatic most of the time. Unless the topic at hand was sex. In that case, she wanted a complete tell-all of every detail, from the first kiss to the last gasp of passion.

"Oh my god, Sally Stresscase! Settle down!" I barked back at her. "Jesus. What am I supposed to do, just start describing our sex life from the first time we did it through now? Because if that's the case, we're going to be here a long fucking time. We do it a lot. A LOT."

"Now, that's more like it!" Jessica nudged Grace with her elbow, and she nodded encouragingly at me.

I buried my face in my hands and just shook my head back and forth. I had a feeling it was going to be a very long night. Eventually, the girls backed off, and we had a good time catching up—after I told them about Vance's sex ninja skills and the stealth orgasms, of course. That took up a good hour's worth of conversation time. Liz, as usual, just sat there listening raptly, but making very few comments. She was the quiet one in our group, always carefully observing everyone, taking note of everything going on around her. She rarely said much, but when she did, it was usually something thoughtful and profound.

We had been laughing and talking for another hour or two and were in the middle of a story about one of Jessica's recent dating disasters when the sound of Vance's ringtone interrupted the conversation. I pulled the phone out of my bag and answered, hoping he was calling to tell me he was already home.

"Hi, sweetheart!" I began. "Are you—"

"Where are you?" he cut me off sharply. "You said you'd be home by nine."

I pulled the phone from my ear to look at the time and saw that it was nine-ten.

"I'm sorry, Vance. I'm still out with the girls. I'll just wrap things up here and will be home in about an hour."

"No, you will say goodbye as soon as we hang up, and you will be home within twenty minutes. No excuses, Mimi. I don't appreciate being taken for granted. I made sure to be home when you said you'd be back, and you couldn't be bothered to even call to say you'd be late. Now, at least do me the courtesy of coming home right away." The line fell silent before I could say another word.

I sat there for a moment, completely flabbergasted. The expression on my face must have told a story, because there was a gentle touch on my arm before I heard Liz' soft voice.

"Mimi, is everything okay?"

I looked down at her hand before bringing my eyes to her face. She was looking at me with concern in her gaze, but I was so shell-shocked, I could only stare back at her for a moment. Finally, I shook it off.

"Yeah, yeah. Everything's fine. That was Vance. He needs me to come home. I'm not sure why, but he made it sound pretty important." I fumbled for words that would explain my need to leave right away, but not cause any undue concern. "He probably just needs my help finding some document for work. I did some straightening up in his office the other day and must have disturbed some organized chaos."

"Well, good luck finding whatever it is," Grace laughed good-naturedly. "I hope you didn't do too much damage. I know how those carefully disorganized piles are. My office is full of them."

We exchanged hugs and promises to meet more regularly. Once out of their direct sight, I practically ran from the restaurant to my car. Watching the time all the way home, I made it from the parking lot to our front door in fifteen minutes.

I entered the house with a stomach full of knots. I shut the door quietly behind me and placed my purse and keys on the table near the door. Removing my coat, I walked into the living room and placed it on the back of the sofa. The room was empty, so I wandered into the kitchen thinking maybe I'd find him there. It, too, was empty. I wandered through the entire house, finding every room the same way. Finally, I found him on the back patio, laying back in a lounge chair, a lit cigar in one hand and glass of scotch in the other. He had removed his coat and tie, his shirt unbuttoned at the throat, and his sleeves rolled up. His shoes were nowhere in sight, but he still had his socks on. He didn't even turn to look at me as I approached.

"Aren't you cold out here?" I asked, rubbing my arms against the chill.

"I'm fine," he answered tersely. "Why didn't you call, Mimi?"

"We just got to talking and I didn't notice how late it had gotten. I'm sorry, Vance. I didn't think you'd be waiting for me."

He turned his head and looked at me with pure venom pouring from his eyes.

"Don't worry. Next time, I won't be."

I gasped at the hatred coming from him. "Vance, I really am sorry. It was an honest mistake. I don't quite understand why you're so upset with me. It could have happened to anyone. Besides, these days I never know when you'll be home. I didn't think I had a reason to be overly concerned with watching the time."

Vance jumped to his feet and gestured at me angrily with his cigar. Smoke wafted in front of my face, causing me to choke slightly.

"Don't try to turn this around on me. You know I've been working my ass off on this deal. Do you think I like stumbling in at all hours of the night after working sixteen-hour days, never stopping for a break, eating takeout at my desk, never seeing you, never talking to you, working weekends, coming home dropping into our bed exhausted, only to get up the next morning and do it all over again? Do you? Then, the one night I manage to make it home at a decent time, I come home to an empty house after you specifically sent me a message saying you would be here!"

With every angry sentence, he took a step forward, backing me across the patio up against the house. Finally, with my back against the wall, he just stood there staring at me with his chest heaving, his hand gripped around his glass of scotch so hard, I feared it might shatter in his hand.

He tilted the glass to his lips and drained it dry of the remaining amber fluid, then angrily threw it at the wall by my feet. I jumped, I was so startled by the action. He smirked as he took a deep puff on his cigar before blowing it in my direction, then turning and walking inside the house. Even in my confused and frightened state, I worried he might get glass shards in his feet since he didn't have shoes on.

I waited outside until I could no longer hear sounds coming from inside the house. I let myself in through the sliding glass door and retrieved a broom and dustpan from the closet in the kitchen and took them to the patio to clean up the mess. Once that was done, I gingerly approached our bedroom to change for bed. He was in there, already changed into a pair of lounge pants and nothing else. He was leaning back against the headboard, staring at the wall. He no longer looked angry. In fact, his expression was... blank. I wanted to try to talk to him but thought it was better not to poke the bear. I would wait until morning to approach him and try to smooth things over.

I silently changed into my pajamas and headed for the spare room. I thought a night apart would be best. I was afraid of the depth of his anger, confused by it since I felt he was completely overreacting, and if I were totally honest, I was angry at the injustice of it all. I hadn't meant to be thoughtless or take him for granted. It was one simple mistake, one time! If anyone was taken for granted, it was me! How often did he come home late from work? Every night, and he never called to let me know what time to expect him. Ever.

I took another look at him before leaving the room, but he still sat there, staring at the wall. It wasn't as if he were ignoring me, but as if he were completely unaware of my presence. I wished I could be just as indifferent. I shook my head and slipped from the room.

I passed the night tossing and turning. I couldn't sleep for replaying the entire scene from the time I entered the house until I went to bed. It was so unlike Vance. It was like the time we went to the charity event for his firm, only much worse. At the gala, he was just a dick. Last night, he was something else entirely. I wondered if Vance would remember this behavior tomorrow, or if it would be like last time. I was unable to sleep whatsoever for all the thoughts running through my head.

The following morning, I got up and made a cup of coffee using our single-cup brewing machine. I thanked God for the invention because if I'd had to wait for an entire pot to brew, I might have lost my mind. I was sitting at the table, sipping my first cup, when Vance wandered in. I did my best to ignore him, feeling more anger at him than anything, but he walked up to stand opposite me at the table and waited for me to look up at him. I continued to ignore him through a few more sips of coffee but finally looked up to meet his eyes. He looked down at me with an expression of remorse so strong, I knew not only did he remember, he heavily regretted how he had acted. I simply looked away and went back to sipping my coffee.

He sighed softly and moved to the coffee machine and made his own cup. After he had his drink, he came back and sat down across from me, waiting for me to look at him again. I finished my cup of coffee and went to prepare another. I was feeling just childish enough to make him suffer for a little while. I made sure to take my time adding cream and sugar, then stirring it well to make sure it was mixed just right. Finally, I returned to the table and sat with my arms crossed, waiting for him to begin whatever he wanted to tell me.

"Mimi, I don't know what to say, other than I'm sorry."

"Let me help you. How about I was a ginormous prick, unrivaled by even an African elephant's dick? Or in the history of dicks? And here's the most important part, I completely and totally overreacted, was horribly unfair to you. I'm sorry, and it will never happen again. I don't know, you may have something else in mind, but it seems to me that's about the only thing or something really fucking close to it that would be appropriate at a time like this." I sat back, taking a sip of my coffee.

His contrite expression was swiftly replaced by a flinty glare for a fleeting second. For that brief moment, I saw the Vance of the night before staring back at me, and I flinched, fearing a repeat performance. Had I gone too far in my outburst? However, he closed his eyes and seemed to struggle for another moment, and when he reopened them, his remorseful look was back.

"You're right, Mimi. I was completely out of line. I was just so disappointed when I got home, I don't know what came over me. I felt so slighted. This new deal at work has stolen so much time from me, it's robbing me of the one thing that brings me real joy—you—and when I came home, and you weren't here, it was just another thing stealing my happiness. I lost it and took all that pain and frustration out on you. It felt like you were being inconsiderate by not calling or texting me to say you would be late, but I understand how you could lose track of time. I was totally out of line.

"Could we please put the incident behind us and start over? I don't want one ugly scene to come between us and ruin what we have," he pled.

"This isn't the first time you've been ugly to me though, Vance. I let the first incident slide by, and you pretended nothing ever happened, but I refuse to do that again. I want to make sure if something is bothering you, we have an adult conversation about it, and you treat me with respect even if you are upset," I said, doing my best to be reasonable.

"What do you mean I've been ugly to you before? When?"

"The night of the breast cancer gala. Of course, it wasn't anything like last night. You were just irritable all day, then extremely rude to me the entire evening. Any time I tried to find out what

202

was bothering you, you brushed me off and grew more annoyed with me."

"I don't remember anything like that." His face twisted thoughtfully. "I was very bored that evening, but I don't recall anything out of the ordinary happening."

I sat there silently remembering his pleasant, normal demeanor the following day. It certainly supported his claim now that he had no memory of how he acted the day before although I couldn't see how that could be possible.

"I'm not making it up, but whether I say it happened or you say it didn't, we're both in agreement that last night did, and my position of how we move on from that doesn't change," I said firmly.

"I understand. I will do my best to be patient and talk with you if I get upset or if something is bothering me. I won't treat you like that again. However, please try to be patient with me while I'm working on this deal. I'm under a lot of pressure right now, and I'm stretched very thin. I'm afraid the stress is taking its toll in a lot of ways."

"What do you mean? What else is going on with you?" I asked, my concern for him growing.

"Well, I've been having a lot more headaches. Since you're asleep most of the time when I get home, you don't see it when they happen. I also forget a lot of things at work. My work is slower because of it, and I have to put forth twice as much effort. I have to leave myself little notes everywhere. It's one of the reasons my days are so damned long.   I'm afraid I've also been short-tempered with my co-workers. I sequester myself in my office as much as I can to avoid any confrontations. I can't wait until this deal is over and everything goes back to normal." He rested his head in his hands. "Maybe I'm just not meant to be a partner if I can't do this level of work. I'll just have to accept I'm only associate material."

I took his hand. "I wish you'd told me you were having these problems. I may not be able to help you with the work, but I can at least help you deal with the pressure by being an outlet for you. You don't have to carry the burden all alone."

"When was I supposed to turn to you?   We hardly ever see each other. We don't even have time to chat on the phone during the day, my time is so consumed by work. Hell, I don't even have time for this conversation. I should be working right now especially since I left 'early'" –he curled his fingers into quote gestures as he said the word early— "last night, but I knew we needed to have this conversation this morning. The only thing getting me through now is the deal is almost closed. Maybe a week or two more of this, and it will be done."

"Then we'll hang in there and see it through. If you have a bad day and I'm asleep when you come home, wake me up and we'll talk about it. I can lose a little sleep if it means being there for you when you need me. I want to be there for you. It's my duty and my pleasure as your wife. I want to share those burdens with you. Likewise, if you have a headache, I want to take care of you. I'll get your pills, I'll rub your temples and help you relax. I'll do anything to make your life easier, Vance," I said as tears began to prickle my eyes. I had no idea he had been suffering. I knew the increased demands on him had to be stressful, but I didn't know how much. I was a terrible wife for not noticing or considering what it was doing to him. No wonder he snapped last night.

I got up and went around the table to sit on his lap and take him in my arms.

"I had no idea things were this hard for you. Don't give last night another thought. All is forgiven. In fact, there is nothing to forgive. You simply reached your breaking point. Had I known things were so bad, I would have been much more sensitive toward you. I promise I will be much more aware of your situation and do my best not to add to your stress."

His arms came up around me and squeezed tight. "I know I can always count on you to make things better, Mimi." He pressed his lips to my temple and whispered against my skin. "I love you so much."

"I love you, too," I said, never meaning it more.

We sat like that quietly, enjoying our renewed connection for a few moments before Vance broke the silence with a regretful sigh.

"I wish I could sit like this for the rest of the day. Maybe even take you into the bedroom for a good long while, but I need to get dressed and head to the office. Can I ask one favor though?"

"Anything," I replied.

"I don't know when I'll be home tonight, but would it be asking too much for you to wait up for me? I want to see your face first thing when I walk in the door," he asked quietly.

My heart melted a little that he would ask for something so simple, but so touching at the same time.

"That is definitely not too much to ask. I will be eagerly waiting for you. Would you like me to have food waiting for you too or maybe something to drink?" I offered.

"No, just you. And if you happen to have nothing on, I might be able to muster the energy to do something about that." He gave me one of his devilish grins.

"I'll see what I can do," I giggled,

He patted my thighs twice before gently easing me up off his lap and giving me a light kiss on the lips. My heart felt much lighter, and I found myself looking forward to the evening.

Vance left the house about nine-thirty in the morning. I wasn't sure what it meant in terms of him getting home since he was usually out of the house by six a.m., and I never knew what time he came home since I was usually asleep when he did. As such, I spent most of the day reading and making sure to take a good nap, so I could stay up late waiting for his arrival. When two a.m. came and went, and he still wasn't home, I began to grow worried. I sent him a text message asking when he thought he might be done. I didn't receive a response.

At three-thirty, I called his cell phone, but it went straight to voicemail, so the thing wasn't even turned on. I thought it could also be a dead battery, but I was aware he had a charger in his office, so that wasn't really a good excuse. I brushed other possible reasons his phone could be turned off from my mind. I then called the direct number for his office phone, but it also just rang several times before going to voicemail.

I continued to wait until six a.m., drinking copious amounts of coffee to keep myself awake. I called his cell phone for the final time, and that time it rang, but there was still no answer. Worry getting the better of me, I decided to drive over to his office to see if I could locate his car, either in the parking lot or somewhere on the route there.

My imagination began to run away with me, fears of him falling asleep at the wheel on his way home, and wrapping his car around a street lamp somewhere invading my thoughts. I grabbed my coat and walked out to my car, only to find him parked in the driveway, fast asleep in the front seat. I panicked because although it was Los Angeles, it was still December and the temperature was far too cold to be sleeping outside. I attempted to open the door, but it was locked. I ran back inside and searched in his desk frantically for the spare key, cursing that it wasn't on my key ring, making a terrible mess as I went along. Once I located it in a side drawer, I dashed back outside and let myself in using the electronic key fob. I knelt on the ground and leaned through the open car door, putting a hand to his cheek to check the temperature of his skin. I was surprised he wasn't frozen solid. His lips had slightly blue tinge, but to my relief were still mostly a light pink. I shook him gently, then a little harder, while calling his name to wake him up. Unfortunately, this accomplished little other than a few heavy breaths and some low grumbling. I slapped his face lightly, hoping to rouse him further and maybe bring some color back into his cheeks, this time eliciting a wave of his hand to brush me away. Encouraged by the response, I slapped his face with much more force, which finally brought him around, his eyes opened wide in shock. He looked at me slightly disoriented at first, then with a furrowed brow asked, "Did you just hit me?"

"Unfortunately, I had to. You wouldn't wake up, and I was panicked."

"Panicked? Why? Is the house burning down? Are you mysteriously pregnant and in labor? Am I late for work?"

"Negative to all the above, except maybe the last one, I'm not sure about that. The reason I was panicked might be answered by the fact if you look around and see where you are, then take note of the fact that I waited for you all night, but you never came home," I said, motioning to his surroundings with a lift of my chin.

His eyes grew wide as he looked around. "I spent the night in my car?" he asked incredulously, wrapping his arms around himself as if just noticing the cold.

"It would appear so," I said. "Let's get you inside and into a hot shower where you can warm up. I'm surprised you're not hypothermic."

I stood and stepped back to let him out as he struggled to stand.

"Vance, why didn't you come inside last night? Did you go drinking after work? Were you drunk?"

He looked slightly dazed as his eyes scanned the front yard. "I have absolutely no idea, Mimi. I don't even remember leaving the office last night." He looked at me with a very troubled expression, and I could have sworn it looked like there were tears in his eyes. He blinked a few times and they were gone. I lifted one of his arms over my shoulders and helped guide him into the house, assuming his legs would be very stiff from the cold and from being cramped while sleeping in the confines of the car.

I got him settled in the bedroom, so he could get undressed while I ran the shower. Once the bathroom was nice and steamy, I helped him into the stall and stood watch while he leaned under the hot spray, bringing his body temperature back to a normal level. I was genuinely worried about his health, not only in the short-term after this night in the frigid air, but the toll his work was taking on him. He needed a few days off to relax and rest his body and mind. He needed lots of sleep, a few good home cooked meals, and a few days of doing nothing but decompressing. I was determined he wouldn't be going into the office that day, no matter what he said, and I was going to call his boss first thing Monday morning and demand someone fill in for him for a couple days. I'd lie and say he had a terrible case of the stomach flu if I had to. I'd tie his stubborn ass to the bed if he gave me any trouble about it. I was going to make sure he rested if it killed me.

Once Vance felt he was sufficiently warm, I helped him out of the shower over his protests he was just fine. I dried him off over more objections and helped him dress in an old, soft, white T-shirt and a pair of lounge pants. He grumbled the entire time that he wasn't an invalid, but with a no-nonsense look from me, he quieted down and allowed me to baby him. I forced him into bed and informed him he wasn't going anywhere that day. It was Sunday, it was the Lord's Day, and he had suddenly found religion at the church of What Mimi Says Goes.

We argued over my plan to call in sick for him for the next two days, but after I threatened him with a divorce, we compromised and agreed he could have work couriered over. He could work on some stuff from home, but nowhere near the amount nor for as long as he would if he were at the office. He made a phone call, then informed me someone would be by that afternoon to bring over a box of files, and he would appreciate it if I would put it in his office, considering I wasn't letting him out of bed.

I made him some soup for breakfast and fed it to him, which amused him greatly. I think he began to enjoy all the attention and being coddled to some extent. It had been a long time since we'd been able to spend any time together and being spoiled by me was something of a novelty. All he had to do was sit back and let it happen, a concept foreign after all these months of being under so much pressure to deliver results.

Finally, I left him alone to get some quality sleep. I checked on him fifteen minutes later, and he was out cold. I smiled to myself, happy he was finally getting some desperately needed rest.

A little after noon, the doorbell rang. I opened it to find a stunning redhead, dressed head to toe in designer labels with a perfectly made-up face, standing on my doorstep, holding a banker's box and wearing a smug look on her face.

"You must be Mimi. I'm Tiffany Strong. I work with Vance. He asked me to bring these files by."

"Oh, hi," I said pleasantly, opening the door wider and motioning for her to come in. "Let me take that from you," I said, reaching out for the box.

"That's okay. I'll just take them back to his office, I know where it is." She started to walk toward the back of the house.

I stopped her and gently took the box from her arms. "No, thank you. Please, have a seat, and I'll be with you in just a minute."

She may have known her way around my house for whatever reason, but I wasn't about to let her go gallivanting around like she owned the place. I placed the box on Vance's chair, not wanting to risk messing up his organized chaos any more than I already had in my search for his car key.

I exited the office to find this stranger standing in the doorway to our bedroom, staring in at Vance as he was sleeping. Good thing he wasn't sleeping naked as he normally did, I thought.

"What do you think you're doing?" I asked. "I told you to wait for me in the living room."

"I just wanted to see if he was okay. It's not like him to not come into the office even if he's sick," she said innocently.

I closed the bedroom door quietly and ushered her back down the hallway, so our talking wouldn't disturb Vance's rest. Once we were back in the front of the house, I turned to her.

"You could have easily asked after his well-being. I don't understand why you felt it was in any way appropriate to make yourself at home in my house."

"I'm sorry, Mimi. I guess I just do feel at home here after all the time I've spent in this house. I didn't mean to offend you. Please tell Vance I hope he feels better soon. I'll—he'll be missed while he's gone." She offered me a weak smile before turning to the door and letting herself out.

I didn't know what she meant by feeling at home in my house, but I wasn't going to put too much thought into it just then. I resolved to discuss it with Vance when he was awake and feeling more rested. Instead, I set about making him a nourishing lunch.

Just as I was taking a fillet of red snapper out of the oven, Vance came into the kitchen yawning and scratching his stomach. He smiled at me, looking much better than he had this morning.

"Mmmm, that smells good, Mimi. Is that for me?" he asked. "I sure hope so because I feel like I could eat everything in this house."

"It is. I also made you a green salad and some pasta in olive oil to go with it. I'll have it plated for you in no time," I said with a smile.

"Aren't you going to eat?" he inquired with a frown, looking around and seeing only enough for one.

"I had a sandwich earlier," I shrugged nonchalantly, "but I'll sit with you while you eat."

We took our places at the kitchen table, and he dug into his food with gusto. It was obvious he was grateful for a home cooked meal after weeks of takeout.

"My god, Mimi, this is delicious. I can't tell you how tired I am of Chinese, Pizza, or anything that comes out of a cardboard or Styrofoam container."

"You know, I was thinking about that. I could always start making dinner and bringing it to you at the office. That way you'd be eating better, and we'd at least have the opportunity to see each other for a few minutes. Surely, you could take twenty minutes or so to stop and eat," I suggested.

He paused, his fork halfway to his mouth before setting it back down again. I could see the wheels of his mind turning as he thought the idea over.

"I might not be able to do that every night as some days are just too crazy, but that just might work two or three nights a week. You don't think that would be too much work for you though? I don't want you going to too much trouble."

"Are you kidding me, Vance? I would do just about anything to have some time with you. Besides, I'm just as tired of having sandwiches for dinner and eating alone. I miss cooking for the both of us. I think it would actually be fun having a picnic of sorts in your office." I smiled encouragingly at him, liking the idea more and more. I wished it had occurred to me earlier.

"Great!" he said enthusiastically. "Let's start doing that as soon as I get back to work. Now, I have something to look forward to that will help me get through the long days."

"Speaking of work," I said as he went back to eating. "Some woman named Tiffany dropped off a box of files for you. I left it on the chair in your office."

He stiffened slightly. "Tiffany came by?"

"Yeah, I thought you asked for someone to bring you some stuff."

"I did," he said as finished his meal, wiping his mouth with his napkin and tossing it on his plate. "I just didn't think it would be her. Did she say anything?"

I paused for a moment, wondering if I should bring up her odd behavior and her implications that she and Vance were close at some point, close enough that she had spent a good amount of time in our house. Apparently, I paused for too long.

"What is it, Mimi? What did she say?" he asked, sounding more than a little concerned.

"Well, she did say that you would be missed, but mostly it's not so much what she said, it's how she acted. She was very comfortable in the house and made it a point to let me know she was. She said she had spent a lot of time here in the past. Also, when I went to put the box of files in your office, I asked her to wait in the living room. When I came out of the office, I found her standing in the doorway of our bedroom, staring in at you while you slept. It was kind of creepy."

"What did she say when you caught her?"

"That she only wanted to make sure that you were okay because you never take time off from work. What is it with this woman, Vance? Who is she?"

"She's an associate at the firm. We used to be friends even went out on a few dates, so she's been over here before. Nothing was ever serious between us, but we stopped seeing each other when I met you. She wasn't very happy when I told her I had met someone else, but we ended things on friendly terms. We've maintained a polite, professional distance since then which is why I'm surprised she'd be the one to bring the box," he explained.

I had a feeling there might be a bit more to the story than he was letting on given the way he stiffened when I mentioned her name, but I didn't press the issue. If he was telling me there was nothing there to be concerned about, then I wouldn't.

"Well, she left easily enough. In hindsight, I think she just wanted me to know there had been something between you two before, no matter how small it was, maybe hoping I'd be jealous. Some women are like that. What matters to me is you're mine. I don't care about what came before me. All I care about is what happened after we met," I said with a smile.

Vance leaned in and kissed me on the lips, then whispered against them, "You. You happened after we met, Mimi Ashcroft, and I've never been the same."

Eleven

I insisted Vance return to bed after he ate his meal even though he was adamant he couldn't sleep anymore. I told him I didn't care, he needed rest, and I was going to make sure he got it. After I cleaned up the dishes from his meal, I returned to the bedroom and changed into a camisole and a pair of soft jogging shorts and joined him in the bed. We spent the rest of the afternoon cuddling and quietly chatting. I was pleased Vance seemed to forget all about the box of files waiting for him in his office. He needed to have at least one day with no work on his mind, and I needed this time with him, reconnecting and sharing affection with him. It felt good to be with him again, and the frightening events of the night before last were just a distant memory.

We talked and laughed and made plans for things we wanted to do, places we wanted to go when the deal he was currently working on was over. He was particularly excited about the idea of a trip to Lake Tahoe, insisting we rent a cabin and spend the time sequestered there, just the two of us with a peaceful, snowy scenery as our backdrop for a romantic weekend.

"Wouldn't you want to get out and do something, at least?" I asked, nestled comfortably in his arms.

"Mimi, there are four things to do in Tahoe in the winter time. Ski, gamble, drink, and fuck. I vote for spending our time drunk, naked, and fucking as much as possible. If we absolutely, positively have to go out, I suppose we could have dinner somewhere, but I was thinking our luggage should only consist of our toothbrushes."

"Well, if we go with your vote," I giggled happily, "we should probably bring along more than our toothbrushes. At some point, we'll require nourishment of some kind, and I don't think the restaurants will appreciate your choice of attire."

"Then it's settled. We'll go to Tahoe with toothbrushes, tequila, and toast the only things weighing us down."

"Sounds like a plan. Although, if you don't mind, I think I'll pack a little more than just toast to eat. You know, in case we get snowed in, or something," I said reasonably.

"Oh, all right, but we're going to work on your sense of adventure," he said, kissing the top of my head.

The following day, Vance slept in late, which made me happy. I was afraid he'd be up at the crack of dawn either itching to get at that box of files, or worse, insisting he needed to be back at the office. While he was sleeping, I made a large breakfast of eggs, French toast, fresh fruit, and coffee. I put everything on a tray and brought it to the room. He stirred as soon as I entered. As I set the tray down on his nightstand, he cracked open an eye.

"What is that fantastic smell?"

"Oh, do you like it? It's my new perfume. I call it Eau de Breakfast."

"I think the only way it could smell better is if it were the only thing you were wearing," he said suggestively.

"Still a pervert and a dork, I see," I teased.

He sat up in bed with a yawn. "And sadly, my dear, you are just a dork. Eau de Breakfast."

I laughed and handed him a fork before placing the tray on his lap. Just then, the doorbell rang. I stood and admonished him.

"Now I want that plate cleared by the time I get back."

"I don't think that will be a problem," he said through a mouthful of food. "This is heavenly."

I opened the door and was astonished to see Tiffany standing there holding a bakery box.

"Hello, Tiffany. I'm surprised to see you here. Is there something I can do for you?" I inquired politely even though I had a sneaking suspicion I already knew what she was up to.

"Hi, Mimi. May I come in?"

Against my better judgment, I stepped back and allowed her to come inside.

"I thought you'd be at work, so I brought Vance some breakfast." She held up the box and shook it slightly while giving me a big smirk. "I got him his favorite. Raspberry jelly."

I'll just bet you thought I'd be at work, I thought to myself.

"Well, Vance has eaten, but I'll be sure to let him know you dropped by," I said, reaching out to take the box from her.

Just then a shirtless Vance came into the room, carrying the tray of empty dishes.

"Thank you, Mimi. That was delicious. I inhaled every—Oh, uh, hello Tiffany," Vance said, looking extremely awkward. I would have sworn I saw his cheeks turn slightly pink. "What are you doing here?"

"I was worried you might still be feeling under the weather, so I thought I'd bring you something to help perk you up." She thrust the box at him even though his hands were full of the tray of dishes, as her eyes moved avariciously over his naked torso. He looked at me uncomfortably.

"Uh, thanks," he said, motioning to the tray in his hands with his chin.

She dropped the box on top of the tray and followed him into the kitchen as he left the room. I followed too, just to see how things would turn out.

"So, you seem to be feeling better," she said. "I guess you'll be back to work tomorrow?" She seemed awfully hopeful.

"I'm a lot better than I was yesterday thanks to Mimi's marvelous skills as a nurse." He looked at me and winked. "But I think I'll need at least another day before I'm back to fighting weight. Maybe two."

"Oh," she said, her face falling. She brightened again, her back straightening. "I can take back the stuff you worked on yesterday if you're finished, and bring you more until you're ready to go back."

"I haven't even opened the box, yet. I've been flat on my back, suffering Mimi's tender, loving care," Vance said suggestively.

Following his lead, I continued, "We appreciate you coming by, Tiffany, but I really do need to get Vance back in bed." Vance turned away and started piling his dishes in the sink. I heard his strangled laughter covered by a poorly faked cough.

I took hold of her arm gently and began leading her toward the door. Vance followed along behind, an amused expression on his face. We stopped when we reached the door, Vance opening it up and leaning against it while I guided her out onto the porch.

"It really was very thoughtful of you to follow up on Vance's well-being, but I promise you, I have all of his needs well covered. You can go back to work and rest easy." I smiled as Vance came to my side and slid his arm around my waist.

"Please give everyone at work my best and let them know I'll be back in a few days. Take care, Tiffany." With that, Vance closed the door on her slightly bewildered face.

We both chuckled as we walked back to the bedroom and lay down on the bed, snuggling up to each other like we did the day before.

"What is her deal?" I asked. "I'd never even heard of her before yesterday, and now, she's been here, two days in a row. Today with your favorite pastries in hand. At a time she thought I wouldn't be home, I might add." Turning in his arms, I looked up at his face. "Why didn't I know raspberry donuts are your favorite?"

"They're not, Mimi." He burst out laughing. "I don't know what gave her that idea. We were in a business meeting a couple weeks ago and I had one, but honestly, that was the first one I'd had in years. While I'm being honest, I have to say I was rather disappointed. I'd thought it was strawberry."

We laughed together for a few moments, then lay there quietly, enjoying the close proximity of each other's body. Vance began skimming his hand across my bare arm as he looked into my eyes, his own slowly filling with desire. I smiled knowingly at him, feeling the stirrings of arousal begin in my own body.

"Don't you have work you need to do?" I asked him teasingly.

"Yeah, but for some reason, it doesn't seem all that important right now. I can think of far more interesting, more pleasurable pursuits."

"Is that so?" I asked, running my own hands over his hard, bare chest, letting my fingernails lightly scratch against his skin. He shivered slightly under my touch.

"Mmhmm. Why don't you let me show you what I have in mind," he said as he rolled over on top of me and buried his face in the crook of my neck, licking along its length until he reached my earlobe. He took the small bit of flesh between his teeth and bit lightly, causing goosebumps to break out over my skin and a delicious thrill to run through my body. Wrapping my arms around his back, I held him tightly to me, as he brought his lips to mine and kissed me tenderly.

"I love you so much, Mimi. It's been so hard these last weeks, working so much and being away from you. I feel like I've been slowly going mad being apart from you. Nothing has been right, I haven't been right without you. Now that I've had time to spend with you, even just this little bit, I feel like I'm grounded again. Like I was very ill and am finally well again. If that makes any sense at all."

"I understand, Vance. You really haven't been well. I can see that now. All that stress has really taken a toll on you physically. I'm glad I insisted you take this time to recharge because you already look a world better than you have in weeks."

"I'd wager I'm about to feel even better...," he said.

I laughed. "Didn't you learn your lesson about making bets in Atlantic City with Pete?"

He chuckled. "We can come up with something to make it interesting if the bet alone isn't enough for you."

"Oh no. I'm not making a fool's bet because you're absolutely right. You're about to feel much, much better," I said before taking control and rolling him onto his back.

I kissed him deeply, running my tongue over his lips before delving inside to let my tongue tangle sensually with his. I slowly made my way down his neck to his chest, trailing my tongue over the grooves of muscle forming his pectorals as I worked over to one dusky nipple. I wrapped my lips around the flat disc and sucked the tiny pebble between my teeth, causing him to gasp and arch beneath me. His hands tangled in my hair, pressing me against his chest, and I felt the bulge of his erection hardening beneath my abdomen. I flicked the skin between my teeth with my tongue rapidly, before taking another long pull, making him tense beneath me again. Finally, I released him and began moving down his abdomen with more tiny kisses and licks over the taut flesh covering those rippling muscles.

When I reached his waistband, I didn't hesitate to slip my fingers inside and drag his pants down his hips. He lifted, eagerly assisting me in removing them, but I only pulled them down far enough to expose the full length of his pulsing cock and his firm, tightly drawn balls. I studied his magnificence for a moment. The sight of him hard and wanting had always taken my breath away, the notion all that desire was for me was more than I could comprehend sometimes. I had always felt humbled and unworthy of something so beautiful, so perfect.

I took him in my hand and licked him from base to tip in one long, slow, torturous swipe. He groaned and jerked against me involuntarily.

"Shhh...," I whispered to him. "Just lay back and enjoy, my love."

I licked him again, pausing at the top to swirl my tongue around the crown, before encircling it with my lips and sucking hard. I inched my way down slowly, allowing my saliva to thoroughly coat the length of his shaft until my nose pressed against his pubic bone and the tip of his cock was firmly in the back of my throat. I slid back up, letting my tongue dance around the length of him, eliciting another soft moan from him. Gradually building up a steady rhythm, I cradled the heaviness of his balls in one hand while my other hand joined my mouth in measured strokes over that gloriously hard piece of flesh. I couldn't get enough of the taste of him on my tongue. I became aware of my own whimpering echoing in my ears as I bobbed my head over him, eagerly devouring his length with enthusiasm.

I pressed the flat of my tongue against his hardness, heightening the sensation as I picked up my pace, my assisting hand gripping him tighter. I worked myself into a sucking frenzy over him as I felt his hands wind into my hair, pushing me down and pulling me up, helping me with my movements, moving me into a faster tempo.

"Yes, Mimi. That feels so fucking good. I love your greedy little mouth and hands, sucking and stroking me like you can't get enough. Make me come, Mimi. Take your prize, baby. It's all yours."

Encouraged by his words, I re-doubled my efforts and worked my tongue over and around his shaft, the way I knew he liked it. Letting it dance and swirl all around his dick with every stroke up and down, I reached my fingers just beneath his balls and began slowly massaging that bit of skin, gradually pressing in to put pressure on his prostate gland. He spread his legs wide and began thrusting his hips up into my mouth, fucking my face. I let go of him with my hand and backed off with the strokes of my mouth, letting him take over. His hands tightened in my hair as he sought his pleasure by using me. I loved it when he did this, just took control and forgot about being gentle or anything to do with my comfort or pleasure. I loved being an observer to him succumbing to his own ecstasy, especially if I was the cause of it.

His fingers curled into tight fists, pulling my hair at the roots as I felt the first spurts of his ejaculate coat my tongue. His moan was guttural as he cried out to the ceiling, his back arching in a spasm of pure bliss. I immediately dove down, driving him deeper into my throat as I sucked hard, milking him of every drop of his salty load. Purring with contentment like a fat cat, I delighted in the flavor of his pleasure. I licked him clean, not sparing any drop of his essence. His hands came under my arms, dragging me up the length of his body to bring me to his lips for a long kiss. He cradled my head in one of his large palms as he looked into my eyes lovingly before a slow smirk took over his face.

"I was right," he said with a twinkle in his eye. "I feel even better than I did before."

"I told you it was a fool's bet," I laughed and swatted his chest. "I knew exactly what I had in mind." I rolled off his chest and snuggled into his side. "Now that I have you here like this, I don't want to share you with that box in your office."

He sighed. "You'll notice I'm not setting any land speed records to get to it. I just want to stay right here like this, forever."

"How about we do this in shifts? You work for an hour while I make lunch. We'll eat, then take a short nap. Then you can go back to it, work for a couple hours and see how you feel after that. If you feel good enough, you can work until dinner. If not, we'll take a snuggle break or another nap until dinner. Then it's quitting time, and we spend the rest of the night either watching television or anything else you want to do that you find relaxing," I suggested.

He considered the plan for a moment. "While I'm not wild at the idea of working on anything but your amazing little body right now, I suppose I should make the effort to get something done. It will look bad if I go back to the office completely empty-handed. They figure if you're not on your death bed, you can at least do dictation."

"Alright. Well, dictate as much as you can, so you're not overdoing it. Let someone else do the hard stuff. If you do that, maybe we can get a few more days out of this. I still have plenty of vacation on the books at work and can take the whole week off if I want to."

"Okay, precious. Let me get cleaned up, and we'll put this plan in action. The sooner we get started, the sooner I'll have you back in this bed, and the sooner I'll be buried inside you."

"I believe the plan was to take a nap," I reminded him.

"Perhaps we should renegotiate the plan."

"Go get cleaned up," I said, swatting him with a pillow. "How does chicken salad for lunch sound to you?"

He swung his legs over the side of the bed, reaching his arms up and stretching his back. I admired the view of his muscles moving beneath his skin. Such a sexy bastard. Sometimes, I still couldn't believe he was mine.

"Chicken salad would be perfect," he said with a yawn. He stood pulling his lounge pants back up and heading toward the bathroom. After cleaning himself up, blew me a kiss before making his way to his office down the hall.

I lay in bed for a moment, just languishing in my contentment and happiness that we seemed to be back on track after weeks of being disconnected. I'd had no idea how much we needed this time together. I really could not wait until his current deal was over and we could go back to being our normal selves.

My moment of reflection was broken by an angry shout from the back of the house.

"Mimi! Get in here!"

Startled, I jumped out of bed and ran down the hall. I skidded into his office to find him standing behind his desk glaring at me.

"What the hell happened to my desk? Everything is a mess. All my papers are scattered, and my drawers are completely disorganized. My system is completely ruined. It will take forever to get everything back into place."

"I'm sorry, Vance. I was in a panic when I found you outside passed out in your car. The doors were locked, and I didn't have the spare key to open them and get you out. I came in here to find it, and in my urgency, must have disturbed everything. I didn't mean to make a mess of everything, I was just so worried about you. The only thing on my mind was getting to you and making sure you were okay," I explained.

He hung his head and pinched the bridge of his nose between his thumb and forefinger.

"Well in your haste, you made hours of work for me. Now our little plan for the day is ruined because you were thoughtless when it came to my stuff. As usual."

"What?" I blurted out, affronted and confused. I couldn't believe he was accusing me of being insensitive toward him when the only thing on my mind had been his welfare.

"Are you telling me that I should have put these stupid papers ahead of your safety?" I said, my voice rising in pitch and taking on a slightly shrill tone. "Because I'll be honest with you. If it happened all over again, I'd do the same thing in a heartbeat. If I have to choose between your life and your stuff, I'll choose you every single time. Your shit can be replaced, reorganized, or whatever. You cannot."

I crossed my arms in front of me, chin out, taking a defiant stance.

"Just get out, Mimi. Forget about lunch, forget about naps or dinner or anything else. I've got to fix your mess and get this work done before it costs me my shot at that partnership, or worse, my job. I should never have let you talk me into taking this time off. It's not worth it."

I took two stumbling steps backward as tears filled my eyes. I thought I had my Vance back, but it seemed as soon as he got anywhere near his work, the mean, and now apparently, cruel man was back. I didn't know what to make of it. I looked at him in shock, wondering just who he was.

"Are you deaf now? Or just plain dumb? I said. Get. Out," he yelled with a wave of his arm toward the door.

I spun on my heel and fled the room, tears falling down my face with alarming speed. A little piece of my heart had broken off. After all the beautiful time we'd just shared, he'd gone and destroyed it all in the space of a few minutes. I couldn't help thinking his work was killing us and had no idea what to do about it.

Unable to remain in the house with him, I quickly dressed and hopped in my car. I drove around for a while, unsure of where to go. I thought about calling Grace or one of the other girls, but I really didn't want to see them while I was so upset. I didn't want to admit that my brand-new marriage was anything but happy. Besides, they were all probably at work. I needed to talk to someone, but there was only one other person I could think of, and I wasn't sure how appropriate he would be. Nevertheless, I found myself parked out in front of Justin's house, just sitting there looking at it. It was only about two in the afternoon, so I'd expected him to be home working, but I didn't see his motorcycle in the drive. He made his own hours, so perhaps it wasn't unusual that he wasn't home now. I rested my head back against the seat and wondered what to do next. I didn't want to get caught waiting outside his house for him and have him think I was some sort of stalker, but I really didn't have a place to go. I didn't want to go see my mom since she would be able to tell something was wrong, and I didn't want to destroy her good opinion of Vance. She adored him, but she was fiercely protective, and it wouldn't take much for her to turn against him if she thought he was mistreating me. I was sure Vance and I would eventually smooth things over, and I wouldn't want to hear her snarky comments about him for the duration over one small fight.

While I was contemplating what to do, the dilemma was resolved when Justin's motorcycle came up the street and parked in the drive with him attached to the seat. He pulled off his helmet and walked over to my car. He bent over and looked in the passenger window, simply raising a brow at me in question as I looked back at him. He looked at me expectantly, so I rolled down the window.

"The fuck you doin' here, Peaches?" he asked looking at his watch. "At two in the afternoon? Don't you have a job or something?"

"Not being at work is a long story. I'm here because Vance and I had a fight and I couldn't think of anywhere else to go."

"Don't you have girlfriends for this kind of shit?" he asked.

"I do, but they're working. I don't want to talk to them about this stuff, anyway. They don't know Vance like you do."

"So, you think I'm going to give you some kind of insight into what that asshole is thinking, do you?"

"Maybe, I don't really know. Please, can I come in?" I plead.

"Fine," he sighed. "No point in leaving you outside here in the cold."

I smiled weakly and got out of the car, following behind him as he walked toward the house. He stopped at his bike and pulled a greasy looking bag out of one of his saddle packs. He motioned to it with his free hand.

"You had lunch yet?" he asked.

"No," I shook my head, "I was just about to make some when Vance got angry. I left the house right after."

"Well, I have a couple sandwiches in here. You can have one if you're hungry."

We went inside, and as I took off my coat and seated myself on one of the slouchy leather sofas in the living room, Justin plated two cheesesteak sandwiches and brought them out, setting one on the coffee table in front of me. He returned to the kitchen and brought back two Coronas, opening them with a bottle opener he had dangling from his keychain.

He took a seat next to me and said, "Dig in. You can tell me what happened while we eat."

I recounted the events of the last few days between bites of my sandwich, beginning with Friday when Vance got angry with me for staying out past the time I had told him I'd be home to the time I found him passed out in the car before Justin said anything.

"Was he drunk on any of these nights?" he asked.

"Not so far as I could tell. He was drinking the scotch on Friday, but he didn't seem like he'd had too much. On Sunday morning, there was no smell of alcohol on him or anything. When I finally got him to wake up, he only seemed very disoriented and confused. Really out of it, like he was just exhausted. He did say he couldn't remember how he got home. He had no idea why."

Justin gave me an odd look but didn't say anything, so I continued with the events that followed. I explained talking him into taking some time off and resting. I went through the next two days and how he seemed to be like his old self again until this afternoon.

"So," Justin begins, "he just got in the vicinity of his work and turned into insta-dick again?"

"That's about right. I think all the stress from that job is killing him. It's unhealthy and it's turning him into someone I don't know."

"From everything you've just told me, it's someone I don't know, either." He sighed and shook his head, slowly stroking his goatee with one hand. "I've known Vance for twenty years, Peaches, and I've never heard him talk to anyone like that before. The fact he's saying these things to you, of all people, someone I know he loves more than anyone in the world, I... there's no explanation for it."

"Let me ask you something," I said as a thought occurred to me. "How much time have you spent around him with his previous girlfriends?"

He paused to think for a while. "Vance never brought women around too much. He had a few we met, don't get me wrong, but I never got the feeling they were serious. He was affectionate with them but only to a point. He wasn't rude to them or mean to them if that's what you're lookin' for, but like I said, he didn't bring them around that often."

I nodded, wondering if there was something to that.

"I can see what you're thinking. That maybe he treats his women differently than other people in his life."

"It's possible, don't you think?" I asked. "There are countless stories of women who are abused and nobody has any clue about it. The guy seems like this great person, an upstanding citizen to everyone else, but behind closed doors, he's another man entirely."

Justin stiffened. "Has he hurt you, Mimi?"

"No, no, nothing like that. Just my feelings. It's that he's getting meaner. He called me dumb today."

"Whoa, now. I really can't imagine that. I want to say it's just the stress from work, but that's going way too far." He rested his elbows on his knees as he ran a hand over his shaved head, clearly frustrated by the thought of his best friend's behavior. "I know this is going to sound really lame, but you two should go on a vacation once this deal is over. Maybe then you can talk him into switching firms. If he makes partner at this place, the pressure on him is only going to get more intense, and that won't be good for either of you."

"That's my fear, too. He said this deal would be over in a week or two. Yesterday we talked about taking a trip to Tahoe. Perhaps then, I can approach the subject of making a change. Maybe he'll be receptive to it, assuming he still wants to go and doesn't stay angry with me."

"I think once he cools down, he'll be fine. Isn't that how he's been ever since this started?"

"Yes," I confirmed, a seed of hope beginning to grow in my chest. Although he'd been mercurial, he would eventually calm down and go back to his usual self. I took this as evidence it was just the stress getting to him. When we had more time to spend together, things would go back to normal.

"Thanks, Justin. You've helped me realize it most likely is just the stress getting to him. I was beginning to think it was something more serious. I just have to find a way to convince him to make a change. To show him that we can't continue on this way because it's hurting us too much."

"Sure thing, Peaches." Justin gave me a hug. "I know how happy you make Vance. If he really knew how this was making you feel, he wouldn't do it. He's just so blinded by his ambition at work right now, he can't see what it's doing to him. We've just got to give the man a little change in perspective. Once you see him through this patch at work and get him out of town, you use every dirty trick you can to make him realize that what you have is worth more than any job can offer him. My suggestion is lots and lots of blowjobs."

"My god." I slugged him in the shoulder. "You are a bigger pervert than he is."

"Those are the most persuasive words in man-speak, Peaches. That's some wisdom, right there."

"Thanks, Justin," I said with a big grin.

"Now, I think I've laid enough knowledge on you for one day. I don't expect you're in a hurry to get home just yet though. You want another beer? You can kick back, relax, and watch a movie. I have some work I need to finish up, but you're free to make yourself at home for as long as you like."

"I think I will if you don't mind. I can't thank you enough for listening and everything. You really are an awesome guy."

"Don't let it get out, darlin'. You'll ruin my reputation as a badass. Beers are in the fridge. Help yourself," he said as he swaggered off to his home office.

Twelve

I awoke to a hand shaking my shoulder. "Mimi, wake up, darlin'. You fell asleep."

I immediately sat up, rubbing my eyes. "I'm sorry, Justin. I just drifted off. What time is it?" I asked, looking around. It was dark outside the picture window in the living room, and I had a sudden sense of disorientation. It could have been eight p.m. or three a.m., and I wouldn't have known the difference.

"It's only about six-thirty. I would have checked on you earlier, but I got caught up in the project I was working on. You should be getting home though. I'm sure Vance has cooled down by now and is probably wondering where you are."

"You're right. He's probably worried since I didn't leave a note or anything," I said, thinking of how he acted when I didn't call to let him know I'd be late. I dug my phone out my purse to check to see if he'd left me any messages, but my phone was blank. Maybe he hadn't cooled off yet after all. In any case, it was time to get home. He was sure to be hungry, and I was determined he'd have another home-cooked meal. Especially, since I didn't get to make him lunch.

I shouldered my bag, gave Justin a quick hug, and dashed out to my car. I made it home in no time, but the house was dark, and Vance's car was missing from the drive. I went through the house, flicking on lights as I went. I looked for a note but didn't find anything anywhere. When I got to his office, I noticed the box of files was missing and my heart deflated. It didn't take a genius to figure out where he was. He had gone to the office. There was no telling when he'd be home now.

I went ahead with my plan to cook him a nice meal, just to make myself feel better. I made sirloin steaks with baked potatoes and spinach on the side. I left a plate for him in the oven while I sat at our kitchen table all alone, eating my food and wondering how to turn things around. I could only hope things would work out as I had hoped after my conversation with Justin. Once this deal was over, and I got him away from all this pressure, things would be fine.

After I finished eating, I cleaned up the dishes, left a note on the refrigerator for Vance to let him know dinner was waiting for him in the oven and went to bed for the night.

I never heard Vance come home that night, but I knew he'd been there because his suit was laying across the foot of the bed when I awoke the next morning and there was still a fog across the mirror in the bathroom from his shower. I decided I would go back to work that day as well since it seemed our time together was over. I went to the kitchen to make my morning cup of coffee and to my horror, I found his plate from the night before, turned over in the middle of the floor, food splattered everywhere.

Two weeks passed much as they had before "the incident" as I was coming to call it in my head. We almost never saw each other with Vance leaving before I woke in the morning and coming home after I went to bed at night. Every afternoon, before I left work, I sent a text message to see if he wanted me to bring dinner like we had planned while he had been off. He always responded he was too busy that day, but maybe the next. It never happened.

One Friday evening just before Christmas, Vance came home from work early in an amazingly good mood, a bottle of champagne in one hand and a bouquet of roses in the other. I was in the kitchen going over cookbooks trying to plan a menu for Christmas dinner. I had invited both of our mothers to spend the holiday with us and was looking forward to a picture-perfect evening filled with family and love. Very Norman Rockwell.

Vance dropped his burdens on the table and scooped me up into his arms, twirling me around the kitchen. I couldn't help but laugh at his exuberance.

"What's gotten into you?" I exclaimed as he twirled me around a few more times.

He stopped and gave me a warm, smacking kiss. I reached up with my fingertips and touched my lips. It was the first time he had shown me any affection since that last day he was off work.

I stared at him, wide-eyed as he smiled down at me, his eyes practically glowing with excitement.

"It's over!" he exclaimed. "We closed on the deal today! All those weeks of hell are finally over."

I gasped in disbelief at first, and then as the realization of what that meant soaked into my brain, I jumped into his arms.

"Finally, I get my husband back!" I yelled at the top of my lungs.

I pulled back and beamed at him. We could go back to our normal, happy lives. We could take that trip to Lake Tahoe, and I could convince him that this job was wrong for us, and he needed to find something that allowed us to put our marriage first.

"You haven't even heard the best part yet, Mimi." he said, grabbing my upper arms and shaking me slightly in his excitement.

"What, what?" I cried, his enthusiasm infecting me like an airborne virus.

He paused, presumably for dramatic effect. "I did it, Mimi. All the hard work paid off. I'm the newest partner at the firm!"

My stomach bottomed out, and my face instantly fell. I tried to recover as fast as I could and gave him a tight smile, but my reaction did not go unnoticed.

His hands fell away from me as if I'd burned him. He took two swift steps away from me, his face twisting into an ugly expression I'd never seen before.

"I thought you'd be happy for me, Mimi." He began to pace the length of the kitchen. "You know this is what I've been working toward. Why I've put in all these long hours. Why I work my ass off. Instead of sharing in my joy like someone who actually loves me would, you look like you've swallowed a bug. Why on earth I thought you'd want this for me too, I have no idea. You've always been so selfish. I was a fool to think this situation would be any different. I should have called Tiffany."

"You wouldn't..." I gasped in absolute shock.

"No, I wouldn't, but I should. No one would blame me with the way you treat me," he spat.

I shook my head back and forth. I felt like I had stepped into some bizarre dimension where everything was backward. When had I ever been anything but good and loving towards him? How could he accuse me of these things?

"Vance, it's not that I'm not happy for you. I know this is what you've wanted. It's just the stress of your job has taken such a toll on you, on our marriage. Forgive me, but I'm worried about what this promotion means for us. You'll be under more pressure, and you'll probably still be working long hours. Your mood has been so erratic lately—I mean just listen to the things you're saying to me. You know me better than that. You know I love you and only want good things for you, for us," I stammered out.

"I have no idea what you're talking about, Mimi. Yes, I've worked long hours, but that's to be expected. You knew I didn't have a nine-to-five job when you married me. But as far as my mood and the things I'm saying? I'm only telling you what I see. You've been a real bitch lately, totally unsupportive of my needs or understanding of my obligations. Like when you text me trying to get me to have dinner with you when you know I have to work. Only thinking about what you want, never about what I need."

He hung his head then, putting his fingers to his temples and rubbing in small circles. He blew out a long breath before speaking again.

"Now you've given me a headache. I can't even go out and celebrate my hard work on my own or with my friends. Thanks, Mimi. Once again, you've managed to ruin everything." He turned and walked from the kitchen, leaving me standing there with my jaw gaping, and my heart bleeding.

Of course, we never made it to Lake Tahoe or anywhere we talked about as we cuddled that day in bed when he was off work. In retrospect, that was the last beautiful day we had together. The last day of our marriage as I had known it to be.

One day bled into the next, a study of loneliness, peppered by unpleasant encounters with Vance on the few days he would come home at a decent hour. When he did, he always let me know ahead of time, so I could have dinner waiting for him when he arrived, but he was always in a foul mood. Whether it was a bad day at work or a rough commute home, he was completely unpleasant.

When he spoke to me, which wasn't often, he always found fault with something. It could be what I was wearing or with what I cooked or how it was prepared. He grew meaner and meaner to the point of being outright cruel. He'd call me fat, even though I hadn't gained an ounce of weight since the day I'd met him. He'd criticize the way I wore my hair, telling me Tiffany's long length and shade of auburn was much more appealing. He made fun of my clothes, insisting they were too boring, that I should dress sexier to "liven things up" if I wanted to keep his attention. As if I wanted any of his attention at that point. My goal was to stay as inconspicuous as possible.

He took to sleeping in the guest room which was fine with me. The less he was near me, the better. One day, on a night he was working late, I took all his clothes and moved them into that room, so he had no reason to ever come into our bedroom anymore. We were roommates as far as I was concerned at that point.

I thought about leaving him. I couldn't see things getting any better since I didn't know how to fix the problems we had, and he certainly didn't seem interested in doing anything other than using me for a verbal punching bag. Still, I was holding on to how things had been between us, and I hadn't stopped loving him. He hurt me, day after day, but some part of me still believed my Vance was somewhere deep inside him, and I only had to figure out how to find him and bring him back to me.

I knew his job was the source of all our problems, his ongoing headaches being more evidence that his job was killing not only us but his health as well. He looked bad—gaunt with dark circles under his eyes. My handsome, happy husband was gone, replaced with a harried-looking, bitter man who did nothing but work and bring me down at every opportunity. I felt if he could find a position in a firm that wasn't so high profile and had a more relaxed atmosphere, he would return to his normal self. I had to believe that, or I would give up altogether.

Then came that final night. Vance had sent me a text message letting me know he would be home early in the afternoon, doing some work from home, specifically advising what he wanted for dinner. He said he had news to share with me, so I should be home as early as I could be, too.

I left work at lunchtime, so I could stop by the market and pick up the ingredients for the meal he had requested. I figured he was in good spirits for a change since he was requesting fried chicken and mashed potatoes, a favorite of his, but not something he usually indulged in. Since he seemed to be in a festive mood, I also picked up the ingredients for a chocolate silk pie, a favorite of his. Might as well go all out and show him I could make the effort. I was downtrodden at this point, but there was still that tiny spark of hope which could be fanned into something brighter with just a hint of encouragement.

When I got home, Vance was already in his office, but he didn't come out to greet me. I changed into a pair of soft pants and a short-sleeved blouse and began working on the pie. By the time it was sitting in the refrigerator, it was time to start preparing dinner.

As I was peeling the potatoes, Vance came into the kitchen and got a bottle of white wine that had been chilling in the refrigerator. He silently popped the cork and poured himself a glass. He pulled another glass from the cabinet and offered it to me, but I just looked at him quizzically.

"Oh, that's right," he said softly. "You still don't like wine."

I shook my head silently and continued peeling the potatoes.

He cleared his throat, then began speaking. "I have news," he said.

"You do? About what?" I asked mildly.

"I've been offered a position in the New York office."

I nodded. "With the 'big boys,'" I said. "That's great. It's exactly what you've always wanted."

"How do you feel about it?" he asked.

I was taken aback for a moment. He was asking me how I felt about something? It was a trap. I knew it. I responded before he could detect any change in my demeanor.

"I just told you. I think it's great," I said with as much enthusiasm as I could feign.

"I'm proud of you, Mimi. I really expected you to object and complain about this. If I had known you'd be happy for me for once, I would have suggested we go out and make a real celebration of it."

"What's not to celebrate? This was always the plan from day one, right? I think you mentioned it the day I met you, even," I said, smiling. "I had a feeling you had good news based on what you requested for dinner, so I went ahead and made you a chocolate silk pie, too. So, even though we're not dressed up or at a five-star restaurant, we can make do with some of your favorites."

He smiled in a way I hadn't seen in a long time—that dazzling Pepsodent smile that used to make my heart melt every time I saw it. Now, it only made my heart ache.

"See, Mimi. When you put the effort in, we can have a nice time together like we used to. Maybe New York will be a new start for us."

I just nodded. It hurt to hear him say what we'd had was simply "a nice time." It had been spectacular, all-consuming, beautiful, and so very special. He reduced it to merely a bland, convenient relationship between two mostly indifferent people in one sentence. That was what we had now when he wasn't being cruel and awful to me. Then to insult me on top of it all by acting as if the demise of our relationship was my fault, it was almost more than I could bear. Nevertheless, I kept my composure and began cutting up the potatoes and putting them in the pot for boiling.

He sipped at his wine while he watched me for a while. I felt very uncomfortable having him in the room, expecting him to criticize or berate me for something at any minute. Instead, he just stood there quietly, watching my every move.

"You look very pretty today, Mimi," he said softly.

I stiffened. He hadn't given me a compliment in ages. I was suddenly suspicious, wondering what he was up to.

"Thank you, Vance," I said carefully, not wanting to do or say anything that might set him off. This was new territory, and I was unsure how I should react. I felt like prey in the face of a new and unknown predator.

"Is that a new outfit or something? Have you done something different with your hair?" he asked.

"Nope. Same plain old me, I'm afraid," I said as I transferred the pot of potatoes to the stove and set them to boil. He came up behind me and rested his hands on my hips, breathing in the scent of my hair. I stood stock still, afraid to move.

"I remember that smell. It's been a long time since I've been close enough to catch your scent," he whispered into my ear. "Perhaps we can get even closer tonight. I believe your new attitude and pleasantness tonight is having an effect on me. It reminds me of how we used to be."

I swallowed, pulling all my strength to me, and turned in his arms. I wrapped myself around him and rested my head on his chest, doing my best to hold my tears at bay. How I wished this hug was like all the others I used to cherish, to take such satisfaction in. Now it was just a hollow impersonation of what we used to have. I squeezed him tightly and looked up at him with fake, but what I hoped appeared sincere affection in my eyes.

"It's very nice, Vance. Unfortunately, if we stay like this, I'll never get this dinner finished and our celebration will be ruined."

He smiled, squeezed me, and stepped away. "To be continued later, then," he whispered suggestively. "I have a few things to finish up in my office. Call me when everything is ready."

"I will," I nodded as he picked up his glass of wine and left the room.

I continued preparing the meal on auto-pilot. I had too many thoughts floating through my head to fully concentrate on everything I was supposed to be doing. I didn't want to go to New York. I didn't believe it would be a new start for us even if it was where everything began. I had no illusions we could recapture any of the magic we had shared before. The way I felt when he touched me tonight hadn't rekindled any feelings of affection or desire. All I felt was sad and cold. What did that foretell for any future we could have together? Here or anywhere else?

Distracted, I made the mistake of frying the chicken while I steamed the broccoli before I mashed the potatoes. When I realized what I had done, I quickly mashed the potatoes and whipped them with the hand mixer for a lot less time than I normally did and didn't make sure they were as smooth they could be in an effort to get everything on the plate while it was still hot.

Once I had everything on the table, I called Vance in to eat. His good mood seemed to have waned a little after working in his office for the last hour, but it hadn't completely dimmed. He examined his plate with a satisfied look.

"I'm really looking forward to this, Mimi. I've been thinking about it all day," he said with a big grin.

He lifted his chicken to his mouth and took a big bite. The look in his eyes changed instantly as he chewed. He wiped his mouth with his napkin, spitting his food into it discreetly. I took a delicate bite of my own food to see what was wrong with it. Other than being slightly cool, I could taste nothing wrong.

He then took a forkful of mashed potatoes and put it into his mouth. That's when all hell broke loose.

Thirteen

After succumbing to my tears, I wipe my face and pull it together. I can't stay another minute in this place. Vance is a danger to me, and every second I stay is a second too long. I'll come back for my things tomorrow while he's at work. I can pick up toiletries I'll need tomorrow at a local store, but I need to get out now and find a place to stay for the night. I turn off the kitchen light and quickly walk through the living room, swiping my purse and car keys off the side table by the front door. I quietly open the front door and slip out into the night. Once the door is closed behind me, I flee as fast as my feet will carry me to the safety of my car and jump inside. I lock all my doors, stick my keys in the ignition and back out of the driveway as fast as I can. I don't care at this point if he hears me leaving. I'm out of the house, out of the immediate reach of his violent hands, and if he wants to get at me now, he'll have to run me off the road.

I drive across Los Angeles, over the hill into the San Fernando Valley, stopping only at the drug store to pick up some cheap shampoo, conditioner, deodorant, a toothbrush, and toothpaste. After driving around a little longer, I eventually check into a Hilton in the west valley. Once safely in my room, I take the hottest shower I can stand, letting the water beat down on my sore muscles for long minutes before reaching for the tiny bar of hotel soap and scrubbing every square inch of my skin. I wash my hair twice before I finish my shower. After drying off and putting my sweatshirt and leggings back on, I'm grateful that I chose such comfortable clothes when I changed in the laundry room. I'll be able to sleep in them, and they won't look any worse than they already do when I have to wear them again tomorrow. My only regret is I don't have fresh underwear with me, but all things considered, I think I can suffer a pair of day-old panties this one time.

I turn off the lights and climb under the covers. The bed is comfortable, but I can't sleep. I keep having visions of Vance tackling me to the floor and mauling me like an animal. Only, in my thoughts, I'm not able to fight him off. It's an endless cycle of what if... what if... what if? I toss and turn for what seems like hours. Around midnight, the muffled sound of "Marry Me" begins playing repeatedly from the depths of my purse. I never changed his ringtone even after things began to fall apart. It was one of the things I held onto, a happy reminder of our past, a romantic memory of the man he used to be. I don't bother to get up and answer his calls or to even shut the phone off. I just let it ring until it finally falls silent sometime after one-thirty. He never leaves a message.

When the sun finally rises, so do I. I order a pot of coffee from room service and make arrangements with the front desk to stay another day. Fully caffeinated, I go into the bathroom and take photographs of my injuries from Vance's attack last night. The bite marks on my neck and five distinct fingerprints around my throat are the most obvious. There are a number of bruises and scratches on my chest and waist where he tore at my clothes, and a few on my arms where I fought against him, but the ones on my neck are those that really tell the story.

Once eight o'clock rolls around, I leave the hotel and drive back over the hill to my office to speak with my one of my bosses, Bob Miller. Both partners at my firm are great men, but Bob, the managing partner, is my favorite. His partner and my direct supervisor, Steve Dickerson is nice, but all business. He's the driving force behind the firm, always out networking, seeking more cases to take on, and the reason behind the continuing success of the company. Bob has the personal touch. He's always taking the time to make sure the employees are happy, that office morale is good, and makes us all feel like we're a family. Either one of them would help me with this problem, but Bob is the one who will care about me in the process and hold my hand figuratively—and literally—if I need it.

When I arrive, I walk straight back to Bob's office, which means I have to traipse past the whole work floor to get there. My appearance gains me some odd looks from the secretaries, but thankfully, no one says anything to me about it.

I stop to check with Sheila, Bob's long-time secretary, to see if he is available. Fortunately for me, he doesn't have anything on the schedule all day. She waves me back, and I go straight in. He doesn't stand on formality. We're never required to be announced or knock, he always maintains an open-door policy for the employees. As I enter the office, he looks up from his computer and his mouth drops in shock.

"Good lord, Mimi. What the hell happened to you? Come here, sit down, and tell me everything this instant."

I fall into one of his guest chairs and look at him for a few moments. I want to open my mouth and let it all fall out, but this is harder than I expected. Finally, I say, "I really don't know where to begin."

"How about who gave you those bruises and that nasty bite mark on your neck, and if you have any other injuries I should know about," he says, pulling a legal pad toward him and a picking up a pen.

I take a big breath and letting it all out in a rush, I say, "Vance did it."

He drops his pen and looks at me in shock. "Vance? How long has this been going on, Mimi?"

"Last night was the first time he was ever physically violent with me. He's been verbally abusive for about the last six months and has been violent in that he started throwing things around somewhere in that time."

"Oh, my dear, I had no idea things were bad at all. You've always seemed so much in love. I wish you would have come to me earlier, so we could have done something about this, got you out of this," he says genuinely.

"I wasn't ready, Bob. Things had been so wonderful between us, it took a long time for me to give up hope they would eventually go back to the way they had been. I kept making excuses for him; it wasn't him, it was just stress from his job making him act this way, once the deal he was working on was over, things would go back to normal. Then, if I could get him away from that firm, everything would be fine. You know how it goes. It's always some external influence rather than something wrong with the individual. Turns out, this is just him. He was on his best behavior the first year of our marriage, I guess. I shouldn't have been so impulsive. I should have listened to the little voice in my head that told me to slow down and get to know him better rather than rushing into things like I did. Live and learn, as they say," I finish while tenaciously clinging to my composure. I'm doing my best to present a strong front and be as matter-of-fact as possible, but inside I'm falling apart as I finally admit to the nightmare my marriage has become.

"What are you going to do now?" he asks gently.

"The very first thing I want to do is file for a temporary protection order and a temporary restraining order. I don't want him anywhere near me or to be able to contact me. He already called me after midnight several times last night. In fact, he called for more than an hour, over and over. I came to see if you could refer me to a good family practice," I say, tears stinging at the corners of my eyes.

"Sure. I know a couple of great people who will do right by you. Do you also want to begin divorce proceedings or file for a legal separation?"

"I hadn't given that any thought yet," I say, refusing to allow myself to break down. "Honestly, I don't know if I'm ready yet. I know I probably shouldn't give myself an opportunity for second thoughts, but I really need time to think about it, to come to terms with it. I'll be doing it sooner rather than later, but I just have to wrap my mind around it."

"I understand completely, Mimi. It's not something you can be hasty about. You made a lifetime commitment, and even though things have broken down beyond repair at this point—since in my opinion physical violence is and should be a deal breaker for everyone—making the decision to break that commitment should be made solemnly and in one's own time," he says with more compassion than I could ever expect from anyone.

Fresh tears fill my eyes with gratitude for this man I have come to love in a fatherly way. I knew I could count on him.

"So, aside from the referral, what can we do for you? Obviously, you're going to need some time off to get into an apartment or some other place to live right away. You let me know how long. I'll arrange to have a temp brought in to cover your job while you're out. Steve will miss you, but once I fill him in, he'll understand. Do you need any money to cover the expenses of getting a new place?"

"Thanks for the time off. That's all I really need. I have enough for a place and movers to get me there. All the stuff I had from before I got married is still in storage, I never got rid of it," I say, running a trembling hand through my hair, my voice not as strong as it had been when I first walked in.

"Well don't hesitate to ask if any surprise expenses pop up."

I nod, as he writes down the names of three top-notch family practice attorneys who can help me with obtaining temporary restraining and protection orders.

After meeting with the first lawyer who could see me that day, providing a statement and printing out copies of all the pictures of my injuries, I am assured the proper paperwork will be filed with the court that afternoon, and Vance will be served before the end of the business day. Once I'm back out in the car, I sit for a while, tapping my index finger against the steering wheel, trying to decide what to do next. Do I go back to the house and pack my things? Do I go apartment hunting? It's almost noon and Vance should be at work. I look down at my clothes and flip-flops. They still look relatively clean, but probably not the best presentation for trying to convince someone to rent to me. That makes the decision for me.

Just to be on the safe side, I call the house phone to make sure Vance didn't decide to work from home for whatever reason. I let it ring ten times, but there's no answer. I feel reasonably safe that I can get in and out without running into him, so I start up the car and point it in the direction of our house.

As I arrive, I notice his car is nowhere in sight. Exhaling a breath I didn't even realize I was holding, I pull in the drive and hustle into the house. I waste no time dashing to the bedroom and dragging out the designer suitcases Vance had bought for me as a gift before one of our trips shortly after we were married. I throw them on the bed and begin emptying my drawers into them, not caring about making sure anything is folded or not. I grab everything from the closet and do the same. I dump the contents of my jewelry box on top of the clothes and zip them up as fast as I can. I grab the small valise from the closet and rush into the bathroom, grabbing all my personal products and make-up, and likewise dump them inside. The sides of the case bulge from all the items I've stuffed inside, but I manage to get it zipped up, anyway. I return to the bags and hook the valise over the telescopic handle of one the suitcases. Pulling both cases behind me, I take one last look around the room. My eyes land on a photo of Vance and me from our wedding.

We both look so happy, Vance is looking directly at the camera, smiling that wide, beaming smile that used to give me butterflies every time he turned it on me. I'm turned slightly into his side, looking down, my eyes hooded with a soft, dreamy look on my face. Impulsively, I grab the frame and open one of the suitcases and stuff it in. I just can't let go of every single memory I have. There was a time when we were blissfully happy, and this photo captures one of the happiest of those moments. Tears prickle my eyes, but I blink them away and resume my trek out of the house, bags in tow. I toss them in the back of my SUV and scurry into the driver's seat as fast as I can. If I left anything else behind, it can be replaced or returned to me later. I have the essentials, and that's all I need for now.

Just as I'm about to back out, Vance's car swings into the driveway. He jumps out of his car, leaving his door open and runs to the side of my car, knocking frantically on the window. I don't think there's been enough time for the papers to have been filed, let alone for him to have been served already, so there wouldn't be much point in calling the police unless he tries to harm me again.

I watch his face as his fist raps against my window. He looks panicked, his eyes scared and nervous. I don't know what he's thinking, but I'm not about to roll down my window, and I know I don't want to hear anything he wants to say. Only mildly concerned about his toes, I shift the car into reverse, look over my right shoulder and back the car down the drive and around his car. I turn into the street and drive away. In my rearview, I see that he has run after me, presumably calling out to me, but I couldn't care less.

A few minutes later, "Marry Me" begins to float out of my purse. I really need to change that ringtone. That song, which used to bring a smile to my face, now only drives a spike of pain through my heart. I reach over and dig my phone out of my purse. I press the button to turn it off, and it goes blissfully silent. Tossing it onto the seat next to me, I continue driving back to the hotel to drop off my luggage.

It's about two p.m. by the time I'm able to turn my thoughts to looking for an apartment. I contemplate putting off beginning my search until the following day but decide I need to keep busy. I'm familiar with the area and know there are several large apartment communities that are fairly upscale. They would have the kind of amenities I would want like a secure perimeter gate and a twenty-four-hour guard. Maybe even an individual unit alarm system. Unfortunately, I failed to grab my laptop in my haste to get out of the house, so I'm going to have to drive the city and find the complexes by memory, hoping they have vacancies rather than doing most of the "footwork" by phone.

I go directly to the one I'm most familiar with and can find with no difficulty. After a short conversation with the gate guard and an I.D. check, he directs me to the leasing office. They happen to have a two-bedroom unit available. I really only need one, but I'll take what they have. It's located in the middle of the complex which the agent keeps referring to as the community, which I suppose is more apt. It's enormous and made up of several large buildings, each with three floors with numerous units per floor. I can't even begin to estimate how many apartments in total comprise this "community."

The unit itself overlooks one of the three pools on the grounds, which are nice. Definitely a better view than the parking lot. The apartment itself is spacious with gray wall to wall carpeting and stark white walls. It appears to be roomy enough to accommodate the furniture I have in storage. The kitchen is small but is attractive with walnut cabinets, black granite countertops, and a gas range. It has double-paned windows which reduce any noise from outside, and it faces east, so it won't catch the afternoon sun. It's a bit of a drive to work and the traffic will be no fun, but it's far from Vance's house. I can definitely live here.

I let the leasing agent know I want it and want to move in this weekend if possible. She beams at me, so she must work on commission. We go back to the leasing office where we fill out the necessary paperwork, and she runs my credit. After about an hour, I am in possession of the keys to my new home and am on my way back to the hotel to make arrangements with movers for Friday.

Finally, I flop on the bed completely exhausted. I have checked all the boxes on my mental to-do list and have earned a well-deserved rest. It dawns on me I haven't eaten a single thing. I've been running all day on the pot of coffee I had this morning. I should order something from room service, but I'm really not hungry and am frankly too tired to even lift the phone to place the order. I look at my luggage and decide I'll unpack some things for the rest of the week tomorrow and fold the rest in the hope I can keep them from getting too wrinkled although that's probably a lost cause. Yawning, I decide to spend one more night in my sweatshirt and leggings, and yes, my day-old panties even though that's super nasty. I'm just too fucking tired to do anything but crawl under the covers and sleep until noon tomorrow.

When I wake the next day, which is indeed just before noon and nearly check out time, I call the front desk again and extend my stay until Friday morning. Having accomplished all my goals the day before, I'm at a loss as to what to do with myself after I complete my unpacking and folding my clothes. I'm still not hungry but decide I should get out and eat something. After a quick shower, I throw my hair up into a ponytail and put on a pair of well-worn jeans and a t-shirt. I slide my feet into the one pair of sneakers I managed to grab in my packing frenzy and head out in search of food with no real destination in mind.

To my surprise, I find myself sitting out in front of Justin's house again. I hadn't planned on coming here. Wasn't even really thinking about anything other than it would be nice to have some company to help keep my mind off everything that's happened, and my car pointed itself in this direction. I question the wisdom of being here because Justin is the last person to take my mind off things. If I talk to him, the conversation is sure to center on Vance.

Just as I'm about to put my car in drive and pull away, the front door opens, and Justin comes strolling down the walkway, his hands tucked into the pockets of his hoodie. He comes up to the passenger window and just stands there looking at me until I roll down the window. I hang my head in shame, defeat, or I don't know what emotion I'm feeling.

"You're sitting out in front of my house again, Peaches. You got something against knocking?" he asks.

"I don't know what it is, Justin. Every time I come here, I always have second thoughts and think I should drive away, but before I can, you catch me."

"Well, you might as well come in. As you said, I've caught you again, and I'm assuming you've got something to talk about. So, come in and we'll talk."

"Actually, I was wondering if you wanted to get something to eat. I haven't eaten in a while and could use a good meal."

His eyes narrow at me. "How long is a while?"

I wince and say in a small voice, "Lunch, day before yesterday."

"I assume you have a good reason why other than you are on some fool diet?"

"Come with me, and I'll explain everything," I promise.

Justin locks up his house then jumps in my car. "Where we going, darlin'?"

"I was hoping you might have some ideas. I'm just hungry but really don't care what I eat. My appetite is a little screwy right now."

"Since it's been a while since you've had anything to eat, we should probably go light on you. Maybe soup and a sandwich or something like that."

Justin directs me to a small, twenty-four-hour diner near his house. It looks kind of questionable to me with its peeling wallpaper and cracked red vinyl booths, but Justin assures me it will pass the health code, pointing to the A rating in the window and insists the food is good.

We take a booth in the back and the waitress is with us almost immediately with menus and to take our drink orders. While we're waiting, Justin finally notices the injuries on my neck and his eyes widen.

"What the hell happened to you, Mimi?" he asks, pointing at my neck.

I look down at the table, not wanting to say what I have to say, unsure how it will affect his friendship with Vance. Maybe it isn't fair of me to tell him. He's one of Vance's best friends after all, and I probably shouldn't be coming between them. But I've made a good friend of Justin, too. I don't want to bad mouth Vance to his friend, but I need Justin to know what he did, maybe to help me make sense of all this even though I know there's none to be had.

Without looking up, I say softly, "Vance happened."

He sucks in a harsh breath and whispers angrily, "You're shitting me."

I quickly look up at him with wide eyes. Does he not believe me? "No, I wouldn't joke around about this or make it up. He got very upset with me the night before last, and when I stood up to him, he attacked me."

"Not that it matters, but what was he upset about?" Justin asks.

"He didn't like the dinner I made for him," I whisper.

"What?"

Just then the waitress comes with our drinks and to take our orders. Neither of us has even looked at the menu, but being that it's a diner, I take a chance and simply order a grilled cheese and fries. Justin orders a burger and onion rings.

"I just can't believe it, Mimi," he says shaking his head. "Vance isn't that kind of guy. He has always taken care of people smaller than him, looked out for people who were vulnerable. I just can't accept he would hurt you."

I feel my stomach drop and tears prickle my eyes. Coming to Justin was definitely a mistake. Vance told me he was fiercely loyal. I should have known he'd take his side.

"I wouldn't lie to you, Justin, but I guess I understand why you don't believe me," I place my napkin on the table and prepare to stand.

"Sit down, Mimi. I'm not saying I don't believe you. I'm just shocked. I don't want to believe it's true even with the evidence staring me in the face. I don't know what's happened to him."

"I guess he's not the guy we all thought he was."

"Now that I definitely know isn't true. I have known him almost my whole life. I know exactly who Vance Ashcroft is, and this is most definitely not him. There's something wrong. Has he been drinking heavily or something? Has he gotten into drugs?"

"He does drink more than he used to, but I wouldn't say he drinks heavily. I've never seen him use any drugs. I suppose it's possible since he spends so much time away from me. I always thought it was because of all the stress he's under, but after all this time, I think it's just who he is, Justin. It's always been in him, he's just been good at hiding it from everyone."

"Well, I'm sure as hell going to find out. If I have to kick his ass, I'll do it. You don't beat on a woman for any reason, so he's definitely got that coming to him. But I'm telling you, something is wrong, and I'm going to figure it out."

"I hope you can for the sake of your friendship. As for me and Vance, it's done. I'll never stay with a man who hurts me, and I'll never be able to forgive him for it. I overlooked the verbal abuse for months, but he threatened to kill me." I leave out the part where he tried to rape me. Justin doesn't need to know the whole dirty business. "I won't stick around waiting for that or anything else to happen."

He nods in acknowledgment. "So, what are you going to do?"

"I've already filed for a temporary protection order and a restraining order. If he hasn't been yet, he'll soon be served with the paperwork. Once I get my head around it, I'll be filing for a divorce."

He places both hands on the table and leans back against the seat, blowing out a breath. "I'm sorry, Mimi. I know how much you love him."

"Loved. How much I loved him," I say firmly. "He killed everything I had left for him the other night."

Justin takes one of my hands in his on the table and just holds it. Neither of us says anything more until the food comes. Despite my lack of appetite, I manage to finish my sandwich and all my fries. Our meal is quiet, both of us lost in thought. As we are walking out of the diner, I clear my throat a little before speaking quietly.

"I want you to know I've enjoyed our friendship. You have always been very nice to me, and it was good to feel a connection to one of Vance's friends. You, more than any of the other guys, made me feel very accepted." I look up at him with the brightest smile I can muster.

"What are you saying, Mimi?"

"I know with this separation, your loyalty to Vance will require you to choose a side. I just want you to know I understand that. I'm sorry we won't be friends anymore, but there won't be any hard feelings from me," I say as we reach my car.

He stops and turns me to face him. "Yes, I will always have a loyalty to Vance, but you are my good friend too, so you also have my loyalty. I won't choose sides. I am going to figure out what's going on, Mimi. Maybe it's too late to fix things for the two of you. It probably is. But I won't abandon either of you."

He pulls me in for a long, warm hug that I really, really need. We stay that way for a few minutes until I pull away, discreetly wiping my eyes. I thank him softly before getting in the car. We drive back to his house silently, and I drop him off with only a short goodbye and a promise to talk again soon.

Fourteen

Friday finally rolls around, and I meet the movers at the storage space. Fortunately, all the stuff is mine. Vance and I never blended any of our stuff in here when we made room for some of my belongings at the house; all his displaced items went into the garage. The movers are efficient, and the space is cleared out within an hour. The longest part of the day seems to be the drive to the apartment because they unload the items in the apartment as fast as they picked them up.

I spend the rest of the weekend organizing the apartment which is a godsend because it keeps my mind busy. Finally, on Sunday evening with everything put away and the furniture arranged the way I want it, I flop on the sofa, one very tired woman. I realize I haven't turned on my cell phone since Monday when I turned it off because Vance was calling. I am loath to turn it on, but I have to. I can't stay incommunicado for very long. There are people who will worry about me, especially if they can't get ahold of me at home. God only knows what Vance has told them if anyone has tried.

I power it up and learn my voicemail is full. Most of the calls are from Vance although those stop on Tuesday, I assume after he received the TRO. I forward through those messages without listening to them, but for some reason, I don't delete them. There are a couple messages from my mom, one from Grace, two from Laurel, one from Jessica, and finally one from Bob. I forward through them all except the one from Bob, thinking I'll get back to everyone during the week, in my own time. I'm not eager to share the news of my split with Vance with everyone. Bob's message is sweet, offering me more time off if I need it, and again letting me know if I need money, he's willing to give me a loan. I'll be back at work tomorrow, so I'll thank him then.

I decide to turn in early, so I can get a start on my life post-Vance. It won't be easy, but I'll persevere until I have achieved a new normal and everything is okay once again. A little voice inside my head wonders if my heart will ever recover, but I squash it and push it aside. Who needs a heart, anyway?

I spend the next few weeks getting through by putting one foot in front of the other and making mental to-do lists like I did the day after I left Vance. It's really the only thing that keeps me sane. If I don't, I will have time to stop and think about what I've lost, how much I hurt, and I know that will be my undoing. So, I continue forth, one step at a time, one task at a time, calling each day completed a victory.

So far, I've avoided telling everyone the news, except for Laurel. I broke down and called her somewhere at the end of the second week and laid it all out for her. It was one giant tear fest on my end, with her vacillating between quietly listening, cursing his name, and threatening some very creative bodily harm to particular parts of his anatomy. Mostly though, she was sympathetic and supportive and even offered to come out for a visit to help me through. I declined, knowing how busy things are at work for her, but promised if things got too rough, I'd tell her right away. She promised to be with me in a flash, bringing along with her sharpest set of kitchen knives.

I'd managed to avoid the rest of the girls at work, which wasn't terribly difficult since we all worked in different departments and on different floors of our building. I simply avoided the lunchroom and ate at my desk or took a late lunch if I had forgotten to bring something with me. I'd come in early and leave late in order to avoid any run-ins at the elevator.

Somewhere toward the end of the third week, however, my luck is up, and I see Grace's extension flash across the LED display on my office phone one afternoon. She'd left a few messages on my voicemail since I left Vance, and I know she's aware I have moved out by the last message she left. I just haven't been able to face telling everyone the truth about what happened. This time she calls though, I know I have to answer if I don't want to damage my relationship with my friend. I take a deep breath and pick up the receiver.

"Hi Grace," I answer.

"Oh, my God!" she practically yells into the phone. "She lives and breathes. I was beginning to wonder if I was ever going to hear your voice again. You have a lot of explaining to do, Mimi."

"I know, but please, go easy on me, okay? This is not the easiest time in my life right now," I say, my voice cracking, much to my irritation.

"Oh, sweetheart. I didn't mean to be insensitive. I'm just worried. When you didn't respond to my messages, I called the house, and Vance said you didn't live there anymore. I just didn't know what to make of it. He wouldn't tell me anything, just told me to ask you and hung up on me. When did you move out, Mimi, and why?"

"It's been about three weeks, now. The why of it is a long story I can't get into while I'm here at work. Maybe we could meet for drinks or dinner?" I suggest.

"Are you busy tonight? I have to work until six, but I can meet you anywhere after that. You just name the place, and I'm there."

I think about it for a minute. I am not eager to relive the last six months for any reason, but she's one of my closest friends and deserves to know what's going on. I don't have anything on my to-do list for the evening. I'd only planned to have a date with a frozen chicken pot pie and a cheesy romance novel I'd been trying to read, but that was probably not the best idea for me, anyway. It was best to face the music if I was truly going to move forward with my life.

"Alright. How about we meet at The Cantina at eight for margaritas? Will that work for you?" I offer.

"I'll be there. Should I bring Jessica and Liz? If you just want it to be us, I'll understand. I can fill them in for you, or you can tell them individually on your own," she offers gently.

I consider it for a moment. I don't want it to become a big gossiping session about my love life, but I also don't want to have to retell the story over and over. I decide that ripping off the Band-Aid in one pull is probably the best way to go.

"Go ahead and give them a call, see if they can make it," I say. "Just let them know it's not going to be a Vance-bashing session, no matter how much they might want to make it one after I tell everything I have to say. Okay?"

"No problem, Mimi. We're your friends and we'll support you any way you need it."

"Thanks, Grace. I'll see you at eight."

As usual, I'm the last to arrive at the restaurant. I take a seat at the table where there is already an enormous margarita waiting for me. I look around at the girls with one eyebrow raised.

"Did somebody bother to order a snorkel to go with this?"

"We thought you might need some extra fortification to get through tonight. Look, there's even two straws," Liz smiles and gestures toward the kiddie pool of frothy, pale green liquid.

"Just in case you need extra encouragement," Jessica chimes in.

"Thanks, girls," I smile and shake my head. "I can always count on you to have my back."

Rather than shining the spotlight on me immediately, we order some appetizers and chat

273

about our days for a little while. It gives me a chance to unwind and sip enough to make a dent in my super-sized margarita. Inevitably, the conversation does turn to me, but by the time it happens, I'm sufficiently lubricated and feel like I can talk about it without falling apart. Too much, anyway.

I explain from the beginning—the small changes in Vance that eventually escalated into his outright hostility and verbally abusive behavior, my continued hope it was just the stress of his job taking a toll on him, that he would eventually return to his normal persona, but the night he attacked me being the final straw, and with it, coming the realization that the person I thought he was, the man I had married was a fictitious character. I had rushed into a marriage with a man before truly getting to know him and paid the price.

"You don't truly believe that, do you, Mimi?" Grace asked. "I know you two married quickly, but you're not a silly girl. You had to be pretty certain of him to have made such a serious decision. Besides, most people show their true colors within three months. It's hard to keep up a façade for a whole year. I think if he were a real beast, he would have shown that side of himself long before."

Liz and Jessica nod in agreement. I look around at the three of them, dumbfounded.

"You can't possibly be defending him."

Liz, our wise and thoughtful one, looks at me sympathetically. "Of course not, Mimi. We all think you made the right decision, the only decision you could make under the circumstances. It's just that something doesn't add up here, and none of us wants to see you begin to question yourself going forward."

"That's right," Jessica agrees. "Your judgment was sound. We don't know Vance like you do, of course, but we've all met him. You even mentioned Justin said this is totally out of character for him and he's known him his whole life. There's no forgiving what he did, I'm not even coming close to saying that you should. I just feel like there's got to be more to this."

I close my eyes to fight back the tears that are threatening, but it's no use. I open them back up and let them flow.

"Nobody wants to believe that more than I do, ladies. I loved this man with my whole being. I hung in there while he was absolutely awful to me because I didn't want to let go of that love for him, of the dream of the life we were supposed to have together, of the happiness he had brought me when things were good. In the end, I have to. I will go mad if I keep clinging to the idea that someday he'll come back to me, that he'll be my Vance again and we'll have that happily ever after I believed in when we got married. Not only that, it's dangerous for me to stay now. He physically hurt me and threatened to kill me. I can't keep loving a man who would do that to me. I have to put it all behind me, stop thinking there's some mysterious reason that made him behave the way he did and just accept it's part of him. My heart is already broken. It will stay that way forever if I keep looking for a reason to justify what he did."

Grace digs through her purse for a tissue, finally producing a whole travel pack. I gratefully accept them and mop the tears from my face. I'm slightly embarrassed for breaking down, but these are my girls. I know they don't see me as weak.

Everyone seems to understand the subject is closed with what I've confessed, and the conversation turns to more mundane topics. I switch to water after I finish my margarita because, let's face it, anything more and I'll be blowing over the legal limit if I'm not already.

We wind things up around eleven and I drive home feeling very tired. I don't know if it's the alcohol or if it's because I finally admitted my feelings out loud, but I'm beat. My confession to the girls was more than I've even admitted to myself before now. I know I told Justin I no longer loved Vance, but that's not true. I will love Vance for a very long time if not forever. But I see Vance as two very different and distinct people now. There's the Vance I met and fell hard for, the man my soul recognized instantly, and Vance, the stranger who entered my life six or so months ago. It hurts my heart and my head to think about it, so I try to push it aside. A little denial goes a long way to surviving a broken heart.

I go back to living with my mental to-do lists but take time to spend with the girls every other week or so. They keep me from turning into a hermit.

Surprisingly, Justin calls to check in on me regularly, too. We don't talk for too long, and we never talk about Vance, but I can tell he wants to. Whenever he even starts to hint he might bring him up in the conversation, I cut him off and find a reason to hang up. It's just too painful to think about him, let alone hear about anything to do with him. I refuse to talk about him from my perspective too. Justin has tried to get me to talk about my feelings, but I won't. I'm trying to move on, and if Justin wants to be my friend, he has to learn to be one independent of any and all things Vance Ashcroft. Still, I'm grateful he wants to be a part of my life, he's a good man and a very good friend.

Three months into my post-Vance life as I have come to think of it, I'm walking out of a Starbucks near my office on a beautiful mid-May Wednesday morning with a latte I sorely need since I dashed out of the house without my coffee. To my utter shock, I run face first into Vance's chest. Fortunately, I manage to hold onto my coffee and not spill it all over myself or him, but it's a close call. I'm startled to see him, not only because he's not supposed to be near me, but because he looks like hell. He's lost at least twenty pounds, his complexion is very pale, and the circles that had started to form under his eyes when we were last together are even darker now. His once gloriously thick and wavy hair now hangs lank and dull over his forehead. My instant reaction is concern for him, but then my anger sets in. I don't even pause to be afraid because honestly, with the state of his physical condition, he doesn't look like much of a threat to anyone.

"What are you doing here, Vance?" I say as I move out of the doorway to let another patron who is trying to leave pass by. "Are you following me?"

He lets go of the door and follows me as I move away. "I need to talk to you, Mimi. I know I'm not supposed to be near you, but this is important. I need you to hear me out."

"There is nothing you can say to me that I'm interested in hearing, Vance. You need to leave," I say as I begin to walk down the street toward my office building.

"Mimi, please. I'm begging you. Please, just give me a chance—

I wheel around and fix him with my most hostile glare.

"A chance? A chance to what, Vance? To explain to me why you hurt me? Why you turned into someone I couldn't even recognize? Oh, wait, maybe how sorry you are? No, Vance. Any time for talking has come and gone. The moment you put your hands on me in violence is the time you lost any right to ask me for anything. I would have given you anything, done anything to make you happy. I tried. I hung in there for months, trying to find a way to make things better, waiting for you to come back to me." I point my index finger at his chest and hiss, "You made damned sure I knew that was never going to happen. So, go. Go and don't come back and bother me again, or I will call the police and have you arrested."

I turn on my heel and march down the street, leaving him standing in the middle of the sidewalk. I go back to the office, but I can't concentrate. The image of his hollow face, his gaunt frame, haunt me. Does he look so bad because I left him? Is it because he is so affected by our break up, he's just not taking care of himself? I snort. It's probably just that damned job of his working him into the ground. He probably doesn't have time to even miss me. The little voice in my head whispers softly, *then what did he want to talk to you about*?

I can't help but feel confused. Part of me, the part that will always belong to him, feels like I should have stayed and heard him out. The look in his eyes was so desperate. Whatever it was, it was vitally important to him. The other part of me feels I did the right thing. I have to protect myself from him, not so much physically anymore by the look of him, but always mentally and emotionally.

His attack may have been effective in breaking that emotional connection I had keeping me tied to him through all the verbal abuse, but I know I still have a lot of healing to do. He still has a lot of power to hurt me that way. If I gave him the opportunity, the access to me, he could easily say something that would shatter the fragile composure I've built over the last three months. I ultimately decided I did the right thing, but for the rest of the day and for several days following, my heart feels heavy.

The following Saturday afternoon, I get a call from Justin. I haven't heard from him in several weeks which is unusual. Normally, he calls every week. We have been getting together for lunch regularly, once we even went to see a movie in an effort to establish a normal friendship.

"Hey stranger," I answer his call. "Where have you been?"

"Hey, Mimi," he says, his voice sounding a little rougher than usual. "Sorry I haven't been around. I've just been handling a few personal things."

"It's okay, Justin. I've been keeping busy. You know, watching paint dry, going to the park and seeing the grass grow. It's fascinating stuff." I try for a bit silliness since he sounds a little off. Justin is a serious kind of guy, but there's something in his voice that makes him sound almost somber. It doesn't help.

"Uh, yeah," he says, ignoring my stupid joke completely. "I was wondering if you wanted to get together for dinner tonight. We haven't seen each other in a while, and I could really use some company."

I'm instantly concerned. I've always had the sense these get-togethers of ours have been about keeping me propped up, making sure I don't fall apart without Vance around. I know we're friends and all, but there's been a lot more taking on my part than giving. Justin's the strong, silent type. If he's reaching out for company, something must be really wrong.

"Sure, Justin. I don't have anything going on. Whenever, wherever you want to go is fine with me."

"I'll pick you up at your place at six. I want to get out kind of early. I'm going a little stir crazy sitting here at home," he says with an embarrassed chuckle.

"If you just want to get out of the house, I'm not doing anything right now. Let me come pick you up. We can go over to the Pier and watch all the people or take a drive up the coast. We can stop for dinner somewhere whenever we get hungry."

He's quiet for a moment as if he needs to think about it. I hear him blow out a breath.

"Yeah, that'd be great. Thanks, Mimi. I owe you one."

"Nonsense. You've been here for me a million times already. I'll be there in a half an hour."

True to my word, thirty minutes later I pull up in front of Justin's house. Before I can even get out of my car, he comes trotting down the walkway and jumps into the passenger seat. He leans over and gives me a kiss on the cheek before settling back and resting his head against the seat back. He seems tense and I can't help but frown as I look at him. Something is very wrong, but I know Justin. I'll just have to wait for him to tell me what's going on, I won't be able to pull it out of him. Instead, I just try to be as upbeat as I can and make things seem a little better.

"Okay, boss man. You're in charge. Do you want to go to the Pier, or take a drive?"

"You make the decision, Mimi. I just want to shut my brain off for a little while. I've had a lot on my mind for the last few weeks, and I really need to get out of my head for a little while."

"Alright. Then we drive up the coast. A little sunshine, a little sea air, some good views of the waves rolling against the shoreline, and you'll be good as new. I promise," I turn and grin at him. "Oh, and we need some tunes. Can't have a really great drive without a soundtrack." I pull my iPod out of the glove box and toss it to him. "There's tons of music on there. Pick some out and just park it in the docking station. We'll be good to go from there."

Justin scrolls through the songs for a while before finally settling the device in the docking station. "Smells Like Teen Spirit" by Nirvana comes blaring out of the speakers, so I assume he's chosen my nineties playlist as the theme for our little excursion.

We drive in silence until we get onto Pacific Coast Highway with the waves rolling gently on our left. It's a mild spring day in sunny Southern California, not too hot, not too cool. We both have our windows down, and I've opened the moonroof, letting in as much fresh air as possible.

Finally, Justin speaks. He talks about his work, how he's been busy working numerous projects, but everything is going well, and he's happy to have the business. I ask about his family, knowing his

282

mother and father are older, and wondering if maybe some health concerns on either of their parts could be the cause of his current stress.

"They're doing great, actually. They're planning to go on a cruise to Alaska this summer. It's all my mom can talk about these days," he says with a grin. "My dad is grumbling because she's shopping for a whole new wardrobe, and they're only going to be gone for ten days."

"Of course!" I laugh. "Doesn't your dad know a cruise is one of the few acceptable reasons to buy an entirely new wardrobe? While most women love to shop, we only get a few outfits here and there. If ever there's a reason to go out and replace everything you have, a cruise is definitely it."

"I'll make sure to tell Dad you said so," he says, grinning even harder.

"Okay, so work is good, family is good. What's got you so stressed? Lady troubles?"

A shadow passes over his face, but only for a moment. He shakes his head with a short bark of laughter.

"Haven't you heard by now, Mimi? I never have 'lady troubles'," he says, making air quotes around the last two words.

"Yes, I know you're supposed to be some great Casanova or something, but in the time I've known you, I've never once even heard you talk about a woman. When I was part of the group, I never saw you bring anyone around, not even casually. Except for those few brief dates with Jessica, I'm beginning to suspect this whole ladies' man reputation is more myth than anything."

"Myth, huh?" he laughs. "Trust me, I have my fair share of dates. I can even show you my address book to prove how many women's phone numbers are in there, so you'll know I can call on any number of women at any time."

"Brag much?" I interject.

"It's not bragging, it's just the truth. I have a lot of superficial relationships. I choose not to have anything serious for my own personal reasons. I don't bring anyone around my friends or family because I don't want anyone to read too much into anything. As soon as you start introducing someone to the other people in your life, they start having other expectations of you and ideas about where the relationship can or should go, and I don't want that. I barely let anyone come over to my house, otherwise, they start redecorating it. I don't need them to start wanting to redecorate my future too."

"You think you're such a catch that every woman is going to start planning your wedding and how many babies you're going to have if you make a little space in your life for her?" I ask dubiously.

"What?" he asks, slightly taken aback.

"I'm serious. I hear this a lot from men who don't want to commit. They keep all women at arm's length because they automatically assume any woman they show any part of their life to is going to immediately fall in love. I suppose it could happen with some needy types, but most of the time, it's a non-event. Meeting the parents, yeah that's a big thing that should be reserved for serious relationships, I think. But letting a girl come over to your house or hang out with your friends? I hate to break it to you, but she's probably not going to think too much of it. Not a normal girl, anyway, unless you do what you do."

"What do you mean?" he asks, puzzled.

"When you make it this big mysterious thing, this off-limits part of your life, sure, a girl is going to take it as a sign something serious is happening when you introduce her to your friends. That's the message you've sent. If you treat it casually, so will she."

"Is that how it was with you and Vance?" he asks quietly.

Pain lances through me at the mention of his name, and the reminder of how things used to be. I'm quiet for a moment before responding.

"Nothing was ever casual between Vance and me. We were serious from the very beginning even if we didn't know it right away." I smile softly as I recall something Vance said. "He didn't want to introduce me to you guys right away though. He said he didn't want you guys to ruin my good opinion of him."

"That little fucker," Justin laughs harshly. "I'd kick him in the nuts if it weren't for...," he stops abruptly.

I'm not sure why, but something inside me tightens nervously.

"If it weren't for what?"

"Nothing," he sighs, running his hands over his face.

"No, it's okay, Justin. You can say it." I don't know why I'm pushing the issue, but I feel like I need to know what he was going to say.

"I was just going to say if it weren't for the fact it doesn't matter anymore. I'm sorry, Mimi. It was a dick thing to say which is why I stopped myself."

For some reason, I was expecting something else. I don't know what, but what he told me makes sense. I don't know why I thought it would be something totally different, but I did.

It's fine." I wave my hand in the air between us. "It's only the truth."

We're both quiet for a moment, before Justin finally says, "I know he came to see you."

A lump forms in my throat. I swallow it away and square my shoulders.

"Then you know I sent him away."

"You need to hear what he has to say, Mimi," he says firmly.

"I can't believe you just said that." I look at him in disbelief. "Knowing everything you know, do you honestly believe he deserves a moment of my time?"

"No, I know he doesn't," Justin's tone gentles. "What I believe is you deserve what he's trying to offer you."

"It's too late for apologies, Justin, if that's what he's looking to give me. I don't want them, I don't need them. I just need to forget him as best I can."

"Mimi, please. Didn't you see what he looks like? Can't you at least take pity on him and give him ten minutes?"

"Jesus Christ, Justin. Of course, I saw him. He looks awful. It's clear he's still suffering away at that horrible job and will probably continue to do so until they put him in the ground. Why is that my problem? I did all I could to try to convince him it was a terrible environment for him. He chose them over me."

"No, Mimi..."

"Why can't you just let this go? Did he put you up to this or something? Oh. My. God. He did, didn't he? Didn't he!"

"Not exactly. He did ask if I would try to help him, but I already decided I would try to talk to you when I found out what he needed to tell you."

"You would do that, knowing exactly how I feel about keeping our friendship separate from anything to do with Vance? You would violate something that important to me?" I ask, feeling very betrayed.

"Yes, Mimi. I feel that strongly about this."

"Then I guess it's good I know where your loyalties ultimately lie. You can't be Switzerland between us. If he asks you to side with him, then that's what you'll do because your ties to him are stronger. I get it, you've been friends your whole life. I'm just the chick who turned up less than two years ago," I say, tears filling my eyes, as I pull off onto the shoulder. Making sure there is no traffic coming in the opposite direction, I make a very illegal U-turn and begin driving back the way we came. I always knew Justin was more Vance's friend than mine, but I still can't help but feel betrayed.

"Peaches, it's not like that. If I didn't think this was important to you too, I wouldn't…"

"Don't, Justin. Just know I never would have asked you to choose between us."

"He didn't! I didn't! Mimi, please, don't shut down. Just listen to me," he pleads.

"Fine," I sigh. "I'll think about hearing him out, Justin, but I won't make any promises," I say with my mental fingers crossed in my head. I'm never going to talk to Vance, and I'm probably not going to talk to Justin again after I drop him off at his house.

"If that's the best I can get tonight, then I'll take it. I won't bring it up again," he says sincerely.

"Thanks. I'm going to head back now if that's okay with you. If I'm going to really think about listening to what he has to say, I'm going to need some time." I try to sound as genuine as possible. Really, I just want to get him home and out of my personal space as fast as I can. I don't know why I feel like Justin has deceived me in some way as if he were never really my friend at all. I know that's not the case. He's in a difficult position trying to be friends with both me and Vance, but maybe some petty side of me hoped if it came down to it, he would pick me over Vance since Vance was so shitty to me.

"I totally understand. I didn't mean to get into this so soon in our time together. I really did want to get out and blow off some steam, but I get that you need your space after all this. I'll just go over to Rosie's and shoot some pool if you decide you want some company later. Just give me a ring and let me know you're coming if you do."

We drive the rest of the way to Justin's house in silence. He knows I'm upset with him, but fortunately, he doesn't try to get me to talk about it. I pull up in front of his house and smile.

"Curbside service, my friend."

"Thanks for getting me out of the house, Mimi. Even if things didn't go the way we planned, I'm glad I got to see you. I hope it won't be too long before I see you again." He leans over and gives me a kiss on the cheek. He lingers a little longer than usual, which strikes me as odd, but he pulls away before I can think anything more about it. He brushes my cheek with the back of his fingers, then steps out of the car without another word. I stay at the curb and watch him walk up to his house. He turns and waves from the door before walking inside and closing it behind him. I can't help but feel like the closing of his front door is a metaphor for so much more.

Fifteen

July comes and with it, a decision I've been postponing for months. I need to file for divorce. The process should be fairly simple. We don't have children, we don't have a lot of joint assets, and we weren't married long enough to have acquired much of any mutual wealth. Vance doesn't have anything I want, and I don't believe I have anything he'd want. He could always make the process difficult just for the sake of being difficult, I suppose. At the end, it sure seemed like he enjoyed making me suffer, so I can't be assured he won't draw the process out for his own amusement. He hasn't tried to contact me since that time about six weeks ago though, so maybe he'll just sign the papers uncontested, and the next six months will go by peacefully with the end result being the dissolution of our once beautiful marriage.

I pick up the phone to call my attorney, and my stomach turns sour. I was about to tell him my decision, so we could start the paperwork, but now just the thought has killed my desire to go through with it. Maybe tomorrow, I'll be stronger. I need more distance from the memories of what used to be, to focus on what it ended up being.

Ever since my falling out with Justin, every night just before I fall asleep, visions of how things used to be with Vance fill my mind. Our first dinner together. Those first phone calls. The trip to Atlantic City. Making love. How wrapped up in each other we were as if no one could penetrate our bubble. My heart aches for Vance more now than it did when he first disappeared and became the stranger I didn't know. I think it's because then, I still had hope. As long as he was there with me, I could make the excuses and believe he would eventually revert to his old self. I no longer have the luxury of denial.

He's gone, it's over, and I'll never again have those wonderful days of laying in his arms, wrapped in his love with our dreams of the future between us. I'd be a dirty liar if I said I didn't want that back. I do. Desperately. On a day-to-day basis, I keep up the façade of a woman who's going on with her life, moving forward and if not healed from a disastrous relationship, then steadily working toward it. In the dark of my bedroom at night, however, I know the truth. I'm devastated. For all my talk about living a life post-Vance, of getting back on track and building a new life for myself, I'm worse off now than I was right after I left. I'm no longer riding on the strength my anger had given me, instead, I'm fully in the depressive stage of grief, but only my pillow and I know it.

I wake in the morning feeling like I have a head and heart filled with lead. It takes monumental effort to follow the method I've used from day one... one foot in front of the other. It's like I'm wearing one of those suits the astronauts wear—big, clumsy, and entirely impractical for everyday use.

Still sitting at my desk, caught up in my thoughts as I am, I don't notice when Steve comes out of his office with a file in his hand.

"Mimi, I need you to run down to the Superior Court and file this—Mimi?"

My head snaps up out of my daze to find him looking at me with a slightly annoyed expression.

"Mimi, you really need to focus. You've been distracted for months now. We all know you've been having a hard time, and we've been very understanding and supportive. The time has come to get your head back in the game, or there will be consequences. Do you understand?"

My heart plummets to my stomach. I know I haven't been working at the height of my abilities, but I don't think I've been fucking up, either. If Steve isn't happy though, I need to get my act together. I need my job more than ever, and he won't hesitate to let me go if he doesn't feel I'm performing to his expectations. He isn't sentimental like Bob, so I can't expect any sense of personal loyalty from him.

"Yes, sir. I promise I will do better. Now please, tell me what it is you'd like me to do?"

Forty-five minutes later, I'm leaving the Superior Court after filing some asset statements for Steve. As I am walking to my car in the large parking structure near the courthouse, I see the shape of a familiar, if loathsome, redhead exiting the car next to mine. She notices me just as I'm looking around for a place to hide.

293

"Well, hello Mimi," Tiffany says, her fake smile firmly in place. "Funny to see you here."

"I don't know why you'd think so. I do work for a law firm too after all. I was just filing some documents with the clerk," I say as I resume walking toward my car.

"Huh. I don't think I knew that. But then, it's not like Vance and I spent a lot of time talking about you."

"That doesn't surprise me. We didn't spend a lot of time talking about you, either," I say sweetly.

"How is he doing, by the way? We really miss him around the office," she asks as I open my car door.

I stop dead and whirl around. "What did you say?"

"I asked how he's doing. Things haven't been the same since he left."

"He left?" I whisper. For a split second, my heart somersaults. Perhaps now we could have a future. Maybe he would be his old self... I give myself a mental face slap and a stern talking to. He attacked you, Mimi. Tried to rape you. Threatened to kill you. There's no coming back from that.

"What the hell is wrong with you, Mimi?" Tiffany looks at me like I am the stupidest person on the planet.

"I'm sorry, Tiffany." I shake my head, trying to clear my thoughts. "You just took me by surprise. I really don't know anything about Vance. We split up in January. I haven't really spoken to him since."

It's unbelievable how she visibly brightens at the information. "Oh, that's unfortunate news. I had no idea."

I nod as I enter my vehicle. "Now you know," I say as I shut the door on her, put my key in the ignition, and drive away.

I maintain a low profile until the second week of August, mostly staying in and licking my wounds. Grace, Liz, and Jessica all call, trying to get me to join them for drinks, shopping trips, movies, both individually and collectively, but I always find some excuse to stay in. Justin calls several times too, but I ignore them all and never return any of his messages. I figure he will eventually get the hint and stop calling. On this particular Saturday afternoon, however, he calls non-stop. I debate turning my phone off, but he obviously needs to speak with me urgently. Even though I don't really want to speak to him, I still care for him. I can at least spare a few minutes of my time.

"Hello, Justin," I say as I answer the call.

"I'm glad you finally decided to answer, Mimi. I need you to meet me as soon as possible. It's urgent."

"Is everything okay?" I ask, suddenly feeling alarmed.

"No, but I can't get into everything right now. I just need you to meet me, and I'll make sure you understand everything later."

"Are you hurt or anything?"

"No, I'm fine. Will you come, Mimi?" he asks insistently.

"Um, yeah, sure. Do you want me to meet you at your house?"

"On second thought, let me pick you up at your place. Are you home now?" he asks, his voice growing more demanding.

"Yes, I'm home, but it's really no trouble for me..."

"I'm not far from your place. I'll be there in twenty minutes. Just let the guard know to let me in." He hangs up before I can say another word.

After making arrangements with the security guard, I spend the next twenty-five minutes pacing the living room of my apartment. I have no idea what's going on. Justin's behavior is beyond curious, but I have this feeling of impending doom I can't shake. I nearly jump a foot when I hear the sharp knock on my door, then run to open it. Justin stands there, looking very tired and haggard. His normally shaved head has a few days growth on it as do his cheeks. His eyes are red-rimmed with dark circles under them.

"Grab your purse and your keys. We'll take your car, but I'll drive," he says, not wasting any time with formalities.

I do as I'm told, offering no arguments or asking any questions. His entire being tells me this isn't the time to be anything but cooperative, so I follow his instructions and hand over my keys after locking up the apartment.

Justin wheels us out of the complex smoothly and efficiently, not wasting a second. He gets onto the freeway in record time. He isn't reckless, but more than one traffic law is broken getting us there. Traffic is light—by Los Angeles standards—given that it's two in the afternoon on Saturday. Forty-five minutes later, we pull into the parking lot at St. Joseph's Hospital. I look at Justin in alarm, but he just opens his door and gets out. I follow suit and continue following him to the front doors, a horrible sinking feeling in my stomach all the way.

As we enter through the sliding doors, I ask quietly, "Justin, why are we here?"

He just looks at me gravely, with the saddest expression I have ever seen on another human being's face.

My own face crumples in response as the reality I have desperately been trying to deny rushes to the forefront of my consciousness.

"It's Vance, isn't it?"

He just nods and leads me to the elevators. I weep silently as we enter an empty elevator and ride up to whatever floor he pushes a button for, I don't notice which.

"What happened, Justin?" I finally gather the courage to ask.

"He's sick, Mimi. He's been sick for a long time, only we didn't know it until recently."

"That's what he wanted to tell me, isn't it?" I ask, fearing I already know the answer.

"Yes," he says simply.

"Oh, no, no, no." I hang my head, shaking it in denial, crying harder.

The doors open, and we walk out onto a patient room floor. As we move down the quiet hall, Justin speaks.

"Before we go in, I have to warn you. I don't know how he'll react to you being here. He could be his normal self and be happy to see you, but he could also be the Vance you know from the last few months you were together. He has a malignant brain tumor..." I gasp in horror. "... that has caused personality changes in him, so you don't always know who you're going to get. If he's hostile, don't take it personally. Just try to stick it out. The real Vance will eventually come around, okay? Be prepared though. He looks even worse than when you saw him last."

I nod in response and do my best to dry my tears as we come to a stop before a room with a closed door. Griffin and Bryant are standing outside with cups of coffee in their hands.

"What is she doing here?" Griffin says to Justin. "You know he doesn't want her here."

"He didn't want her to know at all," Bryant says.

"You both know keeping it from her isn't right. I had to get her before it's too late. They both deserve to see each other and make things right."

I look at Justin, confused. "If that's true if he didn't want me to know, why did he come to see me in May?"

"Initially," Justin sighs, "he did want you to know. He wanted the chance to explain, to apologize, and hopefully, get you to forgive him. When you were so adamant you that didn't want to talk to him, he realized that it was too late, things had gone too far, and you hated him. At that point, he felt you deserved to live your life in peace and move on."

This starts a fresh round of tears, and I need a minute to compose myself. Griffin and Bryant just glare at me as if I'm to blame for everything. I suppose I can't blame them. I should have known something was wrong rather than being wrapped up in my own feelings. I should have known my Vance would never treat me poorly if he could help it. It was like Justin had said all along, Vance wasn't like that. Something had been wrong, I just didn't see it. I shouldn't have lost faith in him.

I finally pull myself together because I have to be strong. He needs me whether he wants to see me or not, and I will be there now even if I wasn't before. I nod at Justin, and he opens the door for me.

I do my best to walk inside confidently, but I fail miserably. Miriam, Vance's mother, is standing by his bedside, holding his hand, and shielding him from my view. She turns to look over her shoulder, and when she sees me, her gaze also turns hostile.

"Get her out of here, Justin. She has no right to be here," she snaps.

A weak voice comes from the other side of her, "Is that Mimi?"

Tired of getting the stink eye from everyone when so much is on the line, I pull myself up to my full height and look Miriam in the eye.

"I'm afraid you're wrong there. I have every right to be here. In fact, legally, I have more right to be here than you do, so I'm going to have to ask you to leave. Now."

I can't help it. I can't take the hostility from these people. They've known about his condition longer than I have. At any time, they could have told me what he was going through. They know most of what he put me through, and no one knew at the time he was sick. Yes, I should have known something was seriously wrong, but if they knew the entirety of what he'd done, I don't think they would look at me as harshly for the way I reacted. Maybe I'm lashing out, but I'm not going to let them get in my way. If I have to be a bitch to all of them, treat them the way they seem to want to treat me, I have no problem with that. Vance is my focus right now.

"You don't have that authority," Miriam sputters.

"I do. I'm still his wife. I'd prefer it if you left quietly without upsetting your son, but I will call security if I have to."

I approach Vance's bedside across from Miriam. He looks... awful. His frame is practically skeletal, his cheeks so sunken in, his eyes look too large for his face. Their once blue gleam is now dull, and his skin tone is sallow and pale. His lips are dry and cracked, nothing at all like the soft, supple, plush skin I used to marvel at. None of this matters as I take his other hand in mine and look him directly in the eyes.

"I'm here, baby."

He gets the softest look on his face as he looks back at me. We share a long moment, just gazing at each other, and I feel our connection blaze to life. Everyone else falls away, and it's just the two of us in our protective bubble, once again. I squeeze his hand gently, not wanting to hurt him. He looks away from me to his mom and Justin. His voice rasps as he speaks to them.

"Can you guys give us some time alone, please? I have a lot to say to Mimi, and I don't want an audience."

Justin smiles and nods. Miriam continues to glare at me, but Justin just takes her by the elbow and steers her out of the room.

"Mimi, you don't know how glad I am that you came. I…"

"Before you say anything more, I want to apologize for sending you away when you came to see me in May. I should have taken the time to listen to you. I should have seen something was wrong, should have known something was wrong all along. If I weren't so selfish, weren't so wrapped up in myself…," I trail off, my throat clogging with tears.

"Mimi, what I put you through is more than anyone should have to take, and yet, for months, you suffered through it with love and grace and dignity. You shouldn't blame yourself for being hurt by the way I treated you and not being able to take it any longer."

"But I should have known you would never treat me that way if you could help it. Combined with your headaches…"

"Why would that make you think it was anything more than the work stress I insisted it was? Thousands of people, if not more, get headaches and turn into assholes when they're under severe pressure. What would ever lead you to suspect it was cancer eating my mind? I hid all the other, more significant signs from you as best I could, mostly by staying away from the house as much as possible. I did a lot of sitting in my office just staring at the wall. I didn't want you to notice the lack of coordination, the times I couldn't find the words I wanted to say. Then the seizures started happening…"

"Seizures? How could you hide seizures from me?" I cry, the tears now flowing freely down my face.

"Do you remember the night you found me in the car? I barely made it home that night. I had just enough time to turn into the driveway and turn off the car. Luckily, my seatbelt had locked up when I swung into the drive, and it kept me from injuring myself as I convulsed. Otherwise, you probably would have been more suspicious than you were or at the very least, thought I'd been in a bar fight of some kind. After the seizure passed, I just sort of knocked out. It's happened after every single one since, I just kind of fall asleep for a while, and when

I wake up, I'm disoriented. It's the reason I started sleeping in the guest bedroom."

"Vance, why would you keep it from me? We could have done something! I would have gotten you help!"

"I didn't want to face it, Mimi. I knew something was seriously wrong. I spent hours on the internet looking up my symptoms and had a good idea what it could be." Vance shakes his head in regret. "Sure, I knew there were other potential causes, but my mind went to the worst and knew there was very little to be done, and what could be done, ultimately wouldn't change the outcome."

"There are treatments though, right? Something they can do to give you a fighting chance? If not cure you, then give you more time?" I ask trying to cling to any shred of hope I can find.

"If I had sought treatment earlier than I did in May, maybe when the headaches started getting worse or when the other symptoms started showing up, I could have received intervention that would have given me more time. It would have been painful though and reduced my quality of life even further. It wouldn't necessarily have prevented the symptoms I did have from occurring. What little they have been able to offer me, I 've declined."

"Vance, if I had known, if you had told me, I never would have left. We could have faced this together like we should have."

"What, suffering alongside me, feeling sorry for me?" he scoffs.

"No! Loving you. Each and every day, I would have spent loving you, understanding what you were going through, and putting you first instead of myself and my little hurt feelings."

Vance's eyes fill with tears, as he grips my hand as tightly as he can manage.

"Mimi... I always wanted you to be first. You and your happiness are and have always been everything to me. When I think of the way I hurt you... especially that last night...," his voice chokes up, "it's my one real regret. From the moment I met you, all I ever wanted was to make you smile that beautiful smile at me. In the end, I was incapable of doing that. When I felt like myself, I would mourn everything I was losing with you. I wanted so desperately to feel our connection, to show you all the love I have inside me for you, but it always seemed like I was less and less that person when we were together. So, when you finally left, I was relieved. I was crushed I had finally driven you away, and I wanted to die right then and there, but I was relieved I couldn't hurt you anymore."

I am touched by the things he's saying, and I understand what he means, but I'm angry too. I feel like I've been robbed. I spent time being angry with him, hating him even, time I could have spent giving him all my love and devotion. It dawns on me then, I'm doing the same thing right now, robbing myself of more time by being angry with him for his choices, when I could be loving him instead. I take his hand between both of mine and bring it to my lips.

"Now that I know, will you let me go back to loving you? I just can't walk away again. I don't care if you're not yourself sometimes. I want to be with you for however long that is, a month, a year, whatever. We promised each other the rest of our lives, Vance. Please keep that promise and give me yours."

Vance sobs and reaches over with his other hand, wrapping it around our joined fists. We stay like that for a while, both of us crying quietly. I've been mourning the loss of our love for a long time. Now, I realize it was never really gone, but it seems like the cruelest of jokes to know I'm going to lose him for real very soon.

"I need to be close to you, Vance," I whisper to him, wiping my tears away. "Would it hurt you if I moved some of your tubes and wires around and crawled up there with you?"

He smiles at me and I see a bit of that twinkle that always used to pull me in.

"I'd pull them all out if it meant I could hold you in my arms again."

"I don't think we need to go to those extremes," I laugh despite the fresh tears that have made their way onto my face. "With a little creativity, I think we can manage it."

After maneuvering his IV line and few of the wires monitoring his vitals, I crawl onto the bed next to him and snuggle up to his side. I lay my head on his chest as he wraps his arm around my shoulders. I can feel how thin he's become through the flimsy cotton gown, but one thing hasn't changed about him. He still feels like home.

We lay there like that for hours, talking softly. We talk about everything and nothing, just like we used to do. We pretend he's not sick and dream about places we'll go, things we'll do together until he eventually drifts off to sleep. I snuggle closer to his side and fall asleep against him, feeling more at peace than I have in the last five months.

I wake sometime later when the nurse comes in with his dinner tray. She looks at me somewhat disapprovingly as I get up from the bed and stretch. She informs me visiting hours have ended, but I politely explain that I'm his wife, and won't be going anywhere. She doesn't believe me, so I have to show her ID. I get another disapproving look from her, and I assume it's because he's been here a while and this is the first time she's seen me here. I don't feel the need to explain.

She does all the regular nurse-like things, checking his machines, his vitals, etc. He wakes up in the process, and she's all sunshine and light toward him, raising his bed into a sitting position as she chats away. I decide she's not so bad even though she wasn't particularly pleasant to me. What these people think of me is of no concern as long as they give Vance the best care they can.

As she's leaving, she lets us know the doctor will be back in the morning when he does his usual rounds. I'm eager to meet him and talk about our options going forward. I may not have been here before now, but I'm going to be an active participant in Vance's medical care from this point forward.

Vance just stares at the tray of what I imagine is bland hospital food. I try to encourage him to eat, but he just looks at me blankly.

"On the best day, I can't imagine this food being even remotely palatable." He says to me. "Unfortunately, my sense of taste has been affected by the tumor. Absolutely everything tastes like shit."

"Well," I respond, "I suppose there's always the option of a feeding tube."

"No," he shakes his head, "I've already signed papers indicating I don't want any measures being taken to prolong my life unnecessarily."

"What?" I gasp. "Vance, you can't mean that."

"Mimi, I'm going to die, and I'm going to do it sooner rather than later. My condition will deteriorate day by day. There's no point trying to fight the inevitable. Forcing nourishment on my body is like trying to hold back the tide with a net."

"Okay, so we don't force it on you. But please, for me, try to eat while you're still strong enough to do so? We don't have to try to reach for more days than you might otherwise have, but we also don't have to try to reduce the time you could have either, do we? I don't want to be selfish, but I'm not in a hurry to let you go."

Vance lets out a sigh and pulls the tray toward him. "Only because I'm not in a hurry to leave you either Mimi, will I consume this vile tray of what can only loosely be described as food. I can't assure you it won't actually hasten my demise, however."

"Oh, just eat it, you big baby," I say removing the napkin from the tray and tossing it at him.

His hands shake as he attempts to take the lid off the bowl of soup they've given him. I come around the side of the bed opposite the tray table and sit down next to him.

"Let me," I say, covering his hand with my own, helping him pop off the top. He relaxes back into the pillows as I dip a spoon into the bowl and come up with a hearty mouthful. He opens his mouth with an amused look in his eyes as I bring it to his lips.

"Blow. It may be too hot to put in your mouth."

"Shouldn't I be the one saying that?"

I groan. "Even now, you're still a pervert and a dork."

"And I'm still just your type," he smirks at me.

I smile and nod because there's no arguing with that statement. Vance has always been the one. Everything about him has been just right for me. If it weren't for this god-awful disease eating his mind, destroying him bit by bit, we would have nothing but beautiful memories of love and togetherness. I'm not naïve enough to think our lives would have been perfect, it's not like we never bickered or argued that first year together, but it was infrequent and there was always that undertone of love softening those moments. Even when things were not so pleasant, they weren't terrible. There was still beauty in every moment we shared.

I feed Vance every morsel of his dinner. He grimaces through some bites, and sometimes, I think he wants to gag, but he's a trooper and finishes it all. It's one of the best gifts he's ever given me because I know that's exactly what it is. Something he's done entirely for my benefit, something just to make me happy.

I lean over and give him a soft kiss on the lips, the first since I set foot in this room, I realize. I pull back and look at him, our eyes connecting, and I feel the desire flame in both of us. Despite the circumstances, the inappropriateness of the location, and the sheer physical impossibility of it due to Vance's health, we still want each other with the same passion we've always had. My heart feels simultaneously full at the notion that nothing has changed that way but so very sad that we will never share another intimate moment of that kind again. If I had known those days I had insisted he take off work to rest after I found him passed out in his car would be the last we spent like that, I would have tied him to the bed and never let him out.

Vance smiles at me wistfully, and I know he's thinking similar thoughts. I push the tray table away and crawl into bed with him again. We may not be able to make love anymore, but I can still have loving, intimate moments with him, and I will take every opportunity I can. I don't care if we're in a lousy hospital with nurses and doctors coming in at all hours. He's mine, and I'm not wasting a single second of the time we have left.

Vance's arms come around me to lay loosely around my waist. I rest my head on his shoulder and kiss his neck. He smells faintly like antiseptic, but his own lightly spicy, musky scent is there under it. I inhale deeply, trying to pull as much of it into my lungs as I can.

Resting my hand on his chest, I can feel his heart, still beating strong under my palm.

Vance kisses the top of my head and whispers, "I love you, Mimi, so very much."

I squeeze him around his waist, as tight as I dare, and whisper back, "I love you more, Vance."

We fall asleep like that, entwined with each other, just the way we were always meant to be.

Sixteen

The next morning, I'm able to meet Vance's oncologist, Dr. Haneef. He gently explains all the tests and scans they've performed over the last few days confirm the cancer is progressing at an advanced rate, and Vance's condition will continue to deteriorate rapidly. The doctor is compassionate, but forthright and honest when he tells us we have to make end-of-life decisions beyond the directives that Vance has already given. He lays out our options such as hospice care, being discharged to home care, or staying in the hospital until the inevitable end comes. We have much to discuss, so Dr. Haneef indicates he'll give us some time to talk and will check back with us after he has completed his rounds.

"I want to go home, Mimi. I know it may sound kind of ludicrous, but I don't want to be anywhere that reminds me of how sick I am," he says once we are alone.

I take the seat beside him and look him in the eyes, nodding. I simply say, "Okay. So, we go home."

"You'd come with me?" He looks a little startled. "You'd move back into the house and stay?"

"Of course, I will," I say. "That's where I belong. Wherever you are, is where I'm going to be. Where your stuff is that's where my stuff will be too. We're married, it's married, all one big happy family." I say, grinning and twirling my hand in the air.

He smiles and shakes his head at me as if there is no hope for me and my particular brand of weird.

"Okay, so we're going home," I say. "We'll talk to Dr. Haneef about getting a visiting hospice nurse to come in and administer your pain medications and take care of any of your other medical needs I can't attend to."

"Yeah..." he begins. "I love you, Mimi, and I know you want to help as much as you can, but there are just some things I can no longer do for myself I don't want you doing for me."

I feel a little stung that he would want a complete stranger attending to his most private needs before me. Doesn't he think I could handle it? While it wouldn't exactly be a pleasure, it would be something I would lovingly do without a second thought.

"Mimi, stop. I can see all the things running through your mind right now. Don't let this hurt your feelings. It's humiliating enough letting a stranger do it, but if I had to let you do it, there would be no possible way to keep my dignity intact. I need to keep what little this disease can't strip from me, okay?"

I am immediately embarrassed. Will I ever stop thinking about myself first? In the last twelve hours, I've come to realize what a self-centered person I am. If I were less me-centric, I wouldn't have lost so much time with Vance. There and then, I resolve to put any thoughts of myself, my feelings, my needs aside and focus on him and whatever he needs before anything else.

"I hate to admit it, but that never occurred to me. Your hospice nurse has the dubious honor of attending to your bedpans, but I absolutely draw the line at sponge baths. No matter how much you might object, that's my territory. You give me any lip on this and I'll make sure I find the biggest, meanest, hairiest nurse out there." I raise an eyebrow at him, daring him to argue.

He laughs outright and shakes his head. "And I was so hoping for a Jessica Rabbit look alike."

I shake my index finger at him. "Keep it up, and I'll see if Bertha from the airport moonlights."

He grabs hold of my finger and brings it to his lips. He kisses the tip softly before letting it go.

"I'm so happy you're here, sweetheart. My body may be weak, but I honestly haven't felt this good in months."

I lean over and kiss his mouth, whispering against his lips, "Me either, baby. Me, either."

Just then, the door opens and Miriam walks in. She seems only slightly less hostile this morning than she did last night in that she doesn't look at me at all. She smiles a little too brightly at Vance, coming over to take his hand and kiss his cheek.

"How are you feeling today, honey?" she asks as she attempts to fluff his pillow.

He stills her with a hand. "I feel great, Mom. Sit down, stop fussing. Say hello to Mimi."

She looks at me finally and nods disdainfully before turning back to Vance and taking the seat next to his bedside.

"When is Dr. Haneef supposed to come in? I was doing some reading last night and there are some things I want to talk to him about..."

Vance puts a hand on her arm, stilling her mid-sentence. When he speaks, his voice is soft and gentle. He knows she's not going to like what he's about to tell her.

"He's already been by, Mom. They're going to release me today or tomorrow. It depends on when we can get all the necessary arrangements made."

"What? Releasing you? Home? No. Absolutely not. You need to remain here until you get better. There's no one to take care of you at home."

"I'll be taking care of him, Miriam," I speak up. "Whatever care I can't provide for him, we'll have a hospice nurse on hand to give him."

"Hospice is for people who have no hope, Mimi. As long as he's here, there's hope," her voice cracks on the last words.

Vance slides his hand down her arm, to hold her hand. "Mom. You have to accept I only have a little time left. Whether I'm here or at home isn't going to change the number of days I have. I want to be home where I'm comfortable, not in a place that's noisy and bright and smells funny. Plus, even though all food tastes bad to me now, the food here is especially awful."

"Vance, it feels like you're just giving up and going home to die. I can't stand the thought of it," she sobs.

"Mother," he says gently, "the only one fighting here is you. It's not that I'm giving up, it's that you're holding onto something that just isn't there. I'm in the end stages of a terminal disease, one that there's never been any cure for. I know it's hard to face, that's why I ignored it for so long, but it's almost time."

She sobs harder as his words become softer but more serious.

"It's going to be soon. I don't know exactly when, of course, but you have to face the fact that before very long, I'm going to be gone. I don't want to leave with the thought you were still clinging to some unrealistic hope I was going to pull through, that some miracle was going to save me. I want you to be ready, so when the time comes to say goodbye, you can give me a kiss like you have every other time we've parted."

I'm overcome by the emotion between the two of them and feel like this is a moment that should be just for the two of them. I stand and kiss Vance's forehead, then whisper to him I'm just going to step out for a little while. He nods in understanding and returns his attention to his mother, who has laid her head on the side of his bed and continues sobbing as he strokes her hair.

As I leave the room, I find Justin hanging out in the hall, leaning against the wall next to the door.

"What are you doing just standing around out here?" I ask, wiping away the moisture still on my cheeks after listening to Vance talk to his mom. "Why didn't you come in?"

"Sometimes it takes a little time for me to work up to it," he says without any hint of embarrassment.

I nod in understanding. "I don't recommend going in right now. Vance just explained to Miriam he's decided to go home, and she's not taking the news very well. I thought I should give them some time alone, so I'm going to the cafeteria to see if I can find some coffee and something that might resemble breakfast. Would you'd like to join me?"

"Sure, I'll take a walk with you," he says as he falls into step beside me.

"You seem to be doing better than I expected you to be," he says after we reach the elevators.

I think about his statement for a moment before responding. "I was a wreck yesterday, but we did a lot of talking which helped. I know a large part of my current state of calm is due to my natural defense mechanism. We have a plan. I'm good when there's a plan. When I left Vance, that's how I kept myself together—by making a plan for myself every single day and following it to the letter. When that plan is finished..." I break off as my emotions swell up into my chest and threaten to overwhelm me. I swallow hard and push them away as forcefully as I can and begin again. "When the end comes, and I no longer have the plan to rely upon, well, then I guess that's when it'll all fall apart."

The elevator doors open, and we walk inside. He presses the button for the ground floor and soon we're descending so slowly, I can barely feel the movement. Or maybe, I really am just numb and don't realize it.

I clear my throat. "Another part of my ability to appear okay right now is that in some ways, I'm better than I was before. It may sound strange since I know I'm about to lose the love of my life forever. But I also got him back, you know? I thought I lost him months ago, with no real understanding why, and my heart was shattered. Now, I know I didn't lose him, exactly. This disease stole him from me in bits and pieces until I couldn't recognize him. I'm angry because if I had known what was going on, I would have understood, and we would never have been apart for those months. I can't do anything to change what happened, but I can make the most of the time we have left, and I'm going to love him as hard as I can. I'm grateful to have that. I'm grateful to you for making sure I have the opportunity to do that. Thank you, Justin. You gave me back something I thought I'd lost forever. I'll always be in your debt."

"You don't owe me anything, Mimi. I couldn't let the worst happen without you knowing what was going on with Vance. Not telling you when you wouldn't listen to him was one of the hardest things I've ever done, but he was so adamant that you be left alone. It went against all my instincts, but you know I'd do just about anything for that guy. In the end, it turns out I'd do just about anything for you, too, even going against the wishes of my best friend. I knew once you found out he was sick, it would change everything for you. I didn't want to know what it would do to you if it was after it was too late."

The elevator doors open, and we step outside into the lobby. As we walk toward the cafeteria, I can't help imagining how horrific it would have been to learn about Vance's illness after he had already passed on, to never have the chance to reestablish our connection and make amends. I honestly don't know if I would have been able to survive something like that, and thanks to the man walking next to me, I would never have to find out. Stopping, I turn and throw my arms around his neck, sobbing in gratitude.

He staggers back a little as his hands grab my waist to steady us both. He lowers his head to my ear and softly hushes into it while rubbing my back, trying to soothe and calm me. I'm sure he's a little surprised at my delayed outburst, but I think he understands why I've suddenly thrown myself into his arms. Just in case he doesn't, I try to explain it to him through my tears.

"Justin, if you hadn't, I don't know what would have happened to me. I don't know if I could have lived through it if I learned none of it was his fault, and I never gave him a chance to say he was sorry or told him I still loved him. I never have to find out because of you." I grip his shirt in both of my hands and look into his eyes. "I love you for that. You had compassion for me when no one else did. When everyone else blamed me for turning him away, you understood and didn't judge me. When everyone would have let us both suffer the ultimate loss

318

without being able to love each other through it, you were there for us to make sure that didn't happen. You are exactly who Vance told me you were the day I met you, the most loyal friend a person could ever hope to have. Even when I questioned that loyalty and wasn't the best friend to you I should have been, you were still there for me, making sure I never had to know that kind of devastation. I love you, Justin, I really do."

Oddly, his face takes on a wistful look before he places his hand behind the back of my head and pulls me close, tucking my face under his chin. He cradles me in his arms, rocking me side to side for a moment before kissing the top of my head and letting me go. His hands slide down my shoulders to my arms before finally taking one hand in his and leading me the rest of way to the cafeteria without saying another word. I think my words must have touched him in some way, and he's just not sure what to say. That's fine as long as he knows I meant every word I said.

We each grab a cup of coffee and bagel which seems to be the most edible thing in the cafeteria's selection of food. We find an empty table near one of the windows and fall into the chairs, not saying much of anything for the first few minutes. Finally, I regain enough of my composure to resume the subject of our earlier conversation.

"What about you, Justin? How are you managing through all this? I know this must affect you more deeply than those other assholes he calls friends."

"Don't be too hard on them, Mimi. They think you hurt him when he was vulnerable, and they're just being protective. They don't know he tried to rape you, that he tried to kill you, so they don't understand your unwillingness to talk to him was just as much about fear as anger if not more so."

"How did you know about those things? I never told you about that. And for the record, he never tried to kill me, he only threatened to," I say, completely shocked that he knows.

"Did he or did he not choke you? Vance admitted as much to me when I went over to confront him after I saw your bruises. Even he couldn't say whether or not he would have stopped if you hadn't fought him off."

"No, no. It didn't happen like that. He let me go. He wasn't trying to kill me, he just choked me for a few seconds. I have to make sure he knows that." I say, immediately worried Vance has been carrying around guilt for something he didn't do.

"Either way, the guys don't know any of that, so they think you were just being hardhearted. Try to keep that in mind when they're being jerks to you."

"I'll try. But don't think I didn't notice that you've deflected the original question. How are you getting through this? Have you guys come together and are helping each other deal?"

"Those guys are my buddies, but we're not exactly touchy-feely types, you know?" he huffs in laughter. "The closest we get, I imagine any guys get, to talking about our feelings is a clap on the shoulder and a 'you good, man?' Nobody is baring their souls, and I'd probably die of shock or wet my pants and run if any of us tried to."

"So, what do you do? You have to let those feelings out somehow, or they'll eat you alive."

"It sucks. There's not a whole lot more I can say about it. Whenever I had a problem and I felt I needed someone to talk to, I went to Vance. He was the guy who always had the time to listen and was able to give me advice that was good common sense. It's not like he can do that now. He's not going to be able to tell me what to do when he's gone. So, I can only deal with it on my own, figure things out when they happen and just keep holding it together. It hurts now, it'll hurt more later, but I have to keep going."

"One foot in front of the other... breathe in, breathe out," I say quietly.

"What did you say?"

"That's what I used to tell myself after I left Vance. Remember how I said I had a plan for every day after I left? Those were the first items on my list every day. Sometimes, they were the only things on the list. I expect they'll make a reappearance on my to-do list again in the very near future," I say, wadding up my napkin and tossing it on the table in front of me.

"Yeah," is all Justin says in response.

When we return to the room, Miriam is still sitting by Vance's side, but he's asleep. She looks much more composed than she did when I left though it's obvious she's been crying. She gives me a sad smile as she stands, motioning for me to join her outside. I'm hesitant since she's been so hostile toward me, but she obviously has something to say. There's really no way to avoid it without causing some kind of scene, so I follow her out of the room.

As the door shuts behind us, she turns toward me and smiles again. I'm a little shocked because I had expected her to drop the pleasant look and give me her animus again. She takes my hand and squeezes it tight.

"I'm afraid I haven't been very fair to you, Mimi, and I owe you an apology. While you were gone, Vance and I talked, and he explained to me in detail why you left him and why you were unwilling to talk to him. I didn't know what he'd done or about the restraining order you had against him. I thought you were just being stubborn and didn't care that my son was sick and suffering. I'm very sorry, Mimi. I can't imagine how hard life must have been for you those months when he was not himself, not understanding why and with no one truly believing you when you tried to tell them what was happening."

"I understand, Miriam. I know now you were only trying to protect your son. I don't have any hard feelings toward you or anyone else. Justin told me nobody else knows what happened."

"I'm glad we have this sorted out. I always thought you two were great together. It broke my heart when you split up, so it gives me some peace to know you won't be apart when the end comes.

"Vance has convinced me going home is the best option for him, so I want you to know I'll be on hand to help out. I know you won't be able to be there twenty-four hours a day since you have a job--"

"I appreciate your offer, Miriam," I can't help but interrupt her, "but that won't be necessary. I'm actually going to give notice at my job tomorrow, effective immediately. I'm not going to lose another minute of the time I have left with him. I have enough money saved to see me through for a while. I'll figure out my future when the time comes."

She looks down at the floor for a moment before looking up at me with a pleading look on her face.

"I want to help you. I know you need to do the majority of caring for him after all the time you lost with him, but please remember, he's my baby, and I need to love him through this as much as you do."

I had imagined it would be just Vance and me in our protective bubble until the end, but listening to Miriam's plea, I realize that would be very unfair to the other people in his life who love him too. They'll need their own time to say goodbye, to show him their love in their own ways, so he passes on knowing just how special he is to so many people. I wrap my arms around her and hug her tightly.

"I promise we'll do this together, Miriam. You're the only person in the world who could possibly love him as much as I do, so I won't take him away from you."

"Thank you, Mimi." She squeezes me tighter before pulling me back and wiping her eyes.

Not having anything else to say, we go back into Vance's room and sit with him while he sleeps. Miriam and Justin decide to go out for lunch and invite me to join them, but I decline, not wanting to leave Vance's side for a minute. They insist on bringing back something for me to eat, and though I'm not even remotely hungry, I politely accept. I can't afford to let myself get sick. I need to be strong for Vance.

He awakens just before Dr. Haneef returns from his rounds. We once again discuss our options for Vance's end-of-life care and inform him of his desire to go home. The doctor supports Vance's decision and tells us he will have someone contact the company the hospital recommends for in-home hospice care. A representative will come within a few hours and make all the arrangements to set up services today, and Vance will be discharged in the morning. I'm impressed and a little overwhelmed with how fast the process moves, but at least Vance will be more comfortable sooner rather than later.

By four p.m., all the arrangements to move Vance home are in place. Miriam is currently at the house, awaiting receipt of the medical supplies, medications, and other paraphernalia he's going to need. The hospice nurse will be waiting when we arrive to help us get him settled. It's surreal to think he won't have an IV line anymore or a team of doctors or nurses on hand should anything happen. I know he has a DNR at the hospital, but to be truly on our own, with absolutely no one who is capable of intervening during an emergency is a very daunting realization because the truth is there are no emergencies. There's only the end.

Vance suffers a terrible headache that night but stubbornly resists the morphine his nurse and I urge him to take. No amount of pleading can sway him from his steadfast determination to tough it out. Just when I think Stranger Vance is going to surface and unleash his wrath on us for trying to nag him into submission, he takes my hand in his.

"Mimi, I don't want to sleep away my time with you, I want to be able to feel you near me. I can't do that if I'm passed out because I took their painkillers. It may not do anything to relieve the pain in my head but laying here holding your hand is better than any medicine this hospital can offer me."

I bow my head for a moment before looking up into his eyes. I can see the pain there, around the edges, making them crinkle and his brow furrow slightly. I rub my thumb between his eyes, just above the bridge of his nose, trying to ease the crease from between them, hopefully, giving him a tiny bit of relief from the ache.

"I can't force you to take the medication, and since you told me how you feel, I'll let it go. I hate seeing you suffer any more than necessary, so tell me what I can do to help make it easier. Whatever you think might work, I'll do it."

"If you would come up here and let me hold you, I think that would go a long way to helping me feel better," he smiles weakly at me.

On this last night in the hospital, in the cramped and uncomfortable hospital bed, wires and tubes strategically strung around it, we snuggle together in the peace and comfort of each other's arms and find relief from the pain that is plaguing us both.

I would love to say that once we get Vance home everything goes smoothly and every day is as good as it can be under the circumstances. As you can imagine, this isn't the case. During the first week back, he has days that are like those two in the hospital after I arrived where he doesn't feel very bad, and we're able to speak heart-to-heart and enjoy each other's company like we did during the early days of our marriage. He's witty, charming, and sometimes, even playful. Other days, he's crabby, bossy, and outright mean when his pain levels are off the charts, and he needs more medication to manage it. It's clear it's worsened to the point he can't stand it anymore because even on his good days, he's never refused taking it again.

As for the rest of us, Miriam and I especially since we're always with him, there's always this dark, oppressive cloud overshadowing everything, this heaviness in the air that, sometimes, threatens to choke us. It's an emotional toll of watching him suffer, of watching the end rush toward us to take our dearest, our most beloved with no way to fight it, stop it, beat it down. It's the feeling of utter helplessness and the knowledge that you'll suffer the greatest loss of your life in mere days, you're just waiting for the executioner's cruel ax to fall without the mercy of being able to close your eyes or hold your breath.

I've resumed an old smoking habit to give me a way to deal with the stress, a way to find some calm in those few minutes I need to take a break when I feel like the walls are closing in on me. I endure the disapproving looks of Miriam as I step outside to get my fix of nicotine a few times a day, but there's nothing to be done about it. I know it's a stupid idea, but we all cope in our own ways. She's been baking cakes and cookies and pretty much eating them all by herself although she does try to foist them off on the boys when they come to visit. I don't judge.

Griffin and Bryant come to visit every few days, and always together. They spend their time with Vance reminiscing about their time as boys, mostly about the mischief they got up to. Sometimes it's about the mischief they got up to as young men as well, but the stories are always entertaining. I stick around for some of them, the ones I haven't already heard anyway because they help me feel even closer to Vance. Otherwise, I try to give them their privacy, their own special time with their friend. I have to admit it's hard though because I am possessive of his good times. I'm greedy and want them all to myself.

Justin comes every day and stays late. He spends an hour or more with Vance, just talking. Sometimes about old times, sometimes about what's going on in his life or in the outside world, sometimes just sitting quietly. The rest of the time,

Justin spends time with Miriam and me, both of us together and individually while Vance is sleeping. He makes it clear he's there to support us all. I have leaned on his shoulder more than once, crying on the days when the pressure has been too much, usually one of Vance's bad days.

On one such evening, Justin sits outside with me on the front steps while I take one of my smoke breaks. My seventh for the day.

"Those things will kill you, you know," he begins.

"I've decided it hardly matters. In a few days, maybe a week, it's going to feel like I want to die, so it really doesn't make a difference if I move the process along a little faster," I respond bitterly.

"You know, you don't really mean that," he says admonishingly, but very seriously.

"I'm not so sure about that, Justin. I'm really not."

"You know he wouldn't want that for you. He wants you to continue on, live your life and someday be happy again, Mimi. We've talked about it, and I'm sure at some point, he'll tell you the same."

"I don't know how the fuck he expects me to accomplish that, Justin. Unless he's got some magic wand he's planning on leaving me, I don't see it happening."

"Time is the great equalizer, Peaches. It will never heal it all, but it makes things easier to bear, that and the love of the people who care about you.

You'll be forever changed, but you'll be new and improved if you allow yourself to be."

"Improved? Improved! How can you be improved by the loss of the most important person in your life? Seriously, Justin. I can't believe you would even say something like that to me. You obviously have no idea what you're talking about, have no idea what it's like to lose someone you can't live without." I start to get up when he stops me. His voice is low, almost dangerous sounding when he speaks.

"For one, Mimi, you don't know me well enough to make statements like that, so I suggest you be very careful and think before you open your pretty little mouth.

"Second, what I meant by improved, I didn't mean by losing them. I meant improved by having been loved by them. Sure, you may have lost that person, but you never lose their love. You get to keep that when they go." He stands. "Think about that, while you're killing yourself slowly, and think again about how if you do hasten your end, how you dishonor that love by bringing it to an end along with you."

He turns and walks into the house, leaving me standing there with my mouth hanging open.

The biggest bright spot, if you can call it that, during the time Vance is home is he insists on me sleeping with him every night, no matter his pain level, no matter his mood. He wants me there next to him, at his side, under his arm. It feels right being back in our bed. We tried to bring in a hospital bed, just to make it easier for him to be elevated during the day when he wanted to sit up, but he insisted on being comfortable in his own bed and having enough room for me to join him when he wanted. So, we're grateful for the invention of wedge pillows and use massive amounts of other big, fluffy pillows to sit him up comfortably. He doesn't seem to mind them and at night, we get to share the warmth and comfort of each other's bodies and have the quiet of the dark to enjoy our connection, just the two of us.

The second week we're home, Vance seems to enjoy a surge of energy. He's alert, happy, and feeling very good. Miriam and I are delighted at this turn of events and spend as much time with him as possible, enjoying every moment with him we can. He makes jokes, always full of innuendo for me, and I smile more than I have in a very long time. It deceptively lifts the dark cloud that's been hovering over our heads, making us feel like maybe the end isn't as close as we thought until the hospice nurse who has been unobtrusively around in the background all this time draws Miriam and I aside. She lets us know that this "second wind" is a very common phenomenon as the end draws near, and we need to do our best to prepare ourselves emotionally.

The dark cloud returns, pressing down even more heavily, and we return to Vance, our smiles now forced and unnatural. The heaviness in my heart is excruciating, but I do my best to enjoy his good humor and lightness. It's infectious, so it eases my burden, and I stay in his company as much as possible because I just can't get enough. So, what if it's an artificial recovery of sorts? It's giving me the best of my beloved, and I will squeeze out every memory I can make from it.

One evening, after a very good day Vance spent teasing me and making me laugh over the silliest of things, he begins to reminisce about when we began to fall in love. I am lying in the bed next to him on my side facing him, my chin propped in my hand while he sits up, his head turned to face me. He's playing with my hair, picking up pieces, then dropping them, occasionally smoothing my bangs back from my forehead.

"Do you remember our trip to Atlantic City, Mimi?" he asks.

"Of course, I do. You nearly got arrested after threatening to burn down Caesar's."

"I did not," he laughs. "I only threatened a few security officers with bodily harm if they wouldn't tell me where you were. Big difference."

"Mmhmm. Stalker."

"Guilty as charged there, but I have no regrets. I got the girl in the end," he grins at me.

"You certainly did. That night as I recall."

His grin widens. "Several times, going into the next day, I believe. But now that I think about it, I don't think it was ever in the end."

Sitting up, I gasp in mock outrage. "Oh my god. Sick as you are, you are still a pervert and a dork!"

"You would think less of me if I weren't."

Settling back down and tucking a pillow under my head, I pretend to think for a minute. "Yeah, you're probably right about that."

"I had a feeling after they detained me because of my response when I couldn't get to you, I was in love with you already. But the following night, when we were at that nightclub, watching you dance... you were so happy and free, I was definitely a goner. I knew then I never wanted to be apart from you. I wanted your spirit all to myself. I thought, if I can have that light turned on me for the rest of my life, I will die the happiest man in all the world.

"I know I put you through a lot of shit because of this disease, and I'm so very sorry. I never, ever wanted to make you feel the way I did, to hurt you, or cause you pain of any kind. Knowing I caused that light to dim for a time is the one regret I'll leave this world with.

"I want you to promise me something. Don't let me dim your light again. Don't let my death diminish that fire inside you. Let it burn, knowing I loved you with all my heart, every minute of every day even through those horrible, dark times when I was unable to show you.

"I know it sounds like I'm asking the impossible. Of course, I know you're going to grieve, but let yourself heal, Mimi. Once you do, keep that fire burning bright for the rest of your life, and... someday..." his voice breaks and he takes a big shuddering breath. "Someday, share it with someone special. That way, I will always be with

332

you because you kept that light burning for me. Promise me, Mimi. I can't leave you without knowing my love is something that has made your life better, and you love me enough to go on and light up the world just for me."

As strong as I've tried to be during these days I've been reunited with Vance, his heartfelt words completely undo me. The tears that began to flow down my face as he was speaking turn into sobs as all my pain and fear and love for him burst forth, spilling all over the sheets, soaking us both in my uncontrollable emotions.

"I don't know how I'll accomplish that, Vance, when you were the one who lit that fire to begin with. My life was nice before I met you, but it was like living in a world of muted colors. When I met you, it was as if everything exploded in front of me into a new world filled with vivid displays of the rainbow, every new sound was like music, and scents became heady and intoxicating. You made me feel high, and I don't know if I will ever feel that way again. Your memory will always burn somewhere deep inside me, but without you, I don't know if anything will ever be as bright again," I choke out through my heavy tears.

"I promise you it can, my love. I know it will take time, but surround yourself with the people who love you, the people who also see that light. Despite what you think, it's always been there, it just needed a little fuel. Nurture it during the times you're feeling down, but as time goes by, look for the opportunities to feed it. Seek out things, people who make you feel good. That's how you'll heal, and that's how you'll keep your promise to me," he says as he wipes my tears away. "Now promise me, Mimi. I need you to."

I don't want to promise. I'm afraid of what it means if I do.

"I'm afraid, Vance."

"I know you are, baby, but if it helps, I'm not. These last days at home, spending time with everyone have shown me that everyone is going to be okay. I have been blessed with a great life, good friends, a wonderful woman who has given me more love than I ever hoped to have and certainly more than I ever deserved. All I need now to make my life complete is your promise that you'll do what I ask."

Hard as it is to imagine that I can ever live up to this promise I'm about to make, I know there's no way I'd deny him this. I can't let him go feeling I didn't love him enough to give him everything I could, so I open my mouth and whisper the second hardest thing I will ever have to say to him.

"I promise, Vance. With all my heart, I promise you."

He gathers me to him and tucks my head under his chin.

"Thank you, Mimi. My heart has always been full for you, to the point of bursting, but I want you to know and always remember it is and has only ever been yours. I never loved anyone until I met you. I may take a piece of you when I leave, but I'm leaving all of me behind with you."

"I love you, Vance. You will always be the one great love of my life, no matter what comes next. Take that with you."

We spend the night, holding each other, alternately crying and whispering words of love and encouragement. The next morning, I wake to the sun shining softly through the blinds. Vance doesn't.

Seventeen

I quietly rise and dress, my eyes on Vance's body the whole time, a numbness stealing over mine, making my movements slow. My old mantra enters my head. Breathe in, breathe out. One foot in front of the other as I leave the room and find Miriam. She's still sleeping. I gently wake her, and by the look on my face, I know she knows. Her face falls, and she buries her head in her hands for a moment. Suddenly, she straightens her shoulders and steels her spine, raising her head high with a stoic look on her face. She stands, and I lead her back to the bedroom. As she enters, a small whimper escapes her lips, and she approaches the bed. She kneels beside it, taking Vance's cold hand in hers as I shut the door to give her some privacy.

I find the hospice nurse sitting in the living room with her knitting. I have to tell her he's gone, but I want to wait for a few minutes in order to allow Miriam her time with her son. The nurse will have to go in and gather his medications to dispose of them immediately lest anyone try to abscond with the controlled substances. I understand this is only policy, but it rankles nonetheless. So, I pass her by as if nothing has happened and go on to the kitchen to make coffee. While I am sipping from my first cup, Miriam's emotion overcomes her, and I can hear her wails echoing throughout the house.

I run to her side, but of course, the hospice nurse is already there. At least she's trying to comfort Miriam rather than just going about her duties. I nod to her to go ahead and wrap my arms around Miriam to lead her from the room. I settle her on the sofa in the living room and just hold her while she cries.

The hospice nurse calls the mortuary and before long, they arrive to pick up his body. I dash into the room before they can claim him and shut myself inside. I sit beside him on the bed, holding his hand for a moment, just studying his peaceful face. I feel a mixture of emotions, tremendous sadness, love, disbelief, but surprisingly I feel a sense of relief. I'm relieved his suffering is over, that the oppressive cloud that has hung over this house is finally lifted, that the agonizing experience of waiting for the end has finally come to pass. As the hospice nurse knocks on the door, reminding me that the mortuary attendants are waiting, I lean forward and whisper the hardest words I will ever say in my life against Vance's lips.

"Goodbye, my love."

Two days later, on a Monday morning in late summer, on what would have been our second wedding anniversary, we have a memorial service for Vance. He wanted to be cremated, always saying he took up enough space when he was alive, and he didn't need to take up anymore after he was gone. The service is attended by a great number of Vance's friends, all the partners from his firm, and his co-workers, including that vile Tiffany who blubbered her way through as if she'd lost her own husband.

The funeral itself, I'm told, was lovely; I mostly tuned out. I did, however, pay rapt attention to the eulogies as they were loving, heartfelt, and sometimes humorous speeches from the people who knew my husband best. I declined to speak as I didn't think I could get through a few sentences without breaking down.

As long as I kept my interactions with people to a minimum, I didn't cry. The numbness that had crept over my body after I left him was back, and I wrapped it around me like a suit of armor. Part of me felt like I had spent all my emotions that last night with Vance, anyway. As if I had given him all I had, and there was nothing left for anyone else to see. Maybe some people saw my demeanor for what it was, maybe some thought me heartless. I didn't much care, either way. My love was gone, and despite what he said about taking a piece of me with him, I thought he was wrong. He'd taken it all.

Justin was there to hold my hand through the church service. He even rode in the limousine back to the house for the gathering after the funeral and stayed close to Miriam and me in case we needed the support. Mostly, I tried to avoid everyone. I did my duty, greeting everyone and accepting their condolences of course, but other than that, I spent my time in the backyard, chain-smoking and drinking Vance's scotch.

Laurel had flown out to help with all the arrangements—and to keep me standing upright if truth be told. She tried to be supportive and keep me engaged, but while I loved her and appreciated her compassion and concern, her exuberant personality was just too much for me to handle. Her way was to try to 'keep my spirits up' by acting positive and philosophical. I really couldn't wait for her to go home. I avoided her throughout the afternoon as much as I could.

Jessica, Liz, and Grace came and eventually found me hiding. They made sure I knew they were all there for me. They were very considerate and said all the things friends are supposed to say under the circumstances, but they weren't pushy and didn't stay too long which I appreciated. I would eventually get in touch with them, but it would be awhile.

Now, it's dark and the scotch has run out. I start thinking it's time to go inside, Miriam will need help cleaning up. Before I can move though, Justin comes out and sits down next to me on the chaise lounge I am occupying

"Got any more of that scotch?" he asks.

"Afraid not although I'm sure there's another bottle beneath the wet bar if you really want some."

"Do you want some more? I'll go in and get it if you do."

"Nah," I say, lighting another cigarette. "I've had more than enough already, but please, help yourself."

"Maybe later." He reaches over and places a hand on my knee. I look down at his hand, then up at his face, slightly irritated that he's touching me.

Holding my hand is one thing. Nobody should be touching me anywhere else.

"How are you holding up?" he asks. "I haven't seen much of you since the service which I'm sure is by design, but I thought someone should check on you to see if you needed anything."

"I'm partially upright," I motion to my semi-reclined position on the chaise lounge, "and following the default plan. All things considered, today is a success."

"Default plan?" he asks, a confused look on his face.

"You remember, breathe in, breathe out..." I say, taking a long drag on my cigarette and exhaling to demonstrate my point.

"Ah, yes. Under the circumstances, I believe it's a sound plan and probably the best that can be expected of any of us."

"Miriam seems to be handling things inside rather well. I don't know how she manages to interact with all those people, listening to their condolences, hearing their stories," I say, shaking my head. "I would want to scream if I had to stand there, smiling politely as every word is another dagger in my heart."

"I think she takes comfort in their memories of Vance, knowing he touched their lives, too. For her, it makes her feel a little less alone."

I nod, thinking it will be a very long time before I ever feel less alone. "That's good. She deserves that."

"She does. Don't you think you do too?" he asks.

341

"What, deserve comfort or to feel less alone?"

"Both, I guess. They kind of go hand in hand, really. Don't they?"

I think about it for a moment before responding. "I can't imagine feeling any less alone, so it's hard to imagine taking comfort from anything or anyone right now. The night before he died, Vance told me to surround myself with people who loved me, but let's face it, anyone who loves me, also loved him. They're going to be grieving too. It's selfish, but I feel too wrapped up in my own pain to share theirs. However, I also made a promise to him that night. I just don't know if I have the strength to live up to it."

"I know what you mean, in a way. My way of coping is to keep it all inside too. Instead of locking myself away though, I try to take on everyone else's pain, so I don't have to deal with mine. Two different approaches, both just as fucked up as the other."

I lean my head back against the lounge and eye him skeptically. "So, what are you thinking? We form a support group of two?"

"Maybe it's not such a bad idea. You aren't overwhelmed by too many people sharing their grief with you, and I don't take on more than I can handle and avoid my own feelings."

I nod. "I'm not wild about not being able to lock myself in my bedroom for the next six months, but in an effort to keep my promise to Vance and because I owe you the world, I'll give it a try."

"That's all either of us can do, Mimi."

The following months blend one into the next. I repeat my mantra several times a day, every day, but the more I try to keep going, the more I sink lower into a pit of despair. The cloud of darkness is back, and every breath I take of the heavy air surrounding me is a weight on my chest threatening to crush my heart. Thanks to Vance's life insurance, I don't have to look for a new job right away, so I don't. I spend my days when I manage to get out of bed, rambling around our house, wrapped in his robe or one of his shirts, reliving our good memories. Sometimes I sit in his office just handling things that belonged to him, taking solace in the knowledge the items once touched his skin. It's like touching him by proxy.

Justin comes over several times a week, bringing me groceries and making sure that certain things are done, like checking the mail, taking out the trash and sometimes even doing a load of laundry or two. I have come to depend on him for far too much, physically and emotionally.

Grace, Liz, and Jessica have long since stopped trying to get me out of the house because I have repeatedly declined their invitations. They still call occasionally to check up on me, but I keep our conversations short. The only person I truly allow to be a part of my life is Justin and I think it's because he is a connection to Vance. That's not to say I don't truly look forward to his visits, I do. They're the only reprieve I have from my agony, dulling it to a lonely ache while he's around. He makes good on our agreement to be a support group of two by consistently showing up and keeping me from wallowing in my sorrow twenty-four hours a day, seven days a week, but I am afraid I'm a dismal failure at living up to my end of the bargain. I don't know what he gets out of our arrangement because I don't really give anything back to him. I don't call him or make sure we get together. He does all the work, and I do all the taking. I have to say though, I don't know how I'd manage without him because he's the only tether I have to the outside world. I know if it weren't for him, I'd probably wither away in my own self-pity until I disappeared.

One night, Justin shows up with a sack of groceries, informing me he's going to cook for me. I'm dubious since we normally have takeout and sit around watching movies. I follow him as he marches through the house and into the kitchen where he takes out packages of steaks and lobster tails from the brown paper bag he brought with him.

"Have you ever made these before?" I ask, eyeballing the food as if it might be poisonous.

He just gives me a look that says I should keep my mouth shut and let the expert work. He finishes unpacking the bag, pulling out a bottle of red wine. I begin to laugh hysterically as I recall Vance's bug-eyed look on our first date when he realized I didn't like wine. Justin looks at me in shock, obviously wondering what has gotten into me but also because I haven't laughed in months. Of course, my laughter quickly dissolves into loud hiccupping tears as the happy memory rips me in two. Justin quickly rounds the kitchen island to where I stand and pulls me into his arms, holding me close and shushing me softly.

When my sobs have died down to quiet sniffles, he pulls back and wipes the remainders of the tears from my face.

"Care to tell me what happened there?"

I try to share the memory with Justin, but I can't really translate the humor in the retelling, and my melancholy doesn't exactly help, either.

"You really had to be there," I say, wiping more tears from my eyes.

"I guess so," he says, looking at me with the softest expression on his face. "Even though it didn't end well, it was good to see you laugh there for a minute."

I smile sadly, visions of that night still playing in my head.

"What about you, Justin? I've been a shitty friend. How you are you coping? What has it been like for you without him?"

Justin blows out a breath and rubs his jaw with one large hand.

"It hasn't been easy. So many times, I've picked up my phone to give him a call to just shoot the shit or to tell him something I know he'd get a kick out of, and realize when I see his name in my contacts, he isn't there anymore. Every time, I wonder why I still have his number in my phone, but I just can't bring myself to delete it. I don't know if I ever will."

345

He goes back to the other side of the island and resumes his preparations for the meal, pulling out pots and pans and all the other utensils he needs. I lean against the counter as he continues to speak.

"I miss the guy, plain and simple. There's no other way to put it. He was my best friend, someone who always had my back. It's kind of like your left arm, you don't really think about it, but you know it's always there when you need it. It was the same with Vance. I guess I took him for granted, and now that he's gone, I realize I should have appreciated what a rare friendship we had. Friends like Griffin and Bryant are great, but they aren't much more than good company. Vance was different. You could talk about stuff that really mattered with him, without feeling like a giant pussy, you know?"

"You mean, like your feelings, Justin?" It feels odd, but I can't help but poke him a little.

"Is that you, Peaches, trying to make fun of me? Careful, now. I might think there's some hope for you after all," he says, brandishing a meat fork at me.

I ignore his comment and try to distance myself from the changing mood of our conversation by asking if I can help prepare the meal. He gives me some potatoes to wash and peel which quickly devolves into an argument over how the potatoes should be prepared.

"You do not have mashed potatoes with steak." I insist. "You have them with chicken."

"What difference does it make?" He looks at me like I've lost my mind.

"Everybody knows you have baked potatoes with steak. Although, since we're having lobster tails, I'm thinking red potatoes probably would have been the more appropriate choice over russet," I say thoughtfully.

"Are the food police going to show up and arrest us if we don't have the right potatoes?"

"Hardy-har. You just be quiet and handle your meat over there, and I'll take care of the vegetables," I say as I grab a fork to puncture the potatoes.

I clap my hand over my mouth just as I hear him mutter, "I seem to be doing that a lot lately."

"You know what I meant!" I shout.

Justin bursts out laughing. "Yes, Peaches, I did. It's just been a long time since I've had a date."

I begin wrapping the potatoes in foil as I say, "Really? That's unusual. How long is a long time?"

"Longer than I care to admit. I've been really busy recently, so there hasn't been much time to meet anyone, and there isn't anyone I've already met that I'm interested in seeing again," he says as he rubs seasonings into the steaks.

"Do you have a lot of contracts you're working on right now? Is that why you're so busy?" I ask as I push him out of the way and pop the potatoes in the oven.

He nods and admits, "I've also been spending a lot of time with my friends lately."

Instantly, I feel guilty. He's trying to tell me that taking care of me like he does is interfering with his social life. I need to stop relying on him so much and let him get back to his own life. He doesn't need to keep babysitting me, but if I tell him that, I know he'll deny that's what he's doing. I can't be this selfish anymore by taking advantage of Justin's good heart. He has a lot to offer someone and currently, I'm eating that up rather than letting him use his time to get out there and meet someone. That's going to change, pronto.

I keep my newfound realization to myself and allow myself to enjoy this last night in his company as much as I'm able to enjoy anything these days. To my surprise, Justin turns out to be a really good cook. The steaks are cooked to perfection, the lobster is succulent, and the potatoes melt in your mouth if I do say so myself. He also brought over a movie, a comedy, of course. He's always looking for a way to lift my spirits, and this time, I manage to muster a couple of chuckles. He looks at me each time like the earth has moved.

At the end of the evening, he gives me a hug at the door as is his norm. I hold on a little longer than usual, uncertain how I'm going to manage a day-to-day existence without relying on him as much as I do. I'm resolved to putting distance between us, so he can get back to his life, however.

As I pull away from him, he looks at me quizzically. "Everything okay with you, Mimi?"

"Sure. I think I'm just a little tired tonight. It must be all that good food making me a little sluggish. It was fantastic though. I'm sorry I ever doubted your skills in the kitchen. You're going to make someone a very good wife someday, Justin Sever."

"Was that another attempt at humor tonight?" he asks, his eyes comically bulging from his head. "I'm going to have to mark this on my calendar."

"Oh hush, you," I say, pushing him out the door. "Have a good night."

"Seriously though," he says as he stands on my porch, "it was good to see you relax and start to enjoy yourself a little. I'll give you a call tomorrow. Maybe I'll even convince you to get out of the house."

"Don't go getting all crazy now."

"Hope springs eternal," he calls out as he walks down the walkway, toward his motorcycle parked at the curb.

I sigh as I close the door and lean against it, squeezing my eyes together to keep the tears that are forming from dripping down my face. It was a mistake to lean on Justin as much as I have, I've only delayed the inevitable. I am well and truly alone now, and instead of learning to live with that knowledge all these months, I feel like I'm back to square one. As if any ground I've gained since losing Vance is gone. I lost Vance, and now, I'm losing Justin.

As I'm lying in bed the following morning, I somehow get it in my head that I need a change of scenery. That maybe if I begin a whole new life, I can escape the ghosts of the past that are always pressing in on me. What were once treasured memories of time I spent with Vance that I gathered around me and clung to with a ferocity of a child with his security blanket, I suddenly cannot cast off quickly enough.

With the decision to leave town made, I have to determine where to go. Getting up, I hurry to Vance's office and boot up the computer. I quickly navigate to a map of California and study it, looking for a city that might be ideal for a quick relocation. Nothing jumps out at me. I figure since I'm being impulsive, I might as well go all the way and make this a real adventure. I pull up a map of the United States, close my eyes and point. I open them when my finger touches the screen. Initially, it lands on an ad for a dating website. I ignore the irony of that coincidence and try again. This time, when I open my eyes, my finger is directly on Arizona. I've been to Phoenix before and thought it was a nice place. Besides, it's not that far from Los Angeles, so if I decide I'm too homesick, I can easily come back. It seems like a smart choice in an otherwise completely irrational decision.

Looking at the clock, I see that it's past nine o'clock, so business hours have already begun. I look up property management companies, so I can arrange to have someone look after the house while I'm gone. I peruse rental listings in Phoenix, but ultimately, decide I'll stay in a hotel for a while and look for a place once I get there. There's no way to tell what a neighborhood is like from a picture on the internet.

I make a list of things I'll need to do to pack up my life here and begin anew in Arizona. It's not as long as I expected it would be. I've withdrawn from the world so much, there's very little beyond closing the house, packing, and letting the few people in my life know about my plans. It's pretty sad really, but I realize I'm already beginning to feel a little better because I finally have a plan to move forward, which is something I just couldn't figure out before.

With such a short list, I figure I can accomplish all the tasks I have set for myself and be on my way within a week. As I'm going over my list again to make sure I haven't overlooked anything, my phone rings in the other room. I run to grab it before it goes to voicemail, only to see that it's Justin calling. I have a moment of indecision before answering. Last night, I had planned to avoid him for a while, so he could go back to his own life without having me to worry about, but if I'm really going to leave, I have to let him know my plans. As good as he's been to me, I can't just go without talking to him about it. That would be too cowardly as tempting as it would be to avoid the lecture I know I'm going to get from him. In the end, I swipe my finger across the screen and answer his call.

"Hey, Justin," I say with more enthusiasm than I normally do.

"Wow, you sound like a different person this morning. What's going on?" he sounds concerned.

"I'm actually glad you called. Do you think we could meet somewhere? Maybe go for a walk?" I think meeting on neutral ground would be best for the conversation I need to have with him, for some reason.

"Uh, sure, of course. I want to think of these as good signs, Peaches, you're sounding better and wanting to get out of the house and all, but I have to say you're worrying me."

"I'm fine, Justin. I've been doing a lot of thinking since last night, and I've come to a few decisions. I just want to discuss them with you today."

We arrange to meet at a nearby park in an hour's time because Justin is too antsy by my turn around in mood to wait any longer. When I arrive, he's already there with a bag of takeout deli sandwiches in his hand.

"Why are you always trying to feed me?" I ask, motioning toward the bag as we walk toward a grouping of picnic tables.

"Because I think you'd shrivel up and blow away if I didn't," he says. "Honestly, Peaches. How often do you eat when I'm not around to feed you?"

A pang of guilt hits me because I'm reminded of how lost I've been since Vance died and just how much I've leaned on Justin. He's absolutely right, I probably would have starved if he hadn't come around as much as he had bearing food. I certainly wasn't trying to do anything for myself.

"Well, you don't have to worry about that anymore," I say with conviction as we sit down. "I've decided to make some changes."

"I think that's great, but I have to ask what brought this on so suddenly? You did seem a bit better last night, but today, it's almost as if you're a new woman or at least, trying to be," he says, unwrapping his sandwich and takes a big bite.

"I'm not sure what started it." I lie as I fidget with the paper wrapping my own sandwich. "It wasn't as if I woke up this morning to some great epiphany. I just decided the reason I've been floundering like I have been is I never made a new plan beyond breathing in and out. I never went back to work, I never tried to do anything but exist from sunup to sundown. It obviously wasn't enough," I pause and take a big breath. "So, I made a new plan."

Justin nods patiently and waits for me to continue, chewing silently on his food. I take a bite of my sandwich as I try to dig up the courage to tell him about my move. The combination of rye bread and corned beef is dry in my mouth and forms a ball of glue-like paste as I chew. I wish I had a drink to help me wash it down, but there's nothing so I have no choice but to either force it down or try to discreetly spit it into a napkin and hope Justin doesn't notice. I take my chances with swallowing and pray I don't choke in the process.

Once I have successfully downed the offending mouthful, I drop my sandwich and look at him for a few moments before saying quietly, "I'm leaving town for a while."

He looks at me, confused. "Where are you going? And what do you mean, for a while? A week? Two?"

"I'm going to Arizona. To live. Indefinitely," I say slowly.

He sits there, staring at me for a few beats, not comprehending what I've just told him. Finally, it dawns on him what I mean, and he explodes.

"You mean you're moving?" he shouts, his eyebrows nearly reaching his scalp as he looks at me disbelievingly.

I look around to see if we've attracted the attention of any of the other people in the park, and he immediately lowers his voice.

"Have you finally lost your fuckin' mind, Mimi? I know how much you've been suffering since Vance died, but running away is not going to solve anything. You can get back on track right here with the people who love you and are here to support you. You already feel alone. How is going somewhere where you really will be all alone going to help matters?"

"There are too many memories here, Justin. Everywhere I look, I see Vance. Everything reminds me of him. I think a change of scenery will help. Going to a place where there's no imprint of him on anything, where nobody knew him, a place where I can put some distance between myself and the past, so I can do the breathing in and out thing without the weight of his loss constantly pressing down on me. Can you understand that?"

He shakes his head and looks me straight in the eye. "Mimi, I promised Vance I would look after you. How am I supposed to do that if you leave?"

I bolt up from my seat. "That's what all this has been about? A promise you made to Vance? I thought we were trying to be here for each other, and while I know I didn't do such a bang-up job of being there to comfort you, I didn't realize you were just satisfying an obligation. I thought you were my friend. You should be grateful then that I'm letting you off the hook. You yourself implied last night that your personal life is suffering from all the time you spend taking care of me. Consider your promise to your dying friend fulfilled. You can get back to your life with a clear conscience because you did what he asked. I'm taking over now, and no longer need you to look after me."

With those words, I turn on my heel and run. Justin calls after me, but I don't look back. I don't know why his admission that he took care of me out of a duty to Vance hurt me so much, but it did. Now, more than ever, I know I need to get the hell out of Dodge.

I put Plan Arizona into gear double time. I pack up all my personal belongings from the house and put them in storage. I don't want to risk a break-in at the house while I am away even though the property management agent will be checking on things. The furniture and heavy items will remain, but the smaller items and valuables should have extra security, I think. I have a night out with Grace,

Jessica, and Liz after informing each of them of my plans. They were concerned at first, but after explaining my reasoning to them, they were all much more supportive than Justin and insisted we go out to celebrate my new adventure before I left.

Telling my mother was harder. While her reaction was better than Justin's, her argument against it was similar. I wasn't able to convince her the move was in my best interest, but she did eventually accept it as something I needed to do for myself and assured me she would be here for me if I needed her. She also promised to visit once I got settled somewhere.

My Skype call to Laurel goes differently. She listens to my plan carefully, without judging me or calling me crazy for wanting a change of scenery, but she lets me know how strongly she disagrees with my plan.

"I understand why you'd want to get away, Mimi. I really do. It's not that your logic makes no sense, but it's flawed. I have to tell you, I agree with Justin. You're running away. Rather than moving your life away from the things that remind you of him, you need to work on finding a way to let go, to truly say goodbye to Vance. Yes, he'll always be a part of you, and he should be, but you have to find a way to accept your memories and hold them dear, not live in them or hide from them.

"If you want to get away for a little while, that's not necessarily a bad thing. Space might be what you need to think clearly and be honest with yourself about what you're doing with your life without Vance. Take an Alaskan cruise. Go on a European tour. Hell, visit a Caribbean Island. Something, but don't pack up your life, Mimi. I think you'll find it to be a mistake and you won't be any happier than you are right now. You'll still have to confront the same issues further down the line."

I feel the wind go out of my sails listening to her because I know she's right. Laurel may be excitable and possess an overabundance of energy, but when she wants to lay the wisdom down, she's usually right on target. I realize maybe some time with my friend is what I need most of all.

"Laurel, what would you say if I came to New York for a little while, then?"

"I'd say 'Hell, yeah!' Now you're talking, Mimi. When would you like to come?" she says with her trademark exuberance.

We make plans for me to fly out that weekend and stay for a couple weeks. She can only take a few days off to spend with me, but I decide exploring New York on my own is not such a bad idea.

I take the time to call everyone and let them know I've changed my mind about Arizona, much to their collective relief. I even call Justin but reach his voicemail. I leave a brief message telling him I changed my mind but will be out of town for a few weeks on vacation and will try to call him when I return.

As I'm packing, I let my mind wander over the things Laurel said to me, and how I might actually go about letting go of Vance. An idea occurs to me, and the more I think about it, the more I know it's the perfect thing to do. I go to Vance's office and look up the necessary information on the internet. I make a few telephone calls and pack all the things I will need to carry out my plan while I'm visiting Laurel. As I'm zipping up the last suitcase, a smile breaks over my face. It's the first genuine smile I've had in a very long time, and it's because I can feel Vance's wholehearted approval of this idea.

Eighteen

The flight to New York this time around takes much longer and is bittersweet. I can't help but reminisce about the last time I flew this route, nearly three years ago. I think about Bertha, Captain Von Sweatyballs, Vance's charming grin, the long talk we had getting to know each other, and about how much hope, how much promise lay ahead of us at the time. It was the beginning of everything, and surprisingly, instead of dissolving into a sobbing mess, I feel humble, fortunate, and oh-so-very grateful. How many people get to have what we had? Yes, it was taken from me too soon, and yes, I went through some very hard and painful times, but my God, we had perfection. I know what it is to have been truly blessed.

I arrive to find Laurel awaiting me in baggage claim yet again, this time without her smartphone visible. She wraps me in a big hug, then helps me grab my bags. She wouldn't be Laurel if she didn't talk my ear off, so she keeps up a steady stream of chatter as we walk to the taxi stand. She informs me she has no grandiose plans this time around, allowing me to set the pace and determine what I would like to do while I'm here. I share my idea with her, and she smiles widely at me. She likes it as much as I do.

We spend the first few days of my visit just wandering around the city, with no agenda. I talk a lot about the good times with Vance, about the bad times with him, about those last days, about how I've felt since he died. Laurel listens to it all patiently if not quietly. She doesn't try to offer me any advice or words of cheer like she did right after he died, she simply listens, and the times when I cry, she holds my hand. It's exactly what I need, right at the moment I need it. One afternoon while walking in Central Park, I comment on her much more sedate demeanor as opposed to her bubbly spirit when she came for the funeral and she looks a little embarrassed.

"I know, I came off too upbeat for the situation. I was trying to stay positive for you, but to be honest with you, Mimi, I was kind of lost myself. I've never known anyone who died before. My grandparents and parents are still alive. So are all my aunts and uncles. I've never lost anyone. I liked Vance a lot, you know that, but he wasn't an everyday part of my life. While I was sad and unhappy such a wonderful person was gone from this world, I wasn't experiencing a loss like you were, like everyone around me was. I really didn't know what to do or how to behave, and I am eternally sorry for making you uncomfortable on top of what had to be the most painful experience of your life. I was hoping to give you something positive to hold onto, but instead, I only seemed insensitive and a little crazy."

I nod in understanding. "I didn't think you were insensitive, I just thought you were being you. Your energy and enthusiasm are hard to contain under any circumstances, and I had neither of those things at the time. I only comment on it now because you've been doing a remarkable job of being very low-key the last few days," I say as I nudge her shoulder with mine and grin at her.

"I have been, haven't I? You know, it's fucking killing me, too. Let's go get a hot dog," she smiles back at me and takes off running toward the vendor a few dozen feet away.

The Thursday following my arrival, we dress up for dinner and go to the little bistro Vance took me to for our first date. We don't manage to get the same table, unfortunately. It's occupied by an older couple who look to be celebrating some happy occasion. I can't be too grumpy about not getting what I want since it seems only fitting that something happy should be happening at that table. Laurel is yet again as patient as Job as she listens to me recount our first date in agonizing detail. If I'm honest, she seems to enjoy hearing about it. She even gets me to try a glass of Riesling with my dinner, and to my surprise, it's not that bad. Its sweet flavor is quite nice. I feel a little wistful that I finally find a kind of wine that I like, and Vance isn't around to enjoy the moment, but I take comfort that I've found it here, in what I consider "our" restaurant.

The following afternoon, I rent a car, and Laurel and I are standing in front of her building.

"Are you sure you want to do this alone?" she asks. "Pete and I would be happy to go with you. He'll be off work around six, and we could leave right after that, or we could go tomorrow morning and avoid the traffic."

"Thanks, Laurel, but I really do need to do this alone. I don't know why, but it just seems like the right way."

"Okay," she says as she gives me a hug. "Just know, I'm only a phone call away if you need me to talk to or if you decide you want me to drive over after all."

I thank her, then hop in the car for the long drive to Atlantic City.

I stay at Caesar's Palace this trip. The vouchers we received have long since been used by Laurel and Pete and a few of their friends, but I giggle to myself thinking about them. Poor Vance being locked up for trying to come to my rescue.

After getting settled in my room, I spend the evening wandering around the casino. I spend some time at the draw poker machines near where we played that first night. Then I stop by the craps table and watch the action. I never did learn enough about the game to place a bet, but I enjoy watching everyone else and thinking about being there with Vance. After a little while, I drift over to "my machine."

Fortunately, it's empty, so I sit down and feed fifty dollars into it. I'm tempted to take out five hundred since that's the amount Vance had given me that night, but I'm not here to completely relive our first days to the letter. I'm just here to visit some happy memories. I go through my investment without ever getting to spin the big wheel. It makes me laugh. I stroke the top of the machine affectionately as I stand up, not bothering to look around to see if anyone is watching. So what if people think I'm crazy, I still do love this machine and probably always will.

The following day, I lay in bed for a while, but that's a little too hard for me to bear. Those memories are just a little too raw to lay alone and think about, so I get up and go downstairs to one of the restaurants for a late breakfast, then spend the day walking around the boardwalk playing games and watching people. I end up with a bit of a sunburn on my nose and shoulders, but I feel a little lighter and happier for having spent the day around people enjoying themselves.

In the evening, I put on my red fringed dress and walk down to the little Cuban nightclub we went to our second night in Atlantic City. I have a few mojitos and decline a few invitations to dance. I considered them, I really did, but it just didn't seem right to me. This is another one of our places, and I don't want to make any other memories here. I want to visit the one I have and leave it at that. I

363

listen to the music for a while, then leave quietly to return to my room.

The following day I spend much like the one before since I enjoyed myself so much. Just before sundown, however, I return to my room and gather the special items I packed and head down to the marina listed in the instructions I received from the company I'd contacted. I meet the captain of the thirty-eight-foot charter vessel on the dock who introduces himself simply as Nick. He advises that we'll be sailing about five miles out from the shoreline for the ceremony, after which we'll circle around a few times and then, per my request, we'll take a short scenic cruise of Atlantic City before heading back into the marina.

It doesn't take long to reach what he calls the burial site. After Nick anchors the boat, we meet at the small platform set up especially for the occasion, and I hand him the urn containing Vance's ashes. Placing them on a small podium before us, the captain gives a very brief but lovely speech about life and death, love and loss, and the returning of one's spirit to nature. Once he finishes, he returns the urn to me. I approach the side of the boat and open it. I close my eyes for a few moments, recalling my last conversation with Vance and my promise to him. I don't know how I'll accomplish it, but I know the love he had given me made me a better, stronger person than I had ever been before. Because of him, I would eventually find my way through, and I'd be able to keep my promise to him. He'd always be a treasured part of me, and just as he'd said, I'd keep that flame he'd lit burning just for him.

With that, I open my eyes and slowly tilt the urn over the side of the boat, letting go of Vance in the place where all our perfection began.

TWO YEARS LATER

"So, when will you be back?" Justin asked as he lifted my small suitcase into the trunk of my SUV.

"We're only going for the weekend. I'll be back before you know it. You won't even miss me at all," I teased. The girls and I were going to Lake Havasu for Memorial Day weekend on a much-needed girls' trip. We were meeting up with some friends of Jessica's who had rented a houseboat and planned on spending our time sunbathing, drinking, and flirting with any handsome men we might find among the frat boys who would be descending upon the lake for the holiday. I was up for the sunbathing and drinking, but not so sure about the men. In the nearly three years that had passed since Vance died, I hadn't really done any dating. I had gone on a few blind dates the girls had set up for me in the last six months but never felt any kind of connection to anyone. Honestly, that was fine with me. I no longer lived in my memories of the past, but I wasn't in any hurry to change my life as it had come to be. Justin satisfied any need for male companionship I had—well, most needs. I'll just say any "special" needs I may have had were fulfilled with the assistance of B.O.B. It was far and away less satisfying than the real thing, but again I was in no hurry. I guess in that respect, Vance had spoiled me. It was going to take a certain type of person to meet my expectations in the romance and sex department, and I doubted his existence. Vance was one of a kind and although I had healed, I didn't think anyone would be able to compare, either. That said, I did feel a certain "itch" so to speak. Wait, that sounds really bad when talking about things down there. Forget I said anything.

"Aww, Peaches, you know that's not true," Justin said while grabbing my hand and holding it over his heart. "I ache right here whenever you're away."

I slapped his chest teasingly. "When do I ever go away?"

"Just last month, you left me to go see your mother."

"For the afternoon! I was back in time for pizza, beer, and movies, just like we'd planned."

"Yes, well I missed you anyway," he said with a smirk.

I just shook my head before leaning forward to give him a kiss on the cheek. At the last minute, he turned his head slightly and my lips landed at the corner of his mouth. A strange thrill I didn't expect ran through me. Justin? Since when did I feel anything like that for him? He'd been my friend for nearly five years, had helped me through the most devastating time of my life, and had become one of the most important people in my world. When I came back from that trip to New York when I'd scattered Vance's ashes, Justin and I had mended fences, and I set about being a better friend to him. The kind of friend he'd been to me, the kind he needed me to be. I finally held up my end of the bargain of being in our support group of two. We grew ever closer, and I'd come to think of him as the big brother I'd never had. Yes, I had always thought him attractive, but was I actually attracted to him and never realized it?

I stepped back hesitantly and looked up at him with new eyes. He smiled at me warmly, and I suddenly felt bashful. Something unusual was definitely going on. I felt flustered and awkward, and... ah hell. I felt like I always used to around a good-looking guy I found myself attracted to. I didn't quite know what to do, so I did the only logical thing I could think of.

"Well... I guess I'll be seeing you on Tuesday. Or maybe Wednesday. Or... um... whenever," I said as I quickly rounded the back of my car and headed toward the driver's side door in full-on retreat.

Justin chuckled under his breath and slowly followed. I hopped in and shut the door, then rolled down the window after starting the engine as fast as I could. He bent down and leaned in my window.

"You take care of yourself and have a good time, Peaches. I'll be here waiting for you when you get back," he said as he leaned forward a little more and planted a soft kiss directly on my lips. I sat there slack-jawed as he straightened with the cockiest smile on his face. He tapped on the roof of the car before turning and starting toward his motorcycle, parked at the curb.

After a few stunned seconds, I called after him "Uh, yeah. I will. I'll call you when I get back!"

He raised his arm over his head, waving in acknowledgment before throwing his leg over the bike and strapping on his helmet. I simply sat there watching as he started the engine and drove off down the street without a glance back.

I looked at myself in the rear-view mirror and saw my eyes were bright and there was a pink tinge to my cheeks. I immediately scrubbed my hands over my face, shook my head to clear it of the daze that had settled over me, and put the car in reverse to back out of the driveway.

It was a very good thing there were several alcoholic beverages in my near future. I had a feeling I was going to need each and every one of them.

Mimi's story will continue...

Books by Heather R. Guimond

Shattered Perfection
Fighting Perfection
Beautiful Imperfection

74089949R00211

Made in the USA
San Bernardino, CA
12 April 2018